UPPING
THE
ANTE

KATE
CAMPFIELD

ALSO BY KATE CAMPFIELD

Going All In

Letting it Ride

Calling Your Bluff

UPPING
THE
ANTE

UPPING THE ANTE

KATE CAMPFIELD

For my Family

CONTENTS

1

BLAKE

They say fake it till you make it, and if that doesn't describe the process of getting a PhD, I don't know what does.

"Congrats, man! You made it!" Miller tosses his head to get his shaggy blond hair out of the way as he raises a glass in my direction and takes a long sip.

I'm not sure I've made it just yet, but I did finish my PhD—blood, sweat, and tears and all that—and get hired at our local college, which is a big step toward making it.

Cam taps his soda to my pint glass, then to Maddox's. "Cheers. Never thought we'd see the day we'd not only be able to celebrate with the esteemed Dr. Grantham, but with Dr. Grantham, *Professor* of Economics and Game Theory at Ardmore College."

I throw back the last sip then set my empty beer glass on the table and snag a handful of pretzels from the bowl in the center of the table. The scent of buffalo wings hits my nose as a waitress walks by, and I wonder if we should order some real food. McFadden's has great appetizers. It's part of the reason it's our favorite bar.

"Assistant professor. Technically, that's the rank. But thanks, guys. Maybe see if I can stick it out for a few weeks before you get too excited."

"You've got this," my brother, Lawton, says. He tosses a pretzel in his mouth. "Did you ever think you'd just be starting your first real job at age thirty-seven?"

I smack him with one hand. "Dude, I've been working."

He holds up a finger. "Technically, you were still a trainee when you were doing your post-doc. And when you were TA-ing classes, you were a student. So this is the first time that it's just a job."

He has a point there, and it annoys me that he's right. Lawton is several years younger than me, and all the way through college, he followed in my footsteps.

But then I chose the ill-advised path of getting a PhD and going into academia, while he went to the police academy. He just got a job up in the mountains of Colorado, working as a small-town cop, and moved up there a few months ago. Supposedly, the winters are brutal, with snowfall measured in feet instead of inches and temperatures rarely rising above zero.

I sent him a pair of long underwear to keep his junk from freezing and falling off.

"Anyway," I say. "Thanks for coming out to celebrate. And I suppose Lawton's right, even if he is a dick. This is my first job where I get a real paycheck."

"So the next round's on you?" Miller holds up an empty glass. "I'll take another Yuengling."

"I don't get paid until I start."

He shrugs. "I'm poor, too, man. I'm just a lowly grad student."

I snort. "Yeah, who's engaged to a future doctor."

Miller grins. "True story. Man, she's so out of my fucking league. I'm the luckiest bastard out there."

"All of your women are out of your league," I say, under my breath.

It's true, too. Maddox is married to Holly, a social worker who has a heart of pure gold, and who happens to be his stepsister, although their parents got married *after* the two of them got together, both of them widowed. She's at home with their nine-month-old son, Rhys, who is about the cutest little fucker I've ever seen.

Cam managed to get with Maddox's sister, Addison, after a decade of crushing on her.

Miller, who I would have voted Least Likely to Settle Down, is engaged to a medical student named Becca. I've met her once, and she's insanely smart. Or at least, book smart. She chose Miller, after all, which calls her intelligence into question just a bit.

Cam elbows me. "Just for that, this next round *is* on you. But for the record, yeah, Addie's way out of my league. Don't think I don't know that."

He pushes his glass across the table toward me.

I shove back from the table. "Lawton, give me a hand. Everyone drinking the same thing?"

Nods all around.

Lawton and I head to the bar, where I hand over my credit card and order four lagers—the proper way to order Yuengling, if you're from Philadelphia—and a soda. I lean against the polished wood while the bartender fills the glasses.

"Hi, honey," an unfamiliar voice says from behind me.

I assume someone is greeting their significant other, so I don't turn around until something kicks me in the calf.

I spin around, looking for the source of the assault, only to see a pair of stiletto heels, one of them tapping against the floor. Long, shapely legs rise from the weaponized shoes. I follow them up, past a knee-length pencil skirt that highlights slim hips, a white button-down tucked into the waistband. The top button is open just enough to give a suggestion of lush tits beneath the no-nonsense top.

I force my gaze away from her chest to take in the rest of her. The woman standing in front of me has a tight smile on her gorgeous face.

And she is *stunning*.

My mouth goes dry as I get a good look at her face. High cheekbones, perfectly sculpted jawline. Light-brown hair that falls in waves just past her shoulders.

"Hi, honey," she says again, her eyes narrowed and flashing, like she's trying to send me a message.

I swallow and try to gather my thoughts.

Jesus, Blake.

I'm in my late thirties. I'm not some teenage boy who would be starry-eyed just from one look at a woman.

I peer over her shoulder, and when I see the man leering at her, it clicks.

"Hi, sweetheart," I say. I drape my arm over her shoulders. "Didn't hear you at first. Sorry, sweetie."

Okay, that may be laying on the pet names a little thick.

"How was your day at work?" Seems like a fair assumption, given her outfit.

I refrain from looking down at her body again.

Is this enough? Am I selling it? Maybe I should lean in for a kiss.

I tilt toward her, hoping she'll give me a signal of some kind. I'm sort of going in blind here.

"It was good." She leans her head away from mine to look over her shoulder at the guy, who finally seems to be getting the hint, his hand stroking his scraggly goatee.

Okay, got it. No kiss.

"Sorry again," she says to the guy, although it doesn't seem like she's the one to owe anyone an apology in this situation. "I told you I was just meeting my boyfriend."

It's starting to make sense. Creeper was flirting and wouldn't take no for an answer, to the point that she needs me to help.

Now I'm invested. I don't know this woman—not yet, at least—but I'm all in on our little ruse. I have no patience for guys like this, the kind who think they're entitled to a woman's attention unless she's already with someone.

"This guy was hitting on you, babe?" I ask.

He raises his hands, stepping back so quickly that

he bumps into another woman who's just trying to make her way to the bar. "Sorry, man. I didn't know she was taken."

"Well, she is," I say firmly, pulling her closer to me.

She's tall, especially with the extra couple of inches from her high heels, the top of her head at my eye level.

"Told you," she mutters.

The creep makes a beeline for the door, his overbearing cologne leaving a trail sandalwood and tobacco behind him as he retreats. I wait until the door shuts behind him before I slide my arm off her shoulders.

"Thanks," she says, shaking her head with a laugh and an adorably crinkled nose. "Some guys just don't take no for an answer, you know?"

"No problem. I'm sorry you have to deal with stuff like that."

The bartender slides the beers toward me, and I lift one and hold it out to her.

"Need a drink to recover?"

She takes the glass and brings it to her lips, taking a sip. She really is gorgeous, her olive skin bright, her hazel eyes fixed on mine, her lips painted a deep red.

"Thanks. Although I really should be buying *you* a drink for saving me."

"Go for it," Lawton says.

I turn around to see him holding up a finger to the bartender, who fills another drink and passes it to him.

"I'll be at our table. Have fun." He gathers four glasses in his arms, leaving one beer for me, and carries them away.

I shrug. "Well, I'll never say no to a free drink, but I have one already. Can I join you while we enjoy these?"

I lift the full glass then take a sip.

She scans the room. "Well, if I'm not taking you away from anything."

I shake my head. "I'm out with my friends. But they came out to celebrate me, so they won't mind me having a drink with you."

She arches one perfect eyebrow. "What are you celebrating?"

"I finished my PhD." I shrug, hoping I'm not coming off as a cocky asshole.

I mean, I am a cocky asshole, but while I'm proud of my academic accomplishments, it makes some people uncomfortable for some reason. Like because I went to school for a million years, I must be extra smart or something.

She doesn't blink, though. Instead, she takes a sip of her beer. "Let's finish these, and I'll get you another one. Seriously, I owe you. There's a table over there."

She sets off toward an empty two-top that's against the brick wall without looking back.

I take the opportunity to peruse the rest of her while her back is to me. Her calves are toned, her shirt is tucked in at her narrow waist, and her ass looks amazing in that skirt, full and round. For a second, I can understand why men like that asshole won't leave her alone.

It's a good thing I'm not in the market for any kind of relationship. But I'm not opposed to one-night stands. If anything, I'm wide open.

I follow her to the table and slide into the seat opposite her.

She holds out a hand. Her fingernails are painted a pale-pink color. "Anyway, hi. I'm Kat."

I return her handshake. Her grip is firm, authoritative. Combined with the pencil skirt, she exudes power and confidence. What does this woman do for a living?

"Nice to meet you, girlfriend. Blake."

She laughs again. "Seriously, thank you. It's such a cliche, you know? Having to pretend to be dating a stranger to avoid some other guy's advances."

I take a long swallow of beer. I feel a little guilty leaving my buddies. In addition to Lawton moving out to Colorado, Miller recently moved to upstate New York and is only in town for a few days.

But then, we're at the bar celebrating me. So if I want to celebrate with this woman, I'll damn well do it.

"Well, on behalf of my gender, I apologize for creeps everywhere."

Kat taps a manicured fingernail against her flawless skin and studies me. "So you're one of the good ones?"

"I like to think so."

She nods, like she's trying to decide whether to believe me. "Well, I'm glad there are some of you still out there."

As she raises her glass to her lips again, I think about her words. I like to think I'm one of the good ones, but since when does being a "good guy" just involve not being a complete asshole and taking advantage of women? Or listening when a woman turns you down?

It's a low bar, guys. It shouldn't be that hard.

"So what do you do?" I ask, digging for something to keep our conversation going.

A small smile plays on her lips as she sets her beer down. "Tell you what. If you guess it, guess *exactly* what I do, I'll tell you. Otherwise, it stays a mystery."

"How many guesses do I get?"

She considers, her finger tracing the edge of her glass as her lips curve. "Three."

"Ten." I can negotiate like no one's business. I'm feeling my victory already.

"Five. Final offer."

I run a hand across the stubble on my jaw. Beautiful *and* sassy. I could like this girl. I *do* like her, enough to want to spend more time with her.

"Okay, then. Let's see. Assuming this is what you wear to work, you're a professional. Some kind of executive, probably."

Her expression doesn't change, the slight smirk never fading as she skims a finger along the edge of her glass. "Specific guesses get a yes or no, Blake. This isn't an open essay where you can bullshit your way to the right answer."

I grin, knowing exactly what she means. It's why I love teaching game theory instead of sociology or religion. "Fair enough. Are you a CEO?"

She shakes her head. "Guess again."

She looks younger than me, but not by much. I'd guess she's in her early thirties, so maybe CEO was a bit of a stretch.

"VP?"

Another head shake.

I tilt my head to the side, trying to read her. "Investment banker."

"Nope. Would I be here at six p.m. if I were an investment banker?" Kat lifts her beer and takes a sip.

At this point, our drinks are starting to get warm, but both of us continue to nurse them slowly. I'm doing whatever I can to draw this out, to spend more time with her.

"Good point." I consider the options. I'm not sure a doctor or nurse would wear heels like hers all day, but maybe... "Healthcare administration?"

She wrinkles her nose. "God, no."

"Is that a no to healthcare or to admin?"

Kat points a finger toward me, her tone flirtatious. "Hey. Technically, that's two guesses. But to answer your question, which is one hundred percent cheating, no, I don't work in healthcare. And not in healthcare admin. Enjoy your freebie. You're down to your last guess."

I keep guessing, loving this game, but as I take the last sip of my beer, I still haven't figured it out. "Come on. Give me a clue."

Kat laughs. "Nope. Rules are rules."

"Yeah, yeah." I set the empty glass down. "Let's see. Model?"

It was the first thing that popped into my head,

honestly, but I thought if I guessed that first, she'd be offended.

By the look that crosses her face, I think that may have been a valid concern.

Kat turns her wrist to check her watch. "Oh, goodness. It's late. I need to get going." She stands from the table and then pushes in her chair. As she takes a step toward the front of the bar, she brushes my forearm with her fingers and making electricity rise in their wake. "It was great to meet you, Blake. Thanks again for saving me."

"Wait." I reach for her arm.

Even if I haven't guessed what she does for work, I'm not ready to let this woman leave, not just yet, and definitely not so suddenly, without learning more about her.

"I'm sorry if I offended you with that guess. It's just that you're stunningly beautiful. It wasn't a line, I swear. I want to get to know you. Do you have something you need to get to? Or are you just ready to leave the bar?"

She shrugs, her body relaxing ever so slightly. "Just ready to get out of here."

I run my fingers up her arm, from her wrist to her elbow and then back down her soft skin. I don't miss the goose bumps that trail behind my touch.

"Can I join you?"

She fixes me with a stare, one eyebrow raised. "Why?"

I shrug as I rise from my seat, standing just a few inches too close to her. Now or never, right?

Even in the bar, I can smell her perfume, something floral. It's too sweet for her—she should be wearing something musky and complex and mysterious, like her. Even from the short time we've shared together so far, I can tell she has an edge to her.

From this angle, I have a perfect view of her hardened nipples, and a quick glance over her shoulder lets me see her gorgeous, round ass. God, the things I want to do to that ass.

Her chest rises and falls with shallow, quick breaths, and she darts her pink tongue out to wet her bottom lip. She hasn't said it, but she's as turned on as I am right now.

"Because I'm attracted to you. I want to spend the night with you." I lean in, letting my jaw scrape against her cheek as I speak directly in her ear. This is a gamble, but I don't have anything to lose. "Because you want me, too."

2

KAT

Everything about him is intoxicating.

I'd chalk my fuzzy brain up to the glass of wine I had while waiting for the Tinder date who stood me up, plus the glass of beer that I almost finished, but I was feeling clear-headed enough until Blake touched me.

The second he put his arm around me in that protective gesture, I started to lose my senses.

It's the only reason I can think of for why, instead of calling an Uber to take me back home, I'm sharing one with Blake, headed to wherever he lives.

"Ardmore," he says, in answer to my unasked question. "Not too far from here."

I swallow hard, his low voice doing something to

my insides. "I live in Ardmore, too. Over by the college."

Going home with a stranger isn't the smartest idea. I get that. But I texted Angela and Naomi—my best friends—Blake's address, which he gave me when he ordered the Uber.

And Blake dragged me along when he went to tell his friends he was leaving. Most serial killers wouldn't give their friends that courtesy. As far as I know, at least.

Blake sits in the middle seat, while I'm on the driver's side, both of us in the back seat of the sedan. I've never seen someone willingly take the middle, but it didn't take long to figure out his game.

His hand rests on his thigh, and since our thighs are touching, his little finger is on my leg, too. He moves it in a circular pattern that has my stomach dropping.

The small movement lights my entire body on fire, and he's barely touching me.

"I can't wait to taste you," he murmurs, sending a new wave of heat coursing through my body and settling between my legs.

Our Uber driver, a little old man whose name is Norbert, according to the app, ignores us, focusing on the road.

"Up here on the left, Norbert," Blake says, not moving his lips away from my jaw.

When Norbert pulls the car into the driveway of a well-maintained, one-story home, I'm practically ready to jump out of my skin with lust.

I don't go home with men, as a rule. The last time I had a one-night stand was during grad school, and even then, I turned it into a relationship. It lasted three tumultuous weeks, and I learned that undergrad frat parties are not the best places to meet guys.

Tonight, I was doing it right, or so I thought— meeting up with a guy for an actual date. We met on Tinder, and we've been messaging back and forth for a couple of weeks. Tonight, we were going to meet for a drink and see where things went.

And then he never showed, the creep hit on me and wouldn't take no for an answer until I made Blake stand in as my boyfriend, and now here we are.

"This is your house?" I ask, then immediately cringe.

That's a dumb question. Of course it's his house, Kat. Why the hell else would we be here?

The Uber backs out of the driveway, leaving me alone with Blake, who just nods in answer to my question.

He reaches over and slaps my ass, making me jump.

"Get that hot little ass in the house, babe," he says, his voice almost a growl. "I have plans for you."

God, do I want to see the plans he has for me.

He smacks my ass again, and *fuck* if I don't love it. I walk toward the front door and pause there while he unlocks it and turns on a light.

The home is exactly what I'd expect from the short time I've known Blake. So far, the vibe I get from him is straightforward, no bullshit. Nothing is subtle here —dark tones of navy and gray, stainless steel, dark wood. Simple, clean lines, a minimalist feel. Clean, empty surfaces without any clutter.

He turns on another light, this one to what must be the living room, which has dark wood paneling with off-white crown molding. A leather couch—no throw pillows in sight. A sleek coffee table holding a single book.

I step farther into the room and read the title— *COLORADO.*

"Is that where you're from?" I ask, looking back at Blake.

My stomach bottoms out at the sight of him rolling up his shirtsleeves. At some point, he undid the top button of his Oxford shirt, revealing a smattering of dark chest hair.

God, he's hot. I'd say he's out of my league, even,

but I'm Kathleen Fucking Milas. As my parents drilled into me from a young age, I'm in a league of my own.

"No." Blake steps toward me, closing in the way he did in the bar, the way that makes me feel his height over me, even though with my heels on, I'm only a couple of inches shorter than him.

He slides an arm around my waist, settling his hand on the small of my back, and I set my hands on his chest. His pecs flex under my hands. He's solid, strong. All man.

His smell wafts around me. It's one of those manly scents, woody and spicy and intoxicating. It's almost indescribable, but I know I'll never be able to forget it. I inhale deeply, pulling more of him into me.

"Kat." Blake uses his free hand to tip my chin upward with one finger, his other hand still on my back, pressing me into him. His bright-blue eyes are hypnotic, standing out in contrast to his dark, close-cropped hair. "Do you want this?"

I nod, breathlessly. Because I do. I want *him*.

"Because I'm warning you now, in the bedroom, I'm...rough. I like control. Are you okay with that?"

My pussy responds with a gush of arousal because I do want him to be rough. To take me however he wants. I spend most of my life being in a position of authority at work, and sometimes I want to not have to think.

"Fuck, yes." I narrow my eyes the tiniest bit, before I give up the control. "One night, though. No strings."

"You're too fucking perfect." Blake's mouth crashes down on mine, hard and demanding.

I melt beneath his power as his lips tease mine. He bites down on my bottom lip, hard enough that I gasp, and he takes the opportunity to slide his tongue into my mouth. I moan as he claims my mouth.

When he pulls back, I gasp for air, leaning against him because my legs don't want to support me anymore.

"Bedroom," he says, nipping at my lip again.

I just nod, following him on shaky legs through the darkened kitchen and down a short hallway.

Blake pushes open a door. A sliver of moonlight from a large window illuminates enough for me to make out a king-sized bed, dark wood furnishings. A framed art print on one wall that I can't quite make out the details of.

He spins me around to face him. I teeter on my heels before I kick them off. In bare feet, he's a good six inches taller than me. It makes him seem that much more dominant as he undoes the buttons of my shirt, one at a time, revealing the lacy, cream-colored bra that matches the thong I'm wearing beneath my skirt.

For the record, the lingerie wasn't for my Tinder date. I happen to like wearing matching sets. It makes me feel sensual, confident. It's my little secret, knowing that beneath my buttoned-up exterior, I'm still sexy and feminine.

And the way Blake is looking at me reinforces all of that.

Pulling the shirt out from where it's tucked into the pencil skirt, he undoes the last button and pushes the shirt wide, holding it with both hands.

"Fuck," he says, thumbs brushing the lace. "Fucking gorgeous."

He runs his hands down my sides to the top of my skirt as my head falls back at his touch. I've never known that just the act of undressing could be so erotic, but then, I've never been with a man like Blake. So alpha, so in control.

Unzipping my skirt, he pushes it down to the floor, and I step out of it.

He growls—actually fucking *growls*—and then he's spinning me, moving us so fast that I'm dizzy as he pushes me up against a wall, my back to him, and brings my hands over my head. He holds my hands there, pinning me against the wall as his other hand explores my body.

His touch is light as he moves his fingers across the swell of my breasts, down my flat stomach, over my hipbone, along the crease where my thigh meets my pelvis.

With every touch, I'm more and more turned on, my underwear a complete lost cause at this point with how soaked I am.

Blake's fingers brush against the crotch of my panties, and I know he feels it too.

"You're so wet for me," he says, his voice low in my ear as his stubble scrapes my cheek. "So fucking wet."

All I can do is moan, every bit of my vocabulary vanished from my mind under his touch.

"I want to fuck you up against this wall, take you just like this." He bites a spot on my neck, just above my shoulder. "But first I'm going to fuck you in my bed. Hard."

He spins me again, walking forward while I move backward until my legs hit the edge of his bed. Even now, my body is completely under his control.

Blake grips my hips and lifts me onto the bed. He hooks his fingers into my underwear and slips them off in one movement, then drops them to the floor.

I shimmy back until my head is on the pillows. They smell like him.

I stare in wonder as he grips the back of his shirt and pulls it over his head, revealing defined muscles and a trail of dark hair that leads down into his pants. He smirks as he undoes his belt and pushes his pants and boxers down in one movement, and as he does, I understand the reason for his expression.

He's big. Really big.

I can't do anything but stare at his cock. Thick, long, heavy between his legs.

"Like what you see?" His teasing tone pulls my attention to his face.

My mouth is so dry that I just nod as he climbs onto the bed, one knee on either side of my legs, leaning over me.

"You want that inside you? You want me to fuck you hard, Kat?"

I've never wanted anything so badly in my life.

"Yes," I whisper.

"Ask nicely, babe. Maybe you'll get what you want."

"Please," I beg.

My clit is throbbing, needing to be touched.

"Please what?" He reaches over, opening the drawer of the nightstand and pulling out a condom.

"Please fuck me." My voice is hoarse as he sheaths himself and leans over me again.

"Good girl." He notches himself at my entrance and slowly, oh so slowly, pushes in.

I gasp at the stretch, just enough to add a twinge of pain in addition to the fullness.

"You okay?" Blake studies my face, holding perfectly still.

I nod, needing more. "I'm good."

He advances an inch, then another, watching me closely as I adjust to his size.

When he bottoms out, I groan, spasming around him. God, he feels so fucking good. I'm so full.

And then he starts moving.

Blake withdraws almost all the way, then slams forward, pressing my hips into the mattress as he fills me up again and again. Stars infuse my vision.

"God, you feel good," he says, pistoning his hips faster, harder. "So fucking good, Kat. You're so tight."

"Blake." I gasp. "Oh God, I'm—"

"You want to come, babe?"

"Yes. Please, yes." I've never begged for anything in my life, but this man has reduced me to a quivering mess.

"Come for me." He thrusts hard, and I topple over

the cliff, my entire body tightening as pleasure rolls through me.

He fucks me through my orgasm, slowing as I recover. When my breathing evens out, he moves faster, bringing me to the peak of another climax.

"I'm right there, Kat. You there with me?"

I nod, my heart pounding as I start to tighten around his girth.

"Come for me again, Kat. Hard."

My body responds to his command, another climax creeping up and over me, pulling me into its spiral.

This time when I come, he does too, both of us gasping in pleasure.

Blake lowers his forehead to mine, both of us breathing hard. "That was fucking amazing, Kat."

I'm still trying to catch my breath, so all I can do is nod.

Blake slips out of bed, taking care of the condom, and comes back with a damp washcloth. He cleans me up so gently I almost forget that he's the same man who completely dominated my body just minutes ago.

"Do you want to stay?" he asks, climbing back into bed and pulling me close.

Every fiber of my being is yelling at me to stay, to

cuddle, to spend every second I can with this man. To let him own my body again, over and over.

But despite the fact that my brain is still clouded from the mind-blowing orgasms, I know I can't.

No strings.

And this isn't the type of guy that Kat Fucking Milas gets involved with. I'm an independent woman, damn it. I don't need to be bossed around.

Even if it was really fucking hot.

I shake my head. "I have to be up early. I need to go."

He's a gentleman about it, picking up my clothes and helping me find my shoe that skittered off beneath his bed in the heat of the moment, and he waits with me for my Uber.

"Kat," he says, as the Uber pulls up. "You were fucking amazing."

"You, too."

He pulls me into a hug and kisses me, sweet and soft, so different from how he was in the bedroom. "No strings, right?"

I take a step toward the waiting car, an unfamiliar pang in my chest. "No strings."

3

KAT

Sweat rises on the back of my neck in a prickle as I look around at the absolute disaster.

Piles of papers on the desk. A book lying open, for God's sake. Another pile of folders on one of the shelves against the wall.

I take a deep breath. It's one thing to let your office go a bit over the summer, when there aren't many students on campus, but there are only a few days left until classes start back up for the fall semester. I'm the first to admit that being neat and organized isn't my forte, but I try my best at work.

So instead of going over lesson plans, I'll be cleaning today, making this place presentable. I mean, the lesson plans are done, but I like to double-check them before I upload them and print. I mentally add that to tomorrow's to-do list.

On the plus side, organizing will hopefully take my mind off the guy. Blake. It's been over a week, but he's still on my mind.

I never go home with men from the bar. Or men at all. But there was something about him that made me agree to go with him, and it was the hottest thing I've done in years. I may or may not have fantasized about it daily since it happened.

I blow out a breath. It's time to forget about that night, at least for now, because there's an awful lot of shit to do around here.

I kick off my shoes under the desk and lift a pile of papers to start going through them.

"Hey, girl!" A knock sounds at the door of my office.

I look up to see Angela's head poking in, the dark curls of her natural hair wild.

"Hey," I say, lifting a pile of papers. "How's it going? Ready for the semester?"

Angela is one of my closest friends at work. She teaches mostly Evolutionary Biology, which is about as far removed as you can get from my Anatomy and Physiology for Pre-Meds classes and still both be in the Biology department.

She nods as she steps into my office and lifts a stack of textbooks from the chair. She sets them on the desk and sits, crossing her leg to tuck a foot underneath her.

The pants she's wearing are brightly patterned. Paired with a lime-green shirt, it's the kind of outfit I'd never be able to pull off. I lean more toward classic cuts, neutral colors. It looks amazing on her, and as always, I'm jealous of her style.

"As ready as ever. You?"

"Those go on the bookshelf, Ang," I say, glaring at the books.

To be fair, though, I'm the one who left them on the chair in the first place. The glare isn't even for Ang. It's for Past Kat, the one who figured that the messy office could be Future Kat's problem.

I hate Past Kat right now. On the plus side, Two-Weeks-Ago Kat took care of anything that could be done remotely to get ready for the semester.

I blow out a breath. "I don't feel ready. I'll get there, though."

She tosses her head back and laughs. "If you ever said you were ready without completely stressing, I'd die of shock. Let me guess, though. Lesson plans are done."

"Yes," I say grudgingly. I pick up the top two books and shelve them.

"You've looked over the class list and double-checked what you're up against."

"Maybe."

She points a finger at me, her long nails a maroon red. "You've printed your syllabus and, not only that, but you formatted it all nice and turned it into a pdf that's already on the course website."

I pinch the bridge of my nose between my thumb and pointer finger. "Yes. But that's not the point. This place is a disaster."

"So?" Angela leans forward, clasping her hands together. "No one cares what your office looks like unless you plan to hold your lectures in here. How are you planning to fit ninety students in this room?"

I take the last book and place it on the shelf, making sure it's in the right spot. Years of schooling equals piles of textbooks, and it's a pain to have to go through all the shelves to find the one I need.

"I have office hours in here. And the department chair might stop by. Or the dean. Or someone else important."

This is what I get for working at home all summer. I timed it perfectly, getting a research project's data collection done at the same time the semester ended, so all I had to do over the summer was crunch numbers and write up a paper.

It seemed so luxurious. Writing in bed. Sitting on the front lawn while making graphs. Attending department meetings via Zoom.

I didn't come into the office once this summer. I was so proud of myself, my ability to take time away, even if I was working nonstop.

And this is the thanks I get—an office that didn't clean itself while I was gone.

"You know this is all your mess to begin with, right?" Angela asks pointedly. "It's not like gremlins came in here and stacked papers a foot high. This is all stuff you were working on back in the spring."

She's right, of course. After the students left for the summer, I spent a week working like crazy to finish everything up, ignoring the building mess, and then hightailed it out of here.

"So is your office perfect?" I ask.

I pick up the seven pens—no, eight—that are strewn across the desk and place them in a coffee mug labelled *I FOUND THIS HUMERUS*, with a picture of an upper arm bone. I can't hold back a snort of laughter.

Get it? Humerus?

It's a running joke between Angela, me, and our other best friend, Naomi, who teaches genetics. We're true science nerds, so every year we get one another gifts with science jokes that we think are hilarious.

Sure, a normal person may laugh at Naomi's mug that says *I USE THIS MUG PERIODICALLY* below the periodic table of the elements, but most would just groan or not understand the jokes at all. Most of them only make sense to people who do this kind of thing for a living.

"What are you laughing at?" Angela asks, ignoring the question about her office.

Her office is, I'm sure, perfect, everything in its place, the way it always is. She even has coasters for our nerdy mugs to keep her surfaces clean.

The coasters were from me. They each have a tongue-in-cheek lab rule, like *Science: like cooking, but don't lick the spoon* and *Hot glass looks just like cold glass until you touch it.*

"The humerus joke." I turn the mug so she can see it.

Angela snorts. "That one is a classic. Anyway, you never told me about the guy you went home with. It's been like a week. You promised me details."

"Okay. So I was supposed to meet up with one guy from Tinder."

"And you went home with him?"

"No. He never showed."

"That asshole." Angela has the good grace to look offended on my behalf.

"Yeah. Well, anyway, some creep tried to hit on me, and I ended up meeting the other guy. And...yeah. It was good."

Angela wiggles her brows. "And? Details. Was there dancing?"

I'm not sure I want to spill all the dirty details, even to Ang. And if I'm going to get into it, I'd rather do it with Naomi here, too, so they can get all of their gossip in the same place.

"How about we just talk about it at journal club?"

Angela nods vigorously. "Yes. And with the semester starting, we need a journal club ASAP."

For those in academia, journal club is a common thing—pick an article from a peer-reviewed journal in your specialty, and you get together with colleagues to review it.

In our little group, journal club is what we call it when we meet at one of our houses for drinks and gossip and to review romance books. The smuttier, the better.

"Can you text Naomi? See when she can come?"

Naomi is married and has a five-year-old daughter, who is about the cutest thing in the world. But it means she has more commitments, generally, than

Ang or I do, so we work around her schedule when we can.

Angela nods, already typing on her phone. "On it. So, are you seeing the guy again?"

I shrug. No, I'm not, but I'd rather wait to get into it.

He made it clear that it was just a onetime thing. We both agreed on that.

Angela's phone buzzes with a notification. "She's free tonight. Your house or mine?"

Why do I agree to these things?

You'd think I'd have learned by now that hosting any kind of event at my place is a recipe for disaster.

I pick up an empty cup from the coffee table and a pair of socks from the couch. I don't remember taking them off, but since I rarely have guests over here other than Naomi and Angela, they must be mine.

How long have they been sitting here? I sniff one of the socks and immediately wish I hadn't.

Also, I remember why I took them off. It was a week ago. Maybe two. I dripped some ice cream on the coffee table by accident while eating in front of the TV, and instead of getting up to grab a towel, I used my socks.

At the time, it seemed well reasoned—I was going to take them off soon and toss them in the laundry anyway, so why not put them to good use?

I shove the socks in the laundry along with the tip-top of the pile of dirty clothes that never seems to get any smaller and add detergent, then I add a little extra.

I'm not taking any chances here. The sweaty-feet-and-sour-milk aroma *cannot* spread to the rest of my clothes.

God, we should have met at Angela's house. The woman keeps her place just like her office—perfect. Everything in its place. She even freaking *dusts*.

Even Naomi's house would have been better. Her daughter—Briar—tries to be part of our discussions, which means we have to censor ourselves, but if I don't have to clean, it would be worth it to refer to our main characters' coital scenes as "dancing."

Briar asked us why our characters liked to dance so much. Angela and I laughed so hard we were in tears, while Naomi calmly explained that we liked to read books about ballet. Her ability to lie with a straight face is next level.

And now we also refer to sex as "ballet" or "dancing" and, occasionally, dating as "ballet class."

By the time I open the door to find Naomi holding a bottle of wine, I've managed to clean up most of the clutter. Some has been shoved into a closet, but the house looks passable.

Plus, the girls know me. It's not like they think I'm a clean freak like Ang. They accept me anyway.

"Come on in!" I say, taking the wine.

Naomi slips off her loafers and tucks a strand of her chestnut hair behind one ear, even though her chin-length hair is in a perfect bob to begin with.

It's prosecco—one of my favorites, and our usual for journal club. We love to experiment with different juices to create the ultimate mimosa.

She follows me to the kitchen, where we uncork the wine and fill the three waiting glasses halfway.

"Did Ang say what she was going to bring tonight?" Naomi asks, sipping from her glass while I pull the bottle of orange-guava-papaya-pineapple juice from the fridge.

"She didn't say, but I'm hoping it's something salty. I'm craving chips or pretzels or something." I fill each glass to the top with the juice. "Cheers."

Naomi and I clink glasses as the doorbell rings, followed by the sound of the front door opening.

"I'm here!" Angela's voice travels through the house.

Her footsteps pad along the hallway to the kitchen in the back. She and Naomi have both spent so much time here that they treat my place like home, which I love.

I'd say I treat their houses like my home, but I try to be on better behavior there than I am in my own place.

We settle in my living room, each of us with a glass in hand. Angela's veggie tray sits on the coffee table between us. It's not chips, but there's ranch dip, and the carrots are crunchy, so it's a close second.

"So what did we think of the book?" I ask, looking between the two of them.

We've been reading a book by Sierra Simone, and let me just say, there was a lot of "dancing" involved.

"Forget the book. Tell us about the guy." Angela points at me with her wineglass.

Naomi swallows her mouthful of carrots. "Oh. Yes. Details, please. I can't believe you told Ang before you told me."

"She didn't tell me shit."

They both stare at me.

I take a sip of my mimosa—orange-guava-papaya-pineapple makes a great mimosa, by the way—and prepare for a dramatic retelling of my wild night.

The late August temperatures are deceiving, a perfect seventy-five degrees and barely a cloud in the sky as we make our way across the quad to the student union for lunch.

This is the key time for campus tours for prospective students—June through August. The admissions office packs them in, offering a view of the campus through the lens of summer vacation and near-perfect weather.

We'll have another few weeks of this before it gets cold, then colder.

It's always mystified me that high school students do their college tours during the summer. I mean, I know that's when they're on vacation, and it's convenient for their parents, obviously.

But it seems almost...disingenuous, somehow. Unless you go to college in a tropical climate, it's going to be cold for most of the school year. Shouldn't you visit your prospective home for the next four years at a time that's representative of how your life will be?

The student union is a hub of campus activity. Right now, before most students come back for the semester, it seems almost dull compared to the usual bustle. There are a handful of upperclassmen here early—orientation leaders, student government representatives, RAs. They cluster around the larger tables, the ones with booth seating.

Angela, Naomi, and I head directly to our favorite spot—The Panini Press.

"What can I get you?" the shaggy-haired worker asks.

He keeps his eyes on the sandwich fixings, not looking up at us.

"Turkey and provolone with avocado," I say.

It still feels strange to order with such abandon, to not worry about my weight the way I did when I was modeling.

"Chicken and pesto," Naomi says. "Extra pesto, please."

"Ham, Swiss, roasted red peppers, and tomatoes," Angela adds. "And three bags of chips and three fountain drinks."

"Three combos, coming right up."

Naomi and I pull out our wallets, but Angela waves us off.

"I've got this one," she says.

I bump her hip with mine as I grab two bags of Lay's. Yes, I got the baked ones. Old habits die hard.

"Thanks, lady," I tell her.

Shaggy sets three empty cups on the counter, pushing them toward us.

"Diet Coke?" I ask, picking up the cups and handing one to Naomi.

"You know it." Angela waits for the paninis while Naomi and I fill the cups—two with Diet Coke for me and Angela, one with lemonade for Naomi.

She says soda rots your teeth, and she's married to a dentist, so she's probably right.

We carry the drinks to a table against one wall and set them down just as Angela arrives with three paninis.

I reach for the chips first, needing the crunch and the salty goodness, while Naomi reaches for her panini.

"So did I tell you what Josh and I did this weekend?" Naomi asks around a mouthful of food.

Angela's eyes widen. "No. Is it dirty?"

Naomi grins wickedly. "Well. On Friday night, we..."

I chew the last bite of my panini slowly as Naomi shares the details, most of it in code, because undergrads aren't much better than five-year-olds, at least when it comes to overhearing things and sharing them in inappropriate situations.

I let my gaze wander around the food court section of the student union to people watch. I especially love checking out what people are wearing, or eating, or how they walk, and seeing if I can guess which academic department they belong to.

The table of men in tweed jackets typing on laptops—English department. Professors working on their novels.

A woman scratching at a stack of papers with a pencil—Math. Probably theoretical, or maybe Physics.

Two dark-haired men in jeans, walking toward the panini station. One of them is from the Econ department, but the other I don't recognize at first. Blue button-down shirt. I sip at my soda, thinking. He looks too casual for the sciences. Too down-to-earth for departments like Physiology or Religion or even Sociology.

God, I love puzzles.

I'm still trying to figure him out when he turns. I get a good look at his face, and it's like a gut punch.

I'm no longer listening to Naomi's story. I can barely hear her over the ringing in my ears.

Because even though I still don't know what department he belongs in, I can easily place him.

It's the guy from the bar.

My stand-in boyfriend.

My one-night stand.

The one I was never supposed to see again.

Heat rises in my cheeks as I remember our night together.

How he played my body effortlessly.

How I let him take control.

It was erotic and hot as hell in the moment, but that was when I thought I'd never see him again.

What is he doing here?

4
____

BLAKE

I take a deep breath as I look up at the weathered brick building. This is it. I clench and unclench my fists, making sure my hands aren't shaking. That's the last thing I need on my first day.

I need a lot of things today, in fact, that nerves would only mess with. I need to meet my new colleagues. Some of them were at the dinner when I was interviewing, but that was a while ago, and not all of the names stuck. More important than that even, I need to get my office in order, and most important of all, I need to iron out my lesson plans for the semester.

I have to give the students a syllabus on the first day with some information about the class I'm teaching on Game Theory this semester. Which means, of course, that I have to know some information about what I'm going to teach this semester.

It shouldn't be too hard, I suppose. I've been teaching this class as a TA for like four years while I was doing my PhD.

But it's different when it's your own class.

I pull open the heavy door of the Economics building and step inside. The hallway is empty, and a door marked *OFFICE* is to my right. I stick my head in.

"Hi. I'm Blake Grantham," I start.

The woman sitting at the desk jumps up, and I wish she'd stayed seated, even if her movement gives me something to focus on other than her bright-blue eyeshadow and false eyelashes.

"Oh, Professor Grantham!" she says, her voice almost unnaturally high-pitched, making me wonder if she's making it that high on purpose. "It's *so* good to meet you. I've heard such great things!"

I'm trying to focus on her face rather than on her outfit, which seems more appropriate for a nightclub than for a receptionist in a college Economics department. A tight leopard-print skirt leaves nothing to the imagination, and if I still wasn't sure about the goods, the fact that her bright-pink blouse is unbuttoned one more notch than appropriate would give me a clue.

"Uh. Thanks." I'm not sure how else to respond, especially since she hasn't introduced herself.

I'm assuming she's the secretary, but you know what they say when you assume.

"Let me show you your office! You're right on the first floor. *So* convenient! I can just bring your mail right on over as soon as I get it."

"Great." I can already tell I don't want to encourage her.

She slides past me into the hallway. "Now, just follow me. I'm Randi. And if you ever need anything —*anything* at all—don't hesitate to ask, okay?"

Her voice is starting to give me a headache.

"Mmm-hmm," I say noncommittally.

Randi slides a key into a door and turns the knob. "This is all yours!" she trills, pushing the door open.

It's underwhelming, but it's a start.

"Thanks, Randi." I hold my hand out for the key, which she passes over. "I'll let you know if I need anything."

"Anytime!" She bats her eyelashes before sashaying back down the hallway.

I look around the space. It's not huge, but it's a damn sight better than the shared post-doc office I'm used to. It's a blank canvas, with white walls and standard campus-issued furniture. It just needs some organization and maybe a few things to add personality, and it'll be solid.

I scratch my jaw as I turn in a circle, taking it in. If I turn the desk that way, set it in the middle of the room, I can sit behind it and have students sit in these chairs. I'll just have them face the desk on the other side. My stacks of textbooks will go nicely on the shelves there. Maybe pick up a filing cabinet to hold important papers.

The chair behind the desk looks like it's seen better days. I sit down, testing it.

It sinks all the way to its lowest setting.

I raise the seat and try again. The chair sinks.

I mentally add *buy new desk chair* to my to-do list.

A knock on the door has me turning around.

"Hello?"

The guy standing in my doorway looks to be about my age, with jeans and a button-down that match mine other than the sleeves—mine are buttoned at the cuff, while his are unbuttoned and rolled up. Even the blue color is similar.

He takes one step into my office and holds out a

hand, a smile stretched across his face. "Hey, man. I heard you joined the faculty. Blake Grantham, right? I'm Jeremy Williams. Macroeconomics."

I return his handshake. "Great to meet you. I'm teaching Microeconomics this semester along with my Game Theory class. Just got here and trying to figure out how to set this place up."

Jeremy holds up a finger. "One suggestion. Write down everything you need—chair, office supplies, furniture, all that—and give it to Randi all at once. Otherwise, she'll be in here all the time."

I chuckle. "I got that sense."

Jeremy looks around the office. "Not a bad spot here. Nice view of the quad. Need help moving stuff around?"

I look at the desk and shrug. "Sure, if you're up for it. I was going to get this desk turned like..."

I gesture with my hands, indicating the direction I want the desk to face—sitting in the center of the room, so when I sit behind it, I'm in direct view of the door.

"Got it." Jeremy steps farther into the office and grabs a corner of the desk while I roll my shirtsleeves up. "So, did Randi already grill you on your dating life?"

I cringe. "No. Thank God."

He lets out a low whistle. "Well, get ready. That cat has her claws out one hundred percent of the time, just waiting to sink them into the next unsuspecting guy."

I grunt as we shove the desk into place. "She's got no chance with me. Not anything on her, but I'm just not in a place for a girlfriend right now."

"She won't care." Jeremy straightens and pushes a hand through his hair. "I told her the same thing for a year. She didn't back off and leave me alone until I told her I was gay."

A snort escapes from me. "Well, that's one way to get a woman off your back."

He nods. "And since I'm bi, it's not entirely a lie. Showing up at a department reception with my boyfriend definitely helped get her off my case permanently." He looks around the office. "I like the desk this way. Need help with anything else?"

***

"How are you settling in?" Randi's voice cuts into my concentration.

"Fine, thanks," I say.

I don't look up. Yeah, it's rude, but this is the fourth time she's been in here. I'm hoping if I partially ignore her, she'll get the hint.

So far it hasn't worked.

After Jeremy and I moved the desk, we moved the bookshelf and found a desk chair that'll work well enough until I get a new one. We left the broken one in the study lounge.

I've been hunched over my laptop, working on this syllabus for a few hours. And every time I think I'm getting into the groove, Randi appears. It's like she has this sense that I'm actually focused, and she needs to insert herself.

"Are you planning to take a break for lunch anytime soon?"

I shrug. "Not really. I'll let you know."

"Okay."

I look up to see her twirling a piece of bleached-blonde hair around her finger. "Thanks, Randi."

How do you tell someone to leave without seeming like a dick?

"Let me know if you need anything! I'll stop by to check if you need coffee or anything, okay?" She wanders off down the hall, and I breathe a sigh of relief.

I wish she'd let me just get my own coffee. I'll have to see if Jeremy has any advice about that one.

My phone vibrates, and I swipe it open to see a new text from Jeremy, who programmed his number into my phone after he helped move my desk.

JEREMY

I'm headed to the student union for lunch. Want to join?

Sure. How do I get out without going by Randi? She invited me to lunch and I told her I had to do work.

crying laughing emoji

Grab your laptop and head toward my office. Opposite end of the hall from the entrance. There's another exit down this way.

I close my laptop and tuck it into my messenger bag, then I slip the strap over my shoulder. I stick my head out my office door and look both ways. Coast clear.

I pull the door shut and head down the hallway, peering over my shoulder to make sure Randi doesn't catch me.

Jesus, it's my first day of my first real, adult job, and I'm sneaking out like I'm playing hooky from high school.

Jeremy is waiting by his office door. He motions

down the hallway, and the two of us creep toward the door like we're afraid of getting caught.

As we step onto the quad, I breathe a sigh of relief. "It's like sneaking out of jail or something. And why the laptop?"

"Plausible deniability. If you do run into her, you just tell her you're headed to the library or to a meeting."

I scratch the side of my jaw. "So am I going to have to do this forever? Maybe agreeing to one date would be easier. Prove we have no chemistry and get her off my back."

Jeremy holds up a finger, shaking his head. "No. Hard no. Trust me. You don't want to end up like Emilio Tavish."

I roll my eyes as we make our way across the lush green lawn of the quad, passing by the massive brick library. "Who's that? Her last conquest?"

From the few hours I've known Jeremy, I've learned that he's a storyteller. Not just the kind of guy who always has a story, but the kind who can take any random event or rumor and turn it into a soliloquy worthy of an Oscar.

"Oh, my sweet child. Let me tell you about Emilio." He flourishes his hand, and I can tell he's picturing a cinematic flashback of some sort. "Emilio, Professor Tavish if you will, was one of the greats. Ivy League educated, brilliant scientist. Recruited by the dean of faculty himself. Anticipated to become a university fixture. There was talk of him being groomed to take over as President of the College one day."

I move to the edge of the sidewalk to allow a group of students to pass us while Jeremy keeps talking.

"First day of the semester, Randi dug her claws into him. Claimed him. Inserted herself into every facet of his day."

"Why didn't he just tell her to go away?" I pull open the door of the student union.

Jeremy pauses and gives me a long look. "Why didn't you?"

I cringe internally. He has a point.

"Exactly," Jeremy says. "He was being nice. And do you know where being *nice* got him?"

I have a feeling I'm about to find out.

Jeremy leads us to a counter with a sign declaring it *THE PANINI PRESS* and orders a panini, then he turns back to me while a guy who looks like he needs a haircut starts making the sandwich. He reminds me of Miller, with his hair in his eyes.

"She started showing up all the time. In his office.

In his classes. Even in the faculty parking lot by his car."

"Yikes." I order a turkey and cheese panini with avocado. "So she turned into a stalker?"

He nods emphatically as he takes his order and places it on a tray. "So he decided to agree to one date. Just to 'get her off his back,' as you said."

This is starting to sound like the opening for a story on *Unsolved Mysteries*. Also, I'm starting to wonder if there's more than a little creative editing on Jeremy's part. If this all really happened, Randi wouldn't have a job.

"And he was never heard from again?" I take my panini along with a bag of chips and follow him to a table.

"What? No." Jeremy sets his lunch down and pulls out a chair. "He told her he didn't want to go out again, but she didn't listen. It changed nothing. So she just kept hanging around him like before. He couldn't get anything done, and he eventually got so fed up that he switched jobs."

I unwrap my panini and take a bite, then I chew and swallow. "Damn, these are good. I'm definitely having lunch here every day." I swallow another bite. "So where does the disgraced Professor Tavish work now?"

Jeremy pops a chip into his mouth and chews. "Oh. He works at Harvard now."

I snort. "Talk about anticlimactic."

"It's the principle." Jeremy looks at something over my shoulder.

I start to turn, but before I can see who's there, a hand lightly settles on my shoulder. "Blake?"

5

KAT

My heart pounds in my chest, and my palms are sweaty.

He turns around, and his blue eyes take me off guard. It's a rare combination with his dark-brown hair, and in the low light of the bar and the bedroom, it wasn't all that noticeable.

But in the bright light of the student union, they're striking, and I'm momentarily speechless.

His eyes widen for half a second before his face creases into a smile, lines at the sides of his eyes appearing. "Kat. Hi."

The nickname snaps me back into focus. "Um. Kathleen, actually."

I hated the name as a child. It seemed old-fashioned, or maybe just too adult for an eight-year-old. I still prefer Kat, but at work, I'm Kathleen.

"Kathleen Milas. I teach Anatomy and Physiology in the Biology department."

A look of surprise crosses his features before he recovers and holds his hand out. "Nice to officially meet you. Blake Grantham. Economics and Game Theory."

I can't say I'm not impressed. Game theory is a complex subject. But beyond coming over and introducing myself, I hadn't really thought through this exchange.

"Shoot, I've got to run," his companion says, shoving the last bite of his panini into his mouth. "Hi, Kathleen. Good to see you."

He holds his hand out to me as well.

"Good to see you too, Professor Williams," I say smoothly, shaking his hand.

We've been on the same faculty committee for four years. He's a nice enough guy, although we've never gotten to know one another more than in passing.

I'm guarded with colleagues, especially the men. Getting the once-over from people who are supposed to respect you as a colleague wears on you after a while. I've learned to just keep a wall up, make sure they know that I'm here to work, not to be eye candy.

It translates into a bit of a reputation for being a hard-ass when it comes to the students, but that's a price I'm willing to pay.

Plus, I know what they call me behind my back, and trust me, I'd rather be known as an ice queen than Hot Prof.

"Hey, why don't you take my seat? Blake has time to chat, right?" He speaks around the food that's still in his mouth as he pulls on a tweed jacket, despite the eighty-five-degree day. "Have fun."

Blake, at least, doesn't look as horrified at the impromptu lunch date as I feel. In fact, he has a smile on his face as he studies me.

His perusal is different than I'm used to. He's focused on my face, his gaze never wandering south, and his expression suggests that he sees me as a puzzle, something that captures his interest, rather than a conquest.

Maybe it's because he's already seen me naked.

"Great idea. Why don't you join me, Kathleen? I'd love some company."

"Oh, I'm sitting with my"—I gesture over to the table, realizing as I do that Angela and Naomi are walking out of the student union—"friends. But they just left, so I suppose I can join you."

So much for them being my backup. Worst wingmen ever. Wingwomen?

Shoot, that was awkward. I've officially lost the upper hand. If I ever had it to begin with.

I take a deep breath. Time to regain control. It's one thing to let Blake take control in the bedroom—it was freaking hot, if I'm being honest. But this is my career. I never would have gone home with him if I'd known we were coworkers.

The last thing I need is this man opening his big mouth and telling everyone about our one-night stand. Especially about the part where I let him have control.

I can just imagine the field day the students would have with that. It may be even more damaging than if they found out about the modeling jobs I took on to pay for college.

"So, Professor Kathleen Milas. How long have you worked at Ardmore College?" Blake takes a bite of his panini.

I fold my hands in front of me, realizing I left the last bite of my own lunch on the other table. I glance over. It's gone, which means one of the girls must have tossed it. Or stolen it. My money is on Naomi, since she hates wasting food.

"I've been here for five years."

He wipes his mouth on a napkin. "Five years? Impressive. You don't look—"

"Old enough?" I ask.

I get that a lot. Sunscreen, retinol, and finishing college in three years will do wonders. But at thirty-two, I'm plenty old to be where I am.

He laughs. It's a deep, rumbling laugh that vibrates through me. "Bet you hear that one all the time, huh? Sorry. They say you should never ask a woman her age. I should have known better."

My stomach rumbles. I touch a hand to my abdomen, trying to force it to be quiet, but Blake pushes his bag of chips across the table.

"Here. Help yourself."

I take one and pop it into my mouth, chewing slowly.

Blake tilts his head as he studies me. "So. Five years in. You must have some good advice for a newbie like me."

I swallow and dart my tongue out to catch the crumb at the edge of my lips. "I'll do my best. Is this your first teaching job?"

He leans back in his chair slightly and holds his arms out to both sides. "First real job altogether. Age thirty-seven."

I laugh despite myself. "First job?"

He shrugs. "Took some time between high school and college, then I took a little break, then grad school and a post-doc. And now here I am."

I'm curious about the break. Plenty of people take time between college and grad school, but almost all of them have a job during those years, and Blake said that this is his first real job. What was he doing during those years if he wasn't working between college and grad school? And what was he doing between high school and college?

Blake leans in toward me like he's sharing a secret. "Do you know the Econ department secretary?"

I know of her, that's for sure. Everyone knows about Randi. She's made no secret of the fact that she's working at the college with the explicit goal of landing a professor.

With her approach to flirting, though, she's likely to land in hot water with HR before she lands a faculty boyfriend.

I don't think anyone's let her in on exactly how much college professors make these days.

"Randi? Sure. You have your first run-in with her?" I reach for another chip.

Despite our one-night stand, the fact that I know exactly what he's packing under those fitted dark-wash jeans, this isn't as awkward as I would have predicted. It's not awkward at all, in fact. Our conversation flows the same way it did that night, like we've known one another for years.

Blake rolls his eyes. "You could call it that. I think she's been in my office four times today."

I crack a smile. "She's a campus legend. One of the frats had a competition a couple years ago to see who could hook up with her first."

He raises an eyebrow as he crushes the foil from his panini into a ball. "How long did it take?"

"All year. She doesn't sleep with undergrads."

It pains me that I know so much about the student gossip mill. I try to stay out of all of that. It's none of my business what the undergrads are doing with their time.

"Interesting." He looks around the student union, his gaze stopping at the gelato counter. "Want dessert? My treat."

"Sure." I'll have to skip dessert tonight, but the gelato here is worth it.

I follow him to the counter, where he looks to me to order first.

I peruse the options but settle on my favorite. "A small vanilla bean, please."

The server scoops it into the bowl and passes it over while Blake studies the flavors, rubbing his chin.

"What do you suggest?"

I take a dainty bite of the sweet dessert. "I stick with vanilla, but from what I've heard, you can't go wrong with any of them."

He orders a chocolate, and we carry our bowls back to the table. I study him as he digs the little plastic spoon into the gelato and takes a huge bite.

"Oh my God," he says, holding his hand in front of his mouth. "This is delicious. I'm going to gain five pounds from this stuff. I won't be able to stay away."

From what I've seen, the man doesn't need to worry about his body at all. His Oxford shirt is tight across his broad shoulders. Heat creeps over my body, remembering the way he pushed me up against the wall, his muscles pressing into me.

No. We are not reminiscing, and we are not ogling the coworker. Focus, Kat.

"It's dangerous," I agree. "I try to bring my lunch so I'm not tempted every time I come in here."

Also so I can work at my desk while I eat it.

He takes another large bite before he sticks his spoon into the remaining gelato and looks at me while he wipes his mouth. "So. Any advice on Randi? Seems like everyone has a story about her."

"No good stories here, sorry." I take another delicate bite and think. "I don't spend a lot of time in that building, though. All I know is that she's perennially on the prowl."

He pulls on the back of his neck. "I don't want to be a dick. But I want to find a way to make it clear I'm not interested."

I shrug. "I don't think interest matters. She'll just try to convince you." I dab at my lips with a napkin. "This is another time it's good to be in a relationship. You have a prop to explain why you're off-limits."

Like at the bar, I silently add, but it's clear from his expression that he knows what I mean.

And he knows that we're not talking about that night because we both agreed. No strings.

I peer at my watch. "I should really get going. I have a lot of work to do to get ready for the semester."

And I need to get away from you before I slip and say something stupid.

Blake nods. "Thanks for joining me for lunch after Jeremy bailed. It's always nice to get to know a new coworker."

I breathe a sigh of relief, grateful that he's seeing it my way. We're pretending the thing in the bar, the thing where I was *Kat, damsel in distress,* never happened, and that our night of mind-blowing sex was a figment of our imaginations. That he only knows me as *Professor Kathleen Milas, coworker.*

I nod briskly. "Anytime. Glad to get to know you."

I offer my hand and give him a firm handshake.

He gives me another grin, one that involves his whole face. "Maybe I'll see you around campus."

6

BLAKE

I close my office door and take three deep breaths to calm myself before I open my eyes, centering myself. Time to focus.

While I know I need to lean into the social aspects of teaching at a university, networking with colleagues and all that, I really, *really* need to get this syllabus done. I don't have time for gelato dates and gossip, even if it's with the woman I've been unable to get out of my mind.

Actually, *especially* if it's with the woman I've been unable to get out of my mind.

On the plus side, it could have been way more awkward. Kat—*Kathleen*—didn't bring up the bar, or the fake girlfriend thing, or the night we shared. It was a cordial conversation between colleagues. Which is good, because that's all I'm looking for right now. Colleagues. Friends. The occasional one-night stand, which will never go beyond one night.

As I told Kat, this is my first real job. Playing poker professionally between college and grad school doesn't really count, even if I made enough to pay tuition the first few years.

At thirty-seven, most people my age are firmly established in their careers and ready to settle down. I'm behind the ball here. And not just because of my time between college and grad school; I started college late, so my entire twenties and thirties have felt like I'm catching up with everyone my age.

Once I'm established as a professor, settled into my niche, maybe I'll look for a relationship or someone to settle down with.

Maybe.

Because getting into a relationship only leads to complications and messy emotional entanglements. Just look at my buddies. They may be in love, but their relationships have upended their lives. And I've seen relationships end up with far worse consequences, too.

Better to focus on what I can control.

A knock at the door startles me.

I step forward, out of the way, and pull it open to find Jeremy.

"How do you know Kathleen?" he asks, without any preamble as he steps into my office.

Doesn't this guy have his own work to do? I mean, I don't mind him visiting, and I could use a friend here. It just seems like he's spent more time in my office than his own today. It makes me curious if the workload gets easier as you get more established. I'm sure he doesn't have to create his syllabus from scratch, or plan out his courses, since he's taught them for years.

"She's a friend of a friend." The lie comes easily, thanks to years of bluffing at poker games.

And it's not entirely a lie. She's an acquaintance, which is the same thing as a friend of a friend in my book. She just happens to be an acquaintance with whom I had the best night of sex in my life.

"You interested?"

I give him a long look. "In?"

He looks into the hall behind him, then he closes the door and steps closer to me. "Dating her. Hooking up. Whatever the kids are calling it these days."

I sit down at my stolen desk chair and lace my fingers together. "No. I'm interested in my career. I don't have time for a relationship."

He looks disappointed. "She's hot. Intimidating as

fuck, but hot. If I break up with my boyfriend, maybe I'll work up the courage to ask her out."

"I have work to do."

He holds up his hands in mock surrender. "Noted. No gossip until work is done."

He offers a mock salute as he exits my office.

I sense Jeremy and I will be good friends. Mostly because he doesn't seem to be offended at the blunt way I just kicked him out of my office.

In general, my friends self-select. I'm a blunt bastard, and I don't pull my punches. It takes a special kind of person to put up with that, usually someone who doesn't take themselves or me too seriously. I'm glad Jeremy seems to be that type.

I pull my laptop out of my messenger bag and set it on the desk. Time to get this syllabus done.

I make it through the first paragraph, outlining the days of the week and times the class will meet—information the students already have before they even set foot in my classroom, but a standard thing to include—before there's another knock at the door, interrupting my concentration.

I try not to let my irritation show. At this rate, I'm not going to get anything done.

I look up, my jaw tightening when I see Randi. She's undone another button of her shirt so it opens practically at the same level as her breasts. One more button and her tits will be spilling out.

"Hi there," she purrs. "Just seeing if you need anything. Coffee, maybe?"

What I need is silence. "I'm all set."

"Just let me know!" She gives me a flirty wave as she bats her eyelashes, disappearing down the hall.

I look down at my watch. The leather of the band is cracked, but I can't bring myself to replace it. It's one of the few things I have from my dad. It still works perfectly, though, and the time displayed tells me the afternoon is getting away from me with all of these interruptions.

Sighing, I scrub a hand down my face as I look at the pile of papers on my desk. I've been here almost five hours today. And all I've gotten done is reiterating the schedule for this class.

A headache starts to form at my temples. Maybe coffee would help, but the idea of voluntarily facing Randi negates any benefit the caffeine may offer.

I rummage in my bag for the Advil and pop two into my mouth, swallowing them dry. I stare at my computer screen and wait for the effect to kick in.

Thirty minutes later, my headache has waned, but my focus is still lagging. I've managed to get the schedule for the exams into the syllabus, so that's something, but there's a lot left to do.

I stand up and stretch. At this point, the need for coffee supersedes my need to avoid the department secretary. Plus, who hides from a coworker? I'll just be my usual blunt self and tell her the truth.

I make my way down the hall, University of Pennsylvania mug in hand. It feels like cheating since I'm working at Ardmore now, but this is the mug that got me through a lot of long nights in grad school. Maybe I should pick up an Ardmore mug to use while I'm here and put the mug from my alma mater on a shelf. I make a mental note to drop by the campus bookstore when I have a minute to check out their selection.

I brace myself as I walk past Randi's office and into the break room that holds the coffee maker, and stare in dismay at the empty pot.

Who takes the last cup of coffee and doesn't make more? Not cool, whoever did that.

I pull open drawers and cabinets to find what I need and get to work. Filter, coffee grounds, water. I dump the old grounds and refill the machine. As it starts to brew, I lean against the counter and breathe in the heavenly scent of coffee.

"Oh, I would have done that for you!"

And there she is.

Randi teeters into the break room on her too-high heels. It's interesting that Kat wears heels that are practically as high as the ones Randi has on, yet on Kat, they look classy. Sophisticated.

On Randi, they don't quite hit that mark. It's a cross between a hooker and a toddler playing with their parent's high heels, tottering around unsteadily.

"No problem. I don't mind making coffee." I shrug, hoping she'll take the hint and disappear.

She gives me a wink. "Maybe someday you'll be making coffee for me."

I furrow my brows. "I'm making coffee now. Do you want some?"

She crosses the room and sets a hand on my chest, her blood-red nails practically digging into me, and speaks into my ear. "I meant you'd bring me coffee in bed."

Abort mission. We need to shut this down.

I clear my throat. "Randi, I'm flattered, but I'm not interested."

She smiles coyly. "Oh, I'll change your mind eventually."

This woman has balls. I'll give her that.

"I'm in a relationship. I'm not looking for anything else." Maybe that will work.

She still doesn't look fazed. "With who?"

I resist the urge to correct her grammar, needing this conversation to end. "Professor Milas."

Shit. That popped out because she's in my head.

But Randi takes a step back, nodding slightly. "Oh. Sorry."

As she flees the room, I wonder if this may not be such a bad thing. Maybe I can keep up the ruse, and Randi will leave me alone.

The coffee pot gurgles as it spits out the hot beverage. I fill my mug and take a sip, thinking. This could work.

***

"You did *what*?" Jeremy asks.

His expression suggests that this is the dumbest idea I've ever had. Or perhaps the dumbest idea anyone's ever had, since he hasn't known me very long.

"Close the door."

He steps into my office for the third—fourth? I'm losing track—time today and closes the door behind him. "Start over. You told Randi you were dating someone?"

I shrug, closing my laptop. I've managed to finish the syllabus for Game Theory, at least. It just needs a quick proofread before I mail it out to the class.

"I told her I was dating someone. And therefore off-limits."

"And she just took your word for it? Man, I'm impressed. She didn't buy that excuse when I tried to use it." He flops into one of the chairs in front of the desk.

I cringe. "Well, not exactly. She asked who it was."

"And?"

I pull at the back of my neck. "Well, I had lunch with Kathleen Milas. Remember? And..."

Jeremy sits up straight. "Oh, no. No, you didn't."

"I told her I was dating Professor Milas." In the relative safety of my office, this move now seems colossally stupid.

The campus rumor mill is a real thing. The last thing I want to do is put Kat in an awkward position.

"Uh, I hate to break this to you, but you fucked up. Royally. It was nice knowing you, kid." He slaps the top of my desk for emphasis.

"I'll figure something out."

He shakes his head. "No, man. Seriously. You

don't get it, do you? You're new here, but you're a man. You're going to get taken seriously no matter what. She doesn't get that luxury. You think her looks are an asset? They're a liability in a career like this. And if you don't pull it off just right, it'll get spun into something damaging."

It feels like I just got splashed in the face with cold water as I realize what he's saying. This could impact her—*will* impact her—more than it will me. And I didn't even give her a say in my stupid lie.

I stand up and pace in the small area between my desk and the window. "Fuck. *Fuck*. How do I fix this? It seemed like such an easy solution. I just wanted Randi off my back."

Jeremy looks thoughtful as he scratches his chin. "Well, it seems like you have two choices."

"And they are?" My voice comes out higher than I intend, the panic taking over.

I've been at my first real job for less than one day, and I've potentially ruined someone's career. Life. Everything. Maybe mine, too.

Fuck.

Perhaps I'm being a little dramatic, but even the short time I've spent with Kat has made it clear that she's someone who takes herself seriously. She's cultivated an image that she sticks to, and it's easy to see why, in the cutthroat ivory tower of academia. I can't imagine she's ever been at the center of a campus scandal.

"One, you come clean to Randi. Tell her you lied. That you're not dating Professor Milas. That you said it as a joke or whatever. She's going to take some convincing, and it might not actually reverse the damage if she's already spreading gossip."

A pit forms in my stomach.

"What's the second option?" *Please, please be better than the first one.*

"You make it true. Convince Professor Kathleen Milas to be your girlfriend."

7

KAT

I tap the stack of papers against the desk to straighten them, then I slip them into a manila folder and slide it into the filing cabinet. Done.

I look around my office, nodding. Everything's in its place, other than the clock that has somehow tilted to the side. I reach up to straighten it, but I can't quite reach.

"Do you have a minute?"

The deep voice startles me, and I almost lose my balance as I spin to see Blake closing my office door behind him. Of course he'd be the one to walk in as I almost fall over.

Smooth, Kat.

"Can I help you?" I run my hands over my skirt, straightening it as I make sure it hasn't ridden up.

He strides across the office until he's standing next to me, then reaches up easily and adjusts the clock, making me realize again just how tall he is.

At five foot ten, I'm as tall as lots of men. I'm not used to being towered over. It's unsettling, somehow. It makes me feel like we're not on a level playing ground, literally, and I hate this feeling.

Is this what short women feel like all the time?

"I have to talk with you." He steps back around me and takes a seat in one of the chairs I have for students who come to my office hours.

I sit down in my desk chair, grateful for the large piece of wood between us. "I see. What can I do for you?"

I didn't expect to see him in my office, but it's not like the location is a secret. Everyone's office location is in the faculty directory. Ideally, though, it's so students know where to go for office hours. Not so we can drop in on one another.

He looks supremely uncomfortable. It's a far cry from the confident man I met in the bar and the one I saw in the student union only a few hours ago.

He clears his throat. "I have a confession."

I lift my eyebrow.

"And I would like to say, first, that I didn't think it

through, and I'm hoping to make things right here." He pulls at the back of his neck.

I give him a nod to continue. No use reacting until I have all the information.

"Uh, I told Randi. You know, the department secretary, the one who works in my building. The one who's always hitting on the professors."

"Yes, I know Randi. What did you tell her?" This is getting weird, if it wasn't already.

"I told her you were my girlfriend."

"You did *what*?" I say, louder than I intend to, then I gather myself. It takes several deep breaths to push down the anger in my chest. "I'm sorry. What exactly did you do?"

He winces. "I was trying to get her to back off. And we'd just had lunch, so you were the first person I thought of. And you said that thing about how it would be easier to be in a relationship."

I force my jaw to relax, because I've seen my angry face, and it's not attractive. Flaring nostrils, clenched teeth, eyes that look like they're about to shoot lasers.

But Blake might deserve to be on the receiving end of that look, because this is going to ruin everything. All my work to be taken seriously in this field, and I'm going to be taken down by this ass clown.

But I tamp down my rage, because if there's

anything that will ruin my reputation even faster than this rumor going around, it's me flying off the handle and giving them the stereotype of the dumb model.

And I'm not a stereotype. I'm better than that.

I realize I'm unconsciously smoothing my skirt and instead lace my fingers together. "Professor Grantham, this—"

"Blake."

I raise my eyebrow. "I'm speaking, Professor."

His mouth hangs open for a second before he snaps it shut. I hold back my smile, but the look of utter shock on his face makes me happier than it should.

"As I was saying, this could have serious consequences. I'm not sure you thought it out properly."

He waits a second after I finish. "May I?"

I nod.

Blake stands from his chair and paces behind it. "I didn't think at all. I'm aware of that, and I apologize."

I'm impressed. Most people deflect when confronted, or they get defensive. He's owning his mistake.

"But the fact remains that this piece of information is out there. Now, you didn't willingly enter this situation, but we're in this together now, and again, I apologize for dragging you into it." He takes a breath and leans on the back of the chair. "I'd like to propose a solution. One I've actually thought through."

"Mmm?" My spine is ramrod straight.

"I'd propose that rather than a rumor we try to sweep under the rug, leading to speculation about one-night stands and the like, we address this head-on. Acknowledge that we're dating, make it out in the open. People can't gossip about the truth."

They can and they will, but his suggestion makes me pause. He does have a point, I realize. Potential rumors of the two of us having a one-night stand or having dated are more damaging, somehow, than the idea of two adults being in a relationship.

I tap my nails on the desk. "To be clear, are you asking me out?"

He shakes his head. "Not exactly. It's more..." He thinks for a minute. "Remember that night? In the bar? Having me available as a boyfriend was convenient. It helped you out. Right?"

I give him a tight smile. He would have to bring that up, wouldn't he? Just another thing I don't need to be floating around campus.

"It did. Thank you again."

"So this is the same thing. We can help one another out."

I'm not sure this is the same thing at all. This seems like a much different, and much larger, proposition. One that I don't have time for, if I'm going to gun for that promotion.

The deep blue of his eyes is hypnotic, and for a second I want to say yes, just to get to know him better, to spend more time with him, but common sense prevails.

I shake my head. "I can't do that. I'm sorry I can't help you out."

His face falls. "I..."

He looks so lost, so worried for a minute, that I crack. Just a little.

"You don't have to walk back anything with Randi. If it comes up again, just...say we broke up. That you're dating someone else by then."

Blake stands up straight and pulls on the back of his neck. He looks more uncomfortable than I've ever seen him, but to be fair, I haven't known him very long.

"Fair enough. Thanks for hearing me out. My apologies for intruding on your day."

I give him a smile to soften the blow, if that's even possible. "Thank you for understanding."

As he walks out the door, I lean back in my desk chair. I should feel more relieved. But for some reason I can't quite understand, I feel almost disappointed.

I knock on the door of Adam Kashman's office. The dean of faculty is the final say in promotions, and I've worked hard to stay on his good side, even if he is a little turd at times.

"Kathleen. Come in," he says, barely glancing up.

I'm not offended because him not looking up is better than his leering at my chest.

These things bought me a degree. But they're not going to be the thing that buys me a promotion. I'm going to do that on my own.

I close the door behind me as I step into his office and take a seat. "Good to see you, Adam. How was your summer?"

He finishes writing something on the paper in front of him, then he caps his pen and sets it to the side. His gaze dips to my chest and, mercifully, back to my face. "It was fine, thank you. Yours? Did you visit your family?"

"My mother lives in Washington, D.C., but no, I

didn't have a chance to visit. I spent the summer working on my research."

The politics are the worst part of academia. Play the game, make small talk, don't let anyone in too deep.

"It was great," I continue. "I was able to make some good progress on a couple of studies and get one paper ready for publication."

"Good, good." He takes his glasses off and cleans them, one lens at a time. "I'm working on faculty committee assignments for the year. Are you okay staying on the Faculty Affairs committee?"

I smile broadly, ignoring the fact that I've been the only woman on the committee for years and likely will be this year. "Faculty Affairs would be lovely."

Lovely may be overselling it a touch. And no one in their right mind smiles this widely when thinking about their committee assignments. It's another admin task that they add to our already overcrowded plates.

Adam returns my smile. "Great. I'll finalize that later today." He sets his pen on the desk. "Actually, I was wondering if I could ask you something."

"Of course."

He clears his throat. "I know we've always had a good working relationship. I'm wondering if"—he clears his throat again—"you'd like to go out. With me," he clarifies, making the whole thing that much more awkward as he steals another look at my boobs.

I blink at him. His bald spot shines in the fluorescent lights of the office, the comb-over doing nothing to hide the hair loss.

How do I answer that?

Hell no is my first instinct. But it's not only rude but will shoot any chance of a promotion to hell.

Saying yes is committing me to dinner with this man, who I tolerate only because of the power he holds over my career. And if I say yes, the options will be that I'll eventually have to break up with him—see said power over my career—or deal with the people who imply, or say outright, that I slept my way to a promotion.

I suppress a shudder.

"Oh, Adam, I'm flattered. But I'm dating someone." The lie comes out way too easily, and I suddenly understand how Blake found himself in this situation.

The flash of disappointment that crosses his face is gone as quickly as it appears. "Ah. Well, perhaps I should have asked sooner, eh? If you ever break up with him, I'd love to take you out."

I need to get out of this office. "Of course. Thanks

for understanding. Looking forward to working with you on Faculty Affairs this year."

I smile brightly as I retreat, but the smile fades as soon as I'm a few feet down the hall. I walk across the quad, right past the Biology building and toward the building that houses the Econ department.

Because in a matter of hours, everything has changed. It's no longer Blake who needs a favor from me. We need one another now.

Thanks to Angela and the magic of texting, I have Blake's office number by the time I walk past Randi's office into the Econ department. She glares at me from her desk, where she's examining her acrylic nails.

I give her a friendly wave. I'm dating someone in her department, apparently. She'd better get used to seeing me.

Blake is standing in his office, his back to the door. It looks like he's contemplating moving furniture or decorating the bland space. Having seen the lack of decor in his home, my money is on rearranging furniture.

I don't even knock, just walking in and closing the door behind me. "I've thought it over."

He startles. "Hi?"

I pull one of the chairs toward me and sit down, crossing my legs at the ankle. "Your proposition. I've given it more thought, and I'd like to proceed with being your girlfriend. Fake girlfriend."

He stares at me, running a hand over his square jaw. The intensity of his blue eyes would make me squirm if I were anyone else, but he can't intimidate me. I've spent too long in academia to cower in front of men who think they hold some kind of power over me.

He keeps his gaze on me as he crosses to his chair and sits, folding one knee over the other. "What made you change your mind?"

I play his game, folding my hands in my lap as I lean forward. "I've come to the conclusion that it would be mutually advantageous."

And not only that, but he's the one who asked for my help with this first. So agreeing to this arrangement gives me some kind of power, or at least puts us back on level playing ground after our night together. And I've checked the faculty handbook, just to make absolutely certain, and there's no rule against dating a co-worker.

He lifts a brow, and I let out a long sigh. Jesus, he makes it hard to keep up the professional exterior.

"Fine. I met with the dean of faculty, the one who's going to be the decision maker on whether I get promoted this year."

A look of surprise crosses his face. I wait for him to bring up my age again.

Instead, he nods slowly. "That's got to be stressful. Exciting, but a stressful time."

He's surprised me a few times. It should make me wary, but somehow, I'm warming to him.

"It is. Both. Anyway, he asked me out. And I...told him I was in a relationship."

A smile plays at his lips. "Ah. You fell into the same trap I did. But with the dean, not a secretary."

I wince. "Yeah. So at this point, my options are pretty much to join Tinder and hope for the best, or to move forward with...whatever this is."

He crosses his arms over his chest, studying me. "Well, I may have started this thing, but I think it can work out in both our favors. I'm glad to have you on board."

Let's not get hasty. "I think we need a few ground rules, though."

Blake unbuttons his shirt cuffs and rolls the sleeves up to his elbows, one at a time, revealing his corded forearms, and I have a flashback to him doing the same thing in his living room, right before we...

"Fair enough. What were you thinking?" he asks.

"Do you have something to write on?" I look around for a notepad.

Blake reaches into a drawer and produces a legal pad and a pen, which he passes to me.

I scoot the chair closer to the desk and start to make a numbered list.

"One. This is for looks only. No real feelings, no physical touch other than what's necessary to convince our colleagues that this is real."

He nods. "Agreed. And this needs to look like a mature, stable relationship. No other relationships while we're committed to this arrangement. We don't need more rumors."

I can live with that. I'm not focusing on anything but my career right now. I'll have time for a real relationship after I get promoted. Probably.

"We'll need to get to know one another enough to make it convincing."

Blake rubs his jaw. "One dinner a week, two lunches at the student union."

"I'm not having dinner with you. This isn't real."

He shrugs, and I realize that despite my best efforts, I'm not fully in control here. It seems to be a pattern I fall into around this man.

"Or another date of your choosing," he says. "We

need to know one another well enough to make it appear real. And the last thing we need is meetings in one another's offices with the door closed. That'll fuel rumors, too."

Crap. He's right. And if there's one thing I've learned in life, it's that appearances matter. They matter more than reality, in fact. Because what other people see *is* their reality.

"Fine. One date a week, when we're both available. I choose the place."

"Works for me. And two lunches." He points to the paper where I'm listing the rules.

I stop writing, my pen hovering. "Why?"

"Same thing. And appearances. Would two people who are dating never be seen together at work?" He grins, and something melts inside me. "I'll buy you gelato."

I add the rule about lunch in neat lettering. "We'll alternate who buys."

Blake crosses his arms over his chest. "Okay, then."

I cap the pen and push the pad across the table toward him. "Anything else you'd like to add?"

He reads through the short list. "We continue until we both agree it isn't working in our favor."

I shake my head. "No. If one of us wants out, this agreement ends."

He pins me with a stare, those brilliant blue eyes baring my soul. I force myself not to squirm. Back straight, hands still, eyes on his. Deep breaths.

Finally, he nods. "Okay. Either of us can end this agreement."

I pull the paper back toward myself and start to add the new rule.

Blake holds up one finger. "But."

I pause, my pen hovering after the number four.

"We will discuss any end to our agreement. Together. No unilaterally pulling out without a discussion."

"Fine." I add it to the list. "Anything else?"

Blake picks up the paper and reads through it out loud, nodding with each number. "One. No touching other than what's necessary. Two. No other relationships. Three. One dinner at restaurant of Kat's choosing and two lunches at student union, per week. Payer alternates. Four. This agreement may be ended by either party following a discussion between both parties." He looks up at me. "Are you sure you're not a lawyer?"

I wrinkle my nose at the idea. "My mom's a lawyer, and it never looked like fun. All that reading of briefs? I'd never have made it through law school. I like questions where the answer is more cut and dry."

Blake's lips twitch.

"What?" I furrow my brow, going over my answer to figure out what was funny.

"No pun intended?"

"Huh?" I think back on what I said about school, about answers being cut and... *Oh.*

"Cut. Because you dissect things for Anatomy, right?" Blake shakes his head. "Sorry. It's been a weird day."

I can't help it. I let out a snort of laughter. The dad jokes get me every time.

Blake's smile broadens, and the lines at the sides of his eyes crinkle, making him look even sexier, if that were possible. Enough that I manage to pull it together.

This is an arrangement. Nothing more.

I stick my hand out. "Well, then. We have a deal?"

Blake shakes my hand, his large palm gripping mine. "Agreed. Give me your phone number, and we can arrange our first lunch meeting."

I dictate it to him while he keys the numbers into his phone.

"I sent you a text so you have my number." Blake stands and turns toward the door as he slides his phone into the pocket of his fitted pants, making my gaze slide to his ass.

I clear my throat. "Well, then. I'll, um, be in touch."

Blake nods and moves to the door. His hand on the handle, he turns back toward me. "One more rule."

I wait silently for him to add in whatever he thinks he can slip by me.

But what he says is, "No falling in love."

I snort. "Well, no fake dating contract would be complete without that, but don't worry. There's no chance of that."

8

BLAKE

"Annika still needs a date." Addison sets a beer in front of me.

I lift it to my lips and take a sip as I peer at my cards. "And?"

She shrugs. "Just saying."

Maddox knocks on the table to check, staying in the game without upping the ante. It's the safe way to play—usually my method. Stay in for as little as possible until everyone else drops out.

Cam pushes chips into the center of the poker table. "Raise. Addie, I told you he's not going to go for it."

Cam's fiancée pouts. "She's my best friend. And since it's a destination wedding, it's not like there's a bunch of single people coming. She's going to be all lonely without a date."

"I don't need a date." I add my chips to the pot.

A king and queen, suited, is too good a hand to tap out now, especially with the community cards showing a nine, ten, and king. At the very least, I have a pair.

"Everyone needs a date. It's going to be a disaster if you don't have one. Seriously, Blake. This is important." Addie's hands fly into the air in a dramatic gesture.

Cam motions for her to come closer to him and then whispers in her ear, something that calms the brewing storm.

She straightens and nods. "I'll be upstairs."

We wait, silent, as Addie heads up the stairs of their home, and a door closes.

Maddox turns to Cam. "Shit, man. What did you say to her? I swear, you're like the Addison whisperer now. I've never been able to do that."

I snort. Maddox is Addie's older brother and overprotective as fuck. It doesn't surprise me that Addie never listens to him after being told what to do her whole life.

Cam shrugs. "I told her our wedding would be perfect and that she didn't need to worry about it. That I'd make sure my friends don't ruin it."

He levels a stare at me.

I set my cards down and hold up my hands, palms out. "Whoa. I'm not going to ruin anything."

"Damn right you're not," Maddox says, taking a swig of his beer. "That's my baby sister's wedding. It's going to be perfect. Even if she's marrying this guy."

He elbows Cam.

For what must be the hundredth time this week, I miss Miller. We started with a group of five poker buddies, all of us rising in the rankings nationally. Then Lawton left to go to the police academy and gave up gambling with some bullshit about legality. And then last year, out of nowhere, Miller moved to upstate New York for a girl.

At the moment, we're down to the three of us. Me, Maddox, and Cam. And our games are few and far between since Maddox is consumed with his new son and Cam is in the throes of wedding planning.

Not saying I'm innocent here. I'm just as distracted by my career as they are with their family things. It just...feels different.

"So if Addie says you need a date, you need one." Cam points at me with a carrot stick, which further reinforces how far we've fallen. We used to have chips and wings at our poker nights. Now the girls make us veggies and dip. "Annika is great. You'll have fun."

I scowl at him. "I'm dating my coworker. So I'll bring her."

This fake-dating thing is working out in my favor so far. I figure we'll conveniently "break up" just in time for the wedding. Honestly, though, after pretending to date for a week, I'm enjoying her company. It wouldn't be the worst thing in the world to hang out with her in the Bahamas for a few days.

Cam and Maddox exchange a glance.

"When were you going to share that with the class?" Maddox asks with interest.

He takes a slice of cucumber from the platter.

I shrug. "It's new."

And fake, but it seems like it's had some benefits so far. I've managed to dodge Randi's advances as well as a forced wedding date.

Cam deals out the fourth community card and looks to Maddox for his next move. "Well, congrats, man. When do we get to meet her?"

"Soon." Better to stay vague.

I've been surprised by how much I enjoy spending time with her, and I get the sense that the guys will like her, too. But I don't want to commit to anything too soon.

We all check, leaving the pot unchanged. Cam

deals the last card, an ace, giving me nothing but my pair.

"Has Lawton met her?" Maddox asks, checking again.

Technically, they've all met her when we stopped by the table at the bar that first night. But she wasn't my girlfriend then.

I nod and knock my knuckles against the table to check.

"What does he think of her?" Cam raises.

I believe he mentioned she was "hot" after he saw her in the bar, but beyond that? Shit. If they ask him and he admits he's never heard of this relationship, he's going to blow this whole thing.

I match Cam's bet, and we turn over our cards, Cam winning with a pair of aces while I work through the options in my mind.

No time like the present.

I stand from the table, taking my beer with me. "Hey, have Addie sit in for me for a round, will you?"

Maddox raises an eyebrow. "You good?"

"Yeah. Just need to do something. I'll be back in a few."

Cam heads for the stairs to get Addie while I go the opposite direction, toward their galley kitchen. The two of them bought this house a couple months ago, moving in together before their wedding in November, and it's changed a lot already. I look at the newly painted cabinets, a white color that stands out against the deep blue backsplash tile.

You can tell Addie was the one who chose it. Cam is a lot of things, but a decorator isn't one of them. Addie has taken this place to a new level entirely.

Leaning against the freshly installed granite countertop, I pull out my phone, trying to gauge how to explain this to Lawton. My brother can see through most of my bullshit, so I consider telling him the truth. On the other hand, his poker face doesn't extend beyond the game. The man can't tell a lie to save his life, and he could blow my cover.

Yeah, he's getting the same story as the rest of them. Setting my beer on the counter next to me, I type out a text to Lawton.

LAWTON

> Hey, how's it going?

Decent. What's up?

> Just realized I never told you. I'm dating someone.

Good luck.

Huh? I thought you were all blissfully in love or some shit.

Kristina is having trouble adjusting to life in a small town. It's been tough. I'm kind of down on love at the moment.

Are you breaking up?

Hell no. I'm all in with this. I'm going to do whatever it takes to make this work.

Well, good luck to you, too, then.

Tell me more about this new relationship of yours.

You remember the girl from the bar?

What girl?

When you were out here visiting. The girl who needed a fake boyfriend.

Oh, yeah. She was hot. Way out of your league.

He's not wrong.

I'm aware of that, asshole. But somehow we're dating.

For real?

Turns out she's a professor at Ardmore, too. I ran into her in the student union.

Holy shit. Definitely out of your league. Hot AND smart?

I'm bringing her to Cam's wedding.

I should probably let Kat know about this plan.

Nice. Glad you won't be the only one sitting at the singles table.

You bringing Kristina?

That's the plan.

Less than three months. I'm looking forward to it.

I can't wait for the Bahamas. By November it's going to be freezing up here.

I slide my phone back into my pocket. I'm still not sure why Lawton decided to move to High Lonesome, of all places. It's like two miles above sea level, tucked into the Colorado Rockies, and way too far away from pretty much anything.

I mean, they have everything they need. It's got

more than I expected for a town that size, with its own small hospital for the town and its surrounding areas. Maybe it's because in the winter, it gets so cold and icy that the two roads leading into town become impassible at times.

I shiver just thinking about it, picking up my beer from the counter. It gets cold in the Philadelphia area, but nothing like Lawton's described in his new neck of the woods.

Pushing off the counter, I wander back into the living room in time to see Addie sweep a pile of chips toward herself and start stacking them into neat piles.

"I should have you sit in for me all the time," I say, perusing her winnings.

Addie beams at me. "What can I say? I learned from the best."

"Damn straight." Maddox raises his bottle toward her before bringing it to his lips.

"No loyalty at all." Cam crosses his arms over his chest in mock protest.

Addie tosses a chip toward him. "Here. Buy yourself some big-boy pants."

I snort, even though those are my chips.

"All my pants are big-boy pants, baby. How else would I fit my big cock in there?"

Maddox smacks the back of his head. "Keep your

dick in your pants, man. No one wants to hear about that."

"Your sister does." Cam's cocky smirk spreads across his face.

"Dude." Maddox's expression is pained.

It took a while for him to come to grips with his best friend dating his sister. He's accepted it, mostly, but only because he doesn't let himself think about them being intimate.

I'm not sure why Cam insists on poking the bear, but it's fun to watch.

I tip my bottle back, draining the last of the beer. "Moving on. Addie, you want to join?"

Pushing back from the table, she shakes her head. "No thanks. It's fun to beat these two, but I have more wedding planning stuff to do. And I heard you have a date now."

Nodding, I take her place at the table. "That I do."

"Good. It better be someone who fits in with the group. I don't have time for drama."

Addie is nothing but drama, if you believe Cam, but I'll keep that one to myself.

"You'll like her. She's a teacher. You and Annika can bond with her over lesson plans and stuff."

Eyes widening with excitement, she brings her

hand to her mouth. "Ooh, I like her already! What does she teach?"

"Technically, she's a professor. She works with me. Teaches Biology."

Addie eyes me suspiciously. "I thought you were anti-dating or something."

Shrugging, I rack my brain for a response that makes sense. I've made way too big a deal over the last two years about how I'm not looking for love, how I only do one night with a girl and no more. I'll need a good reason to do a complete 180.

"Maybe she's the one," Maddox says, studying my face, like he's going to get any information from my expression.

"Maybe. She's just...different." That sounds believable. Isn't that what people say in romance novels and shit? Like, the right one is *different*, whatever the fuck that means.

I should ask Miller. He's always reading Harlequin romances that his mom sends him.

Addie still doesn't look like she believes me, but she heads for the stairs. "I want to meet her before the big day," she says over her shoulder.

"Noted." Waiting until she's out of earshot, I turn back to the table and pick up the deck of cards. "Now, let's play poker."

This hand is a winning one from the initial deal of pocket cards. Two aces.

I raise on the first round, and I keep raising when the flop shows another ace along with a queen.

When the river's final card is another queen, handing me a full house with aces high, I push my whole pile into the center, going all in.

I'm going to up the ante, raising the bet as much as I can, because I have a winning hand. With the cards, and with Kat.

As long as she keeps playing along.

9

BLAKE

"Welcome to Econ 405, Game Theory." Rolling up my shirt sleeves, I survey the small lecture hall.

There are about thirty students, which isn't too bad for a senior-level class, and for now, they seem invested, all of them with laptops open in front of them or pens poised over open notebooks. The lecture hall is modern, with long continuous surfaces in front of each row of chairs instead of individual desks.

Writing my name on the board, I introduce myself. "I'm Professor Grantham. This is a senior-level class, and make no mistake—it's tough. But my goal this semester is to have some fun while we explore the world of game theory and how its principles apply to things we do every day."

I pick up a stack of papers from the desk at the front of the room and start to pass out the syllabus. "The syllabus has all the information you need regarding required texts, assignments, and exam dates. This is also available in pdf format on the course website. Please note my email address if you have questions, as well as my office hours listed on the front page."

The class is silent as they pass the papers down the rows, and I start to sweat. I need some engagement here, something to get them invested.

Pointing at one of the students in the front row, I say, "What's your name?"

He looks startled. "Uh, Brad. Brad Kingsbury."

"What do you know about game theory, Brad?"

He taps his pen against the desk, thinking. "Well, it's about games, right?"

Smart-ass.

But I nod, encouraging him. "True. It's about how we make decisions, essentially." Sweeping my gaze over the assembled students, I raise one hand in the air. "Who knows how to play poker?"

A few smiles from them as hands shoot into the air. It's easily the majority.

"Good. And to get more specific, who knows Texas Hold'em?"

A few hands drop, but most remain in the air. This is the most popular version of poker played in the United States—by far—so I'm not surprised that almost everyone who knows poker knows this version.

I point to a woman in the third row. "What do you know about Hold'em?"

"Well, you start with two cards each. Then five community cards, dealt out with the first three at once, then the next two, one at a time. And each of the players gets to bet several times."

"Perfect." Turning to the board, I erase my name and write four numbers. "Is it a game for one player, two, or more than that?"

"More than two."

I write *Players* next to the number one.

Turning back toward the class, I point to another student. "What things can players do?"

The students are all leaning forward in their chairs, all of them eager to talk about poker.

The boy I'm pointing to nods as he speaks. "Well, you can stay in or fold. You can match the bet before yours, or you can raise it."

"Exactly." I write *Actions* next to number two. "And how do players know what to do?"

A girl in the back row raises her hand. "Professor?"

I point to her.

"Uh, your, um, fly is open."

Fuck. Just when I thought it was going well. I keep my poker face impassive as I reach down and pull up the zipper. Better to own it, right?

"Thank you. What's your name?"

"Annabelle. Or just Anna." Her face is beet red.

"Thank you, Anna. Do you want to take a stab at my question as well?"

"Players can decide what to do based on information they have. Like, what cards are in their hands and what's showing on the table. And some people are good enough to tell what other players might have based on their expressions or actions."

I turn back to the board and write *Information*. "Perfect. And there's one more piece that plays into all this. What's the reason we play poker?"

"Money!" someone yells behind me.

Turning, I search for the source. There's a boy in the back, a few seats down from Anna, who looks out of place. While the rest of the students are, for lack of a better descriptor, the math nerds you'd expect to see in a high-level Econ class, this guy looks like he got lost while looking for football practice. The smirk on his face is a dead giveaway that he's the one who yelled out the answer.

Focusing on him, I take a few steps up the aisle between the desks. "Money is exactly why we play. Poker is big business, and people can make a killing. There are people who make entire careers out of it."

The jock's smirk fades as he realizes that he got it right, despite his best efforts.

"And the amount of money is a factor in deciding what to do, too, right? You choose how much to raise and how far to push your luck based on the *payoff*." Walking back to the board, I write *Payoff* next to number four, then tap each word. "Players. Actions. Information. Payoff. These are the elements that are needed to determine if something is truly a game."

I stride back to the center of the room, giving all of the students a good view. This is the moment. Either I'll win them over, or I may as well quit now.

"Poker has all of these elements. That's why it's a game, the way we consider it in game theory. Now, in contrast, my wardrobe malfunction. Can that be considered a game?"

A few twitters of laughter, but most of them are hanging on my next words.

"This had a few elements, right? I had the information that my fly was down when Anna so kindly pointed it out. I had actions available to me—

pull it up, or leave it down. Turn away, or zip it up right in front of you. But were there players?"

Heads shake *no*.

"And was there a payoff? Did I stand to win anything?"

More heads shaking.

"So while I had some decisions to make up here, my fly incident does not meet our rigorous definition of a *game*. And once we define a game in this way, we start to see a framework for how we might categorize games. Are they win/lose? Do players work together or against one another? Can another player's actions influence your own, and should they?"

Computer keyboards tap as students start to take notes, and I breathe a sigh of relief. I thought I was ready after helping to teach as a post-doc. If every day is this stressful, I'm not sure I'm going to last the semester, let alone an entire career.

"I would have bought you lunch."

Kat looks up, a panini halfway to her mouth. "No need."

I'm aware she can buy her own lunch, but that's

not the point here. "I'm going to grab something, and then I'll join you. Need anything else?"

Chewing her bite, Kat tilts her head to the side in thought. She swallows and dabs her mouth with a napkin before she finally says, "A Diet Coke, please. Thanks."

It's 11:15, and the food court is mostly empty. It only takes a few minutes for me to order a ham and cheese panini, a Diet Coke for Kat, and a regular Coke for me along with a bag of chips. I carry the load to the table on a tray and set it down in the center.

"How was your first day of class?" Kat asks, reaching for her soda and bringing the straw to her lips.

Unwrapping my panini, I wonder if I should tell her about the wardrobe malfunction. "It went well, I think. Students seemed invested, actually answered questions."

"That's the beauty of teaching senior classes, huh?" Kat sets the drink down and props her chin up with her hand, elbow on the edge of the table. "They're always more interested when it's their major and a class they chose, rather than something they're taking to check off a box and meet a graduation requirement. My Advanced Physiology class is always more fun than the basic A and P that I teach for non-science majors."

I take a bite, savoring the saltiness of the ham as it blends perfectly with the Swiss cheese. With the mustard, it's the perfect blend and my go-to sandwich. The Panini Press makes them better than anywhere else I've tried.

"Is Advanced Physiology your favorite to teach?" I'm curious to know more about this woman.

I need to know enough to convince people we're actually dating, but I find myself wanting to really understand what makes her *her*. Not just favorite color and her birthday, but how she defines herself, what makes her smile. Because her smile is gorgeous when it's real, like right now.

Her face shines as she starts to tell me about her Advanced Physiology class, how she created the lab sessions, how she structures the semester. She comes alive, and I find myself itching to watch her in action. I wonder if she'd let me sit in on one of her classes sometime.

"So, anyway," she says, shrugging. "That's why. It's my baby, that class. And the reviews from students I've had over the past few years have just reinforced that it's probably my best class."

"That's inspiring." I pop a chip into my mouth and chew slowly.

She's opened up, just a little, and I feel like I need to offer something, too.

"I hope I can get to that point with Game Theory. As of right now, all they're going to remember is how my fly was down for part of class."

Kat stares at me for a minute. Then her lips twitch, and a snort escapes before she erupts in laughter.

"Oh my God," she says. "That's too funny. On your first day? How did you figure it out?"

Deadpan, I eat another bite of my panini before I answer. "One of the students raised their hand and told me. It was classic."

Kat wipes a tear from her eye. "Oh, man. Yeah, they'll be telling that story for a while. Thank God they're seniors, right? They'll all be gone by next year, so hopefully the story will leave with them."

Honestly, if the story can make Kat laugh like this, I just might keep on telling it.

Reaching for my soda, I angle my head toward her. "So how about you? Classes go okay? No wardrobe malfunctions on your part?"

Nodding, she sips on her Diet Coke, those perfect lips surrounding the straw. "Went smoothly. It's my sixth time teaching this course, I think? It gets easier with repetition. You don't have to make brand-new lesson plans for every class."

We talk lesson plans for a few more minutes as I finish off the last of my panini and students start to fill up the food court.

Kat glances down at her watch. "I should get back for my office hours. This was fun, Blake."

It has been fun, more than I expected. All of our time together. I figured this would be more of putting on a show, acting for the benefit of people around us, but over the past week, I've found myself actually enjoying Kat's company.

I don't know why I'm surprised. That first night when I met her, I didn't want to stop talking with her. Combined with how gorgeous she is, it's dangerous when you're not looking for a relationship.

Standing from the table, I brush a crumb off my pants. "I'll walk you back."

She considers this but doesn't protest. We walk together past the student mailroom and out to the quad, where the sun is shining brightly and groups of students dot the grass. Brick buildings line the quad, tall and stately, and once again, I'm in awe of how lucky I am to have this job.

"Thanks for the conversation," Kat says, unlocking her office door.

I lean on the doorframe as she steps inside the small room. "Me, too. Lunch again on Thursday?"

Kat pulls out a small book from her purse and flips it open, running her finger down the page. "Thursday, I have a committee meeting at lunchtime, but I can do Friday, if that works for you. 11:15?"

I can't stop the grin that spreads over my face. "Looking forward to it."

10

KAT

"What am I going to do?" I hiss.

I have no idea how I didn't think of this until just before the faculty meeting. This is going to be a disaster.

Naomi shrugs from her usual spot on Angela's office couch, clearly not grasping the gravity of this situation. "I think you can just do what you normally do at faculty meetings. Actually speak up when the dean asks questions and make the rest of us look bad. Why?"

I throw my hands in the air. "But what about Blake?"

Both of them stare at me blankly.

"What does that have to do with faculty meeting?" Naomi peers at me, confused.

"*Everything*." I pace around Angela's office, stepping over the stacks of books that haven't quite made it back to the bookshelf. "I told the dean I was dating someone, and that's why I couldn't go out with him. It seemed like a good option at the time."

Angela picks up a mug from the desk (this one proclaiming *SCIENCE DOESN'T GIVE A FUCK WHAT YOU BELIEVE*) and sniffs the contents before making a face. "I think this coffee is from last week."

I feel like she's not taking any of this seriously. Neither of them are.

Since Blake and I came to our agreement three weeks ago, we've had lunch together in the student union twice a week, and I've had at least one complete meltdown per week about the situation.

In that time, I've learned several things. Normally, during this time of the semester, all I'm focused on is figuring out which students need extra attention and what kind of class I'm looking at. Do they need cold, hard facts, or do they need things to be described with a little more color? I've always prided myself on being able to get a quick handle on the type of class I'm working with.

What I haven't gotten a handle on, though, is how

this arrangement with Blake is going to go. This seems to surprise everyone who finds out, but I don't have a lot of experience dating.

I've spent my entire life focused on getting to the next step—finishing high school, graduating from college, getting my PhD, getting tenure, and meanwhile, working to make each of those things possible. In academics, there's always another stepping stone to reach for, and when your goal is to get to the next one as quickly as possible, it doesn't leave a lot of time for dating.

But Blake is making it...easy, so far. He's serious, especially about his classes, and I respect him for it. But even outside of class, he carries himself with a quiet confidence. It's like he's so sure of his place in the world, how he fits into it, and how he moves through it.

It's exactly the image I try to project to the world, too. But while I put on the armor of confidence, it seems like it's just a part of Blake's personality.

I blow out a breath. "I'm going to get going. I want to get there early."

Angela frowns at the week-old coffee. "I'm going to get a fresh cup. I'll see you there."

I focus on the click of my heels against the

linoleum as I walk through the interconnected buildings. When I mentioned this to Blake and we planned to meet up before the meeting, it all seemed fine. It *was* fine, until today, when I realized that this is a make-or-break moment.

Adam will be there, of course. He runs these meetings. And he's going to put two and two together when he sees Blake and me together.

It has to be convincing. If Adam sees through it, I'm screwed. No promotion—that's a given. They may even take my tenure away or send me in front of the disciplinary board for something like this. I don't know. I've never looked into the etiquette and rules for dating another faculty member because I never pictured being in this situation.

And as my dad always says, it's not what the truth is. It's what people believe the truth is.

Turning the corner, I see Blake leaning against the wall next to the doorway to the lecture hall. His lips turn up when he sees me, and he pushes off the wall to take a few steps toward me.

"Hey, Kat. Kathleen for the purposes of this meeting, right?"

My palms are sweaty.

"Hey. I..." I look up and down the hallway, my gaze lighting on an open classroom door halfway down the corridor, and I point to it. "Can we talk in there?"

"Sure." Blake follows me down the hall, nodding to a math professor who passes us.

He steps past me into the empty room, hands in his pockets. He looks far too relaxed for the shitshow we may be walking into.

Shutting the door, I turn to him. "We need to have our stories straight."

He frowns, his brows knitting together. "I thought we did. You and I met outside of work—not a lie, for the record—and we're dating. No one needs to know that much more about it."

I don't think he understands how much I have riding on this. I need him to be on point, to sell this.

"The dean of faculty runs this meeting. I told him I'm dating someone, remember? He can't see through anything. Everything I've worked for is riding on this, Blake." My stomach twists.

This whole thing was a mistake, wasn't it? One mistake, one misstep. That's all it takes for someone's career to come crashing down. I've seen it before, more than once.

Stepping toward me, Blake places his hands on my upper arms. His touch is light but firm as he holds me in place.

"Kat."

When I don't look up, he says my name again, then takes one hand and presses his fingers under my chin, forcing me to look directly into those intense blue eyes.

"We've got this. Trust me." His deep voice washes over me. "Follow my lead, and I'll take care of everything. Got it?"

I'm momentarily stunned into silence, and all I can do is nod.

Blake presses a kiss to my forehead, muddling my thoughts further. Taking my hand, he leads me out of the classroom and down the hall, where he holds the door open for me to enter the lecture hall before him. His hand brushes against my lower back while we head up the aisle to a seat.

If I thought I wasn't ready to share our little ruse with the full complement of the Ardmore College faculty, I was completely unprepared for how his touch makes me feel. The warmth of his hand settles at the base of my spine.

My breath quickens slightly. I swallow hard, reminding myself that this isn't real.

But Blake is doing a damn good job of selling it.

"Committee assignments are on page three." Adam's voice is muffled by the entirety of the lecture hall flipping through the sheets he passed out to find the referenced page. "Most of you maintain the same assignments from last year, and we appreciate your hard work. If yours changed, I tried to speak with some of you ahead of time."

I know what my committee assignment is—Faculty Affairs—but I turn the page to double check. There it is in black and white—Kathleen Milas, Faculty Affairs. I let out a small sigh of relief.

An elbow nudges me, and I look to my left to see a smile playing at Blake's lips. Following his finger, I see what he's pointing to. A few rows above my name—Blake Grantham, Faculty Affairs.

We're on the same committee. With Adam chairing it, nonetheless.

I inwardly groan. It's not that I'm opposed to spending time with Blake. I'm enjoying it, honestly. A lot.

Leaning toward me, Blake whispers in my ear, "Worried about spending more time with me?"

His lips graze the shell of my ear, sending a zing of electricity through me.

I inhale through my nose, holding my breath for a

few seconds before exhaling, and then repeat the process. I know my body is reacting to his closeness because he's the last man I've been with, and other than him, I've been in a dry spell for a while.

That's all it is. That and hormones and nerve endings. I know enough about physiology to understand exactly what chemical is spiking in my brain right now—dopamine, and possibly oxytocin— so I know better than to fall for it.

But seriously, we're at a faculty meeting. I don't need to walk out of here with wet underwear.

I give him a subtle shake of my head, but from the smirk on his face, he's not buying it.

Another pulse of heat goes through me when his fingers tap my leg, just above the knee. "If you don't mind spending time with me, I have a favor to ask."

His breath is hot against my cheek. He's doing a good job of selling this ruse, that's for sure.

"What?" I breathe, doing my best to focus on what Adam's saying at the front of the room.

Something about getting grades in on time and volunteering to mentor different student groups.

The soft vibrations of my phone from inside my purse grab my attention, and when I look at Blake, he nods toward it. I reach into my purse and pull the phone out. There's a new text message, and I swipe the phone open to read it.

> **Blake**
>
> Any chance you'd be my date for my friend's wedding in a couple months?
>
> I kind of already told them you'd be there.

He did *what*? I type out a response and hit Send.

> When? Where? How do you know we have the time off?
>
> It's Thanksgiving weekend. They scheduled it that way because it's just friends and family, and most people have time off. It's in the Bahamas.

I consider. This is further than I planned to take things with this fake relationship. Going to a wedding together seems much more like a *real-couple* thing.

But then, we're in this to help one another out, right? I don't mind hanging out with Blake. And it's not like I had plans for the holiday, anyway.

Despite my hormones trying to push for more, I can see him turning into a good friend. And if I can help him out and go to the Bahamas? Two birds, one stone, right? Maybe it would be okay.

> I'll check my schedule but if I'm free I'm happy to go.

> What's the dress code? Should I bring a gift?

> Island casual. So I think like sundresses and stuff. They told me to wear shorts. And I'll take care of the gift.

The idea of Blake in shorts has me grinning. He's so buttoned up at work. But then, so am I.

It's leggings, for the record. All leggings, all the time, outside of work.

Oh, you think leggings aren't pants? Keep your negativity to yourself, sister.

They're comfortable, they make my ass look fantastic, and really, what more do you need?

> Okay. I'll check my planner after the meeting.

> Also, she wants to meet you. The bride.

> … and my friends. I apologize in advance, they're assholes. I mean, nice guys. They just like to give one another shit. And that includes me.

And as far as they're concerned...
this is real.

I tap my finger on the edge of the phone as I think about Blake with his friends. I wonder how different he is.

When Angela and Naomi and I hang out, not only are we in leggings, but it's like we're entirely different people outside of work, and if I'm honest, I'm intrigued to know what Blake is like outside these hallowed halls of academia.

"That's all from me. Any questions or other business?" Adam says, drawing my attention back to the meeting.

I have no idea what he said in the last ten minutes or so. I can guess—it's the same every month, more or less—and I'll get the rundown from Angela or Naomi.

Adam dismisses the meeting, and we all stand and gather our things.

I turn to Blake. "You want me to meet your friends?"

Shrugging, he lifts his messenger bag and slips the strap over his head. "They're asking to meet my girlfriend. Addie especially wants to meet you. She's the bride."

"Well, yeah. Of course I have to meet the bride if I'm going to the wedding. I don't want to crash."

I wouldn't want people I've never met at my own wedding someday. I don't want one of those huge weddings, where it's half a wedding and half a networking event. When it's my turn someday, I want friends and family only. Like Addie, apparently.

Blake chuckles as we make our way down the aisle toward the door, his hand on my lower back again. "You're not crashing. You're my date. She's just nosy. They all are."

"Professor Grantham," a voice interrupts as we reach the door. "Adam Kashman. Dean of faculty."

He extends his hand to Blake.

"Good to see you, Dean Kashman." Blake shakes his hand. "I remember meeting you at the recruitment dinner. How've you been?"

It's impressive to watch, the confidence in Blake's posture. He doesn't look the least bit intimidated by the man who holds all the power over his career. But then, maybe I'd be less intimidated if I towered over Adam by at least eight inches.

"Good, good." Adam lifts his chin in my direction. "Kathleen mentioned she was dating someone."

Blake nods in answer to the unasked question. "It's

new, and we're trying to be fairly subtle, but yes, Kathleen and I are dating."

Adam runs a hand over his jaw, his gaze bouncing between Blake and me.

Finally, he nods. "I like you two together. It's giving me a few ideas."

Oh, crap.

11

———

BLAKE

For what it's worth, I've now made it through an entire month of classes without another wardrobe mishap, but it may be because I check my fly obsessively before I head to each class.

My gamble on the first day paid off, though. The way I managed to play off being called out on my fly being unzipped on day one is now the stuff of campus legend, and I'm firmly established as a "cool" professor.

We'll see how cool they think I am after I grade this exam, though. I drop the stack of papers on my desk with a satisfying thud and push a hand through my hair.

"This a bad time?"

Turning around, I see Dean Kashman at my office

door. He seems like a squirrelly kind of guy, the type who made it to where he is in life through back-room deals and being sneaky, but maybe I'm being judgmental.

"Not at all. Just getting started on some grading. Come on in." I settle into my desk chair as he steps into the space.

This chair finally got delivered last week. It's a high-backed leather chair, its armrests at the perfect height, and it rolls on its casters effortlessly. If it were possible to be in love with a chair, this would be the one.

Dean Kashman sits in one of the two chairs on the opposite side of my desk and crosses one leg over the other, his ankle on the opposite knee. "How are things with Kathleen?"

A gossip session was not what I anticipated when the dean of faculty appeared at my door.

I keep my face impassive. "Good, thanks."

He nods once. "Good. As I said a couple weeks ago, I think the two of you make a cute couple. She's a nice girl. It's given me an idea."

Oh boy. I hope he cleared this with Kat first.

I also hope she's never heard him refer to her as a "nice girl." I can just imagine how that would go over.

"A crossover class, Biology and Econ. You two can co-teach. Economics of the American Healthcare System." He looks at me expectantly.

I scratch my jaw. "Interesting concept. Intriguing, even. But I teach Game Theory. I'm not sure I'm the best person to be teaching something like that."

He waves his hand in the air, dismissing my concern. "You have a degree in Economics, and this will be more of a non-major's course. I see it appealing to pre-med students, mostly. A non-science that's relevant to them."

He has a point, and I can see a class like this being particularly popular. But I'm not sure I'm the one most qualified to teach it. The one with the least on his plate as a new faculty member, sure. But not the most qualified.

More importantly, I'm not sure about co-teaching with Kat. From our time together so far, I know we work well together. That's not the issue. It's whether Kat would agree to it.

I press my lips together, trying to come up with a response that toes the line between remaining professional while still turning him down. "Hmm. Well, I'm not sure she'd want to co-teach a class with me."

Put it on her to make the decision.

Dean Kashman raises one eyebrow. "You wouldn't want to co-teach a class with Kathleen? I thought you two were dating. It seemed like things were going well."

Alert. Alert. Alarm bells go off in my head. Is he sensing that this isn't real?

If anyone gets wind of the fact that this relationship is a ruse, our careers are tanked. Done for. Cooked. We'll be dragged in front of the Honor Council for violating professionalism, being untrustworthy, and God knows what else.

I know how hard Kat's worked to be where she is, how close she is to her goal of being promoted. I'm not going to be the one who takes her down with me.

I lean back in my chair, trying my hardest to appear casual. "Oh, things are going very well, thanks. We're looking forward to a vacation together over Thanksgiving break."

He schools his features quickly, but not before I catch his eyes widening for half a second. He doesn't think this will last, does he? Good old Dean Kashman is waiting in the wings for Kat and me to break up so he can swoop in for his chance.

I fold my arms over my chest. "Of course, I'm happy to work with her, although I know her course load and research are time-consuming. You know how it is when your career is taking off."

He clears his throat, trying and failing to hide an expression of discomfort. "I see. Of course."

"If Kat is on board"—I use her nickname deliberately—"then I'd be happy to teach with her. But the ball is in her court."

Dean Kashman nods. I have him where I want him, which is pretty damn convinced that Kat and I are solid.

"I'll check with Kathleen."

"Thanks." I reach for the top paper in the pile of exams and pull it toward myself, picking up a red pen as well. "Could you shut the door on the way out? I have a lot of work to get done."

He pulls the door shut as I set down the pen and pick up my phone instead, sending a text to Kat.

Kat

Heads up, Kashman is headed your way.

Kat

Well, that was interesting.

He ask you about teaching a class together?

Yes. On US Healthcare Economics, of all things. What does that have to do with Anatomy? Or Game Theory, for that matter?

I told him that, but it was almost like he was looking for clues that we're not solid.

What did you tell him?

That you were super busy and that I'd defer to you.

I told him I'd talk with you about it.

Are you in your office?

Yes. Come on over.

"Heading somewhere important?"

I cringe at the voice. Randi has been poking her head into my office less frequently since she learned I had a girlfriend—and because I learned to keep my door shut—but she's like a fruit fly. You think you've gotten rid of it, but it keeps popping up when you least expect it.

"Headed to a meeting," I say.

The less information I feed her, the better.

Randi taps her acrylic nails—hot pink this week—against the coffee mug she's holding, the Ardmore College crest partially visible. "Do you need me to make coffee? Or file anything?"

"I'm all set. Thanks."

Maybe she isn't like a fruit fly. Maybe a more apt comparison would be herpes. Not only does it never really go away, but it comes with an unfavorable reputation, and appears at inconvenient times. Or so I've heard.

Yeah, that may be a little harsh. She's backed off a lot since I told her I'm dating Kat. Apparently, the reputation Kat has for being a hard-ass works for this situation as well as keeping her students in line.

"Hey, Randi." Jeremy appears behind me, clapping a hand on my shoulder. "You mind making some coffee for me?"

Talk about a true friend.

"Looks like you're busy, Randi. I've got to run. Good seeing you." I mouth a *thank you* to Jeremy behind Randi's back for falling on that grenade and take off before Randi can try to dig her talons into me again.

The path from the Econ department to Kat's office is second nature to me now. I've made this trip so many times over the past weeks. Turn right, head down the sidewalk, another right, and I'm at the Biology building. Kat's office is the third door on the left once you enter the building, and I hear Angela's voice before I knock on the mostly closed door.

"How is he in bed?"

I bite back a smile, waiting to hear Kat's answer.

"Um, how is that an appropriate question to ask at work?"

"It's an appropriate question to ask my best friend."

"Over tacos and margaritas, maybe. Not when we're in my office. You'll notice that Naomi is in her own office, minding her own business, Ang."

So Kat likes margaritas. I file this information away for later. Maybe I can take her to the Mexican place I like that's over in University City.

Angela's voice grows louder. "I'm just saying, you're my best friend. I tell you everything. You've been dating Blake for what, a month? I've seen the way you look at one another. There's no way you're not fucking."

An exasperated sigh from Kat. "Maybe I want to keep some things private, Ang. He's a coworker, too. He probably doesn't want gossip all over campus."

"I bet he has a big dick. You can tell from how big his hands are."

I smile to myself. She's not wrong.

"We are not talking about his dick."

"Oh my God. It's tiny, isn't it? Is that why you don't want to talk about it? It's okay if it is. It's how you use it, or that's what I've heard. The motion of the ocean or whatever."

I choose this moment to knock on the door that's cracked open.

"Come in?" Kat's voice sounds strangled. Probably trying to come up with a response to the "motion of the ocean" comment.

Pushing the door open, I give the women a dazzling smile. "Hi, Kat. Angela."

Angela has the good grace to look slightly embarrassed at being caught discussing the size of my package. "Hi, Blake."

"Having a nice conversation?" I say innocently.

They exchange a glance.

"Just talking about a class I have coming up. You know, teaching stuff," Angela says.

I stifle a laugh. "Ah, well, sorry to interrupt. Can I talk to my girlfriend for a minute?"

Angela practically sprints out of the room, and once I close the door, I let the laughter out.

"Did you hear that whole thing?" Kat asks.

Sitting in one of the chairs in front of the desk, I shrug. "Part of it."

She drops her head into her hands, elbows on the desk in front of her. "She's one of my best friends, but sometimes she takes it a little far."

"I don't care if you talk about my dick. Just don't let her think it's small."

Raising her head, Kat narrows her eyes at me. "I don't want to talk about your dick."

"It's not small. Remember?"

She rolls her eyes. "Sure. Whatever."

"You want to check? Remind yourself?" I motion to my groin.

I've got nothing to hide.

Despite our appearing together in public, Kat and I haven't done anything remotely close to physical since that one night. It was part of our initial agreement, after all. This "relationship" is just for show.

But fuck, it's getting hard. Pun intended, because every night I have a boner thinking about her legs in those pencil skirts. The way her high heels make her calves look long and slender, the way the fabric skims along her thighs and her round ass. The way her pussy felt clenching around my length.

If anything, my only regret is that I can't sleep with

her now. Normally, I'd be the first to charm her right into my bed, but I don't do more than one night.

And with this, there would be strings. So many fucking strings. So as ironic as it is, my fake girlfriend is the one woman I can't have.

"No thank you," Kat says primly, but I don't miss the way her pulse quickens in her throat at the thought of my cock.

So I'm not the only one affected here.

"Care to move on from dicks to curriculum?"

"Please." Kat pulls her ever-present legal pad toward her and lifts a pen. "So, if we were to do this, what would we cover?"

"You sure you want to move forward with this? I told Adam that the ball was in your court." I study her face, but it's unreadable.

For someone who has made an awful lot of money reading expressions, it bugs the hell out of me that I can't read Kat. Occasionally she slips, but she has a poker face to rival the most seasoned players.

Nodding, she writes something at the top of the page. "As annoying as it is to come up with an entirely new class for next semester, I see Adam's point. This would be a unique course, and a real selling point for the college."

"Fair enough." Leaning forward, I cover the hand

that holds the pen. "But let's have fun with it. I don't want to come up with a concept while we're in your office. Let's do it over dinner. Mexican?"

Kat bites the inside of her cheek. "You heard the entire conversation, didn't you?"

"I did. And it's got me craving tacos and margaritas. What do you say?"

12

KAT

"Oh my God." I walk into Angela's office, closing the door behind me, and flop against it dramatically. "He heard the *whole thing*."

Naomi looks up from the paper she's reading on Angela's couch, her bare feet tucked underneath her. "So he heard Ang talking about his dick?"

"What was that?" Angela looks up at me over her reading glasses.

I swear she wears them just to be taken more seriously at times. It would help more if they weren't pink with orange polka dots, but it does add a little something.

"The conversations about how big his dick is. Seriously, Ang. This is what happens when you gossip at work."

Shrugging, she turns back to her laptop. "So? Was he offended?"

"I don't think so. Honestly, sometimes I can't tell with him. He's hard to read." Pushing away from the door, I kick my heels off and cross the room to join Naomi on the couch.

The loveseat is perfectly positioned beneath the window, and if I have reading to get done, the lighting doesn't get any better. It's almost certainly why Naomi is here now.

I sit down and tuck my legs beneath me, mirroring Naomi. "We're making up a curriculum for a new class together. Adam's idea."

This gets their attention.

"Really? What's the course?" Naomi asks, tapping her pen against her lips.

"Economics of the American Healthcare System. It's not really a niche that either of us has much experience in, but it's intriguing, right?"

"Yeah." Naomi chews on the top of her pen.

She goes through a box of BIC pens a week, throwing them away when the caps are chewed into unrecognizable patterns. I've pointed out that it's a waste of perfectly good pens, but it seems like it falls on deaf ears.

"I think it would be super popular," she says. "It would do wonders for your career."

"My thought exactly."

Angela nods. "It would be great for your career. For both of you. But I still want to know about the sex."

I groan. "I told you. Not now."

"It's not like he's going to show up at my office, is he?"

I gesture toward the door. "Maybe not, but anyone else could. The department head. The dean. One of our other coworkers. You want to be known as the girl who likes dicks?"

"It wouldn't be completely inaccurate."

Naomi snorts.

I can't hold back my smile either. "Keep it in your pants, lady."

"Fine." Angela plucks a new pen out of the box in her top drawer and tosses it to Naomi, who has disposed of her chewed-up pen. "But I want a real gossip session, then. Let's get margaritas tonight. Or tequila shots. Whatever will get you to actually talk to your best friends about your relationship."

Tequila shots are *not* going to happen, and not just because of that one night back when I was a college student and had too many of them. It was the one and only night I did shots, and let's just say tequila tastes even worse on the way back up than it does on the way down.

But beyond the memories of puking, tequila is like a truth serum. Most alcohol is for me, and that's why I don't drink much. If I do tequila shots, or more than one margarita, it's entirely possible that I'll blurt out the truth about my entire relationship with Blake.

I shake my head. "Not tonight. I'm having dinner with Blake."

"Just dinner?"

I ignore the question, because honestly, I don't know. "If you want to come over Friday, we can gossip. I'm not making margaritas, but I can pick up a bottle of wine."

Sticking the new pen into her mouth, Naomi nods. "That works for me. I can even bring the wine if you want."

Angela considers. "And you'll order takeout?"

Jeez. Set your oven on fire once, and no one ever wants you to cook again. "I'll order takeout. Italian?"

I sigh with relief as I step out of my heels and toss them into the closet in my entryway. Beauty is pain, or whatever the saying is, and the pulled-together professional look is worth it for what it gets you in your career. But damned if I'm going to assault my feet any more than necessary, and shoes don't belong in the house.

I slide my feet into my fuzzy slippers and pad across the small house to my bedroom, where the skirt and button-down shirt are the next things to go. I pull on my go-to leggings, the ones that have a small hole in the crotch after being worn so often.

I really should throw them away, but they're too comfortable to give up. Besides, it's not like I wear them in front of anyone. I could walk around with no pants at all in my house, and no one would know the difference.

It only takes me a few minutes to settle into my post-work routine, and soon I'm seated cross-legged on my extra-deep sofa, a can of lime La Croix on the side table and a pile of papers to grade in front of me. I lift the remote and hit Play on an episode of *The Bachelor* from earlier in the week.

Now, before you make a comment about reality shows or anything like that, I would like to point out that when you work hard all day, sometimes you need something light and fluffy to decompress afterward. And that something like fifty percent of *The Bachelor* viewers hold a master's degree or higher.

Also, I don't give a fuck what anyone thinks of my television viewing habits. Or my smutty romance books, for that matter.

My therapist once pointed out that the common thread in both of these hobbies is that they tend to have predictable happy endings, and asked if I'd considered that I was focusing on those happy endings so I wouldn't have to worry about my own.

I found another therapist, one who appreciates the fine literature that is the romance genre.

Uncapping my pen, I start to go through the first test, marking points off here and there while the girls on the TV gush about the male lead.

"He was my *soulmate*!" one of them says tearfully.

I glance up at the screen. Mascara runs down her cheeks. I wonder if the contestants choose not to wear waterproof mascara, or if the producers insist on it. The smeared makeup adds a certain level of drama.

I circle a red B at the top of the page and set it face down in a separate pile. My phone vibrates, distracting me from my dual TV-watching and grading.

BLAKE

Does 6 work for you for dinner?

Sure. Where? I can meet you.

I'll pick you up. Send me your address.

I can drive.

I'm sure you can. But I know where we're going and it's in the city, and parking's a bitch. Just let me pick you up.

Please.

I chew on the inside of my cheek. I like to drive myself for dates, when I have them, which is rare. But in those cases, I usually don't know the guy well and don't know if I'm going to want to spend much time with him.

With Blake, I'm pretty sure he isn't going to kidnap or murder me, and I know we'll have a good time. I always do with him.

Plus, it isn't a date. Not really. And he said please.

There's also the concern about letting a coworker see my house. Not that I'm ashamed of it. Not at all. I've spent hours picking out decorations and making this place mine.

I look around. It's not like it's *dirty*. It's just clutter. Plus, the living room is all he'll see from the doorway, and most of the mess is in my bedroom and the kitchen.

For some reason, though, I don't think I mind Blake seeing my house and getting to know this side of me. Maybe because we have this agreement, and because it was largely his idea. We're keeping one another's secrets for now, and mutually assured destruction is a powerful motivator to keep things to yourself.

Fine.

I text him my address and check the time—5:15. Enough time to get a few more papers graded before I get dressed and put those goddamn heels back on.

Knock. Knock.

I pause *The Bachelor*, right as he's about to hand out the second-to-last rose of the night. The dramatic music has risen almost to its peak, and I wonder if I heard right, but then it comes again, a knocking at my front door, louder this time.

"Oh, *fuck!*" I shriek, realizing what time it is.

I jump up, knocking the half-full can of La Croix off the table. I dive to catch it before it spills, but all I manage to do is land on the ground next to the can, my ass right in the liquid that's already absorbing into the carpet.

"Shit!"

I take a deep breath to calm my racing heart and rub my elbows. Normally, I don't get so absorbed in things that I run late. Or dive off the couch.

Another deep breath. The La Croix is just water. It'll be fine.

I pull open the front door just as Blake is raising his hand to knock again. "Hey. Sorry, I got lost in grading tests. Come on in. I just have to change."

Blake steps into my house, his gaze traveling around the living area. "I like your place. Very different from your office."

Looking around, I see what he means. There's color here, a lot of it, with splashes of deep reds and yellows, in contrast to the neutrals of my office. The carpet is a plush maroon that feels amazing between my toes.

When I focus back on Blake, his eyes are on me, his gaze heated.

"I like this side of you," he says.

I don't know how to respond to that, or how to respond to the look in his eyes. The look that says *I want to kiss you* or *I want to push you up against the wall and have my way with you* or possibly *get on your knees and take my cock in your mouth.*

My stomach bottoms out as I think through the possibilities, but when I meet his gaze again, the look is gone, and I wonder if I imagined it. Probably. That would be my luck, imagining sexual desire when really, this is all a business arrangement.

"Did you know you have a hole in your pants?"

I glance down, and my face heats.

My dive off the couch turned the small hole in my leggings into a sizable one. It's no longer discreet, visible only when I sit spread-legged.

Now it's extending right into the front of the leggings, like some kind of reverse camel toe. The lace of my thong is prominently on display, the pink and green pattern obvious against the navy blue of the spandex.

"I'm going to go change quickly," I say, covering my crotch with one hand, even though he's already seen it all.

When I said I was okay with him seeing this side of me, I meant the laid-back, colorful me that I keep at home. Not the hot mess in wet, ripped leggings.

"Take your time," he says, a small smile playing at his lips.

I don't take my time, rushing through the process

of pulling on a dinner-appropriate outfit and freshening up my makeup. I cringe when I pull off the leggings. The hole is the size of my head.

Into the trash they go.

Farewell, my friend. You were the best pair of leggings a girl could have.

I smooth my hair with my hand, making sure the hoodie didn't move any strands out of place, and then decide to run a brush through it anyway.

"Okay. Ready." I emerge from my bedroom to find Blake sitting at my kitchen table, next to the stack of mail that I need to go through.

My face heats as I realize he's seen the mess, but he's not looking at the clutter.

His eyes are fixed on me.

His gaze skims down my body, slow and heated. As his eyes linger on my curves, I'm glad I picked this dress. It's something I'd never wear to work—too tight to be taken seriously, too bright, too *everything*.

It's a holdover from my modeling days, and while I've tried to leave most of that in the past, I couldn't let this dress go. It's one of my favorites.

Blake's gaze lingers on my chest for half a second too long, and a triumphant feeling rushes through me. I wasn't imagining the look earlier.

I'm not the only one interested.

But my eyes are going to stay on the prize for now. Promotion. That's why I'm here, and Blake is in this for his own reasons. If real feelings get involved, it could jeopardize everything. We can't chance that.

"Shall we?" Blake stands, and I try to ignore the way his body looks in jeans and a gray and blue Ardmore College T-shirt, the fabric stretched across his broad chest and showing off strong arms.

Strong enough to pin me against the wall as he—

"Kat." Blake's deep voice pulls me from my perusal of his body.

Not as subtle as I thought.

"Yes?" Why is my voice squeaky? Darn it. I clear my throat. "Yes."

There. Professor voice.

Blake takes two steps to stand right in front of me, then one more until he's close enough that I can feel the heat coming off his body. Those strong arms wrap around me and pull me into him.

Without my heels, I'm struck once again by how much shorter I am than he is, by at least six inches. It's a strange feeling when I've spent so much of my life as tall as the men I work with, or at least trying to with my too-high heels.

"You seem stressed. Just relax. This is going to be fun." His voice rumbles through his chest.

Stressed? Me? Never.

But what else can I say? *Sorry, not stressed, just thinking about you naked.*

"I'm fine." I push off his chest. "Sorry, just stressed about running late."

And wondering if he can feel the sexual tension that surrounds us.

"Ready?" He steps back and offers his hand.

I take it, the warmth of his palm enveloping my hand as we walk to the front door.

I pause to slip on my heels, then I follow him out to the car he's parked in my driveway, a black F-150.

I lift my eyebrows in surprise. "You drive a pickup truck?"

We took an Uber to his house from the bar the first night we met, and the truck must have been in his garage. It's definitely not what I would have pictured him choosing.

Grinning, he shrugs and pulls the passenger door open for me. "I've always wanted one. And living in the city, it wasn't exactly practical. I'm not sure it's practical now, to be honest, but I have room to park it in my garage now."

I study him. Maybe I should feel overdressed, wearing a bright-red bodycon dress while he's in jeans and a T-shirt, but he just wears them so *well*. And with the way he carries himself, it doesn't seem to matter what he wears. He can command any room no matter what his outfit is.

"What?" Blake says, his lips quirking. "You look like you're deep in thought."

I let a laugh bubble up as I pull my seat belt down and across my body. "Just thinking it would be nice to have the confidence of a man every now and then. That's all."

Blake leans over, taking the seat belt from my hand and inserting the buckle into the clip. His arm brushes mine in a way that may be intentional.

"You have every reason to be confident in everything about you, Kat. And my confidence is from another place entirely, if you recall," he says with a smirk.

His face is so close to mine that the heat of his breath brushes my cheek. His eyes are dark, the bright-blue irises overshadowed by his dilated pupils.

My breath hitches in my chest.

And then he's closing my door, rounding the truck to the driver's side, and climbing in to start the engine, leaving me with an ache between my legs that I can't ignore.

13

BLAKE

I can't take my eyes off of her tonight.

I thought the pencil skirts were my thing, the way they show off her legs and ass. But then seeing her in her comfortable state, the way she dresses when there's no one to impress? That was an entirely different side of her, and a side I'd like to get to know better.

It didn't hurt that she had a hole right in the crotch of her pants. I considered not mentioning it, but I remember how I felt when I got called out for my fly being down.

Besides, I didn't know whether she was planning to wear that to dinner and figured she should know. I wouldn't have cared if she wore her comfortable clothes to dinner. I'm not into her for her clothes.

Wait. Scratch that. I like her as a *friend*. This isn't a real relationship. We're on the same page here. I can appreciate her assets without needing to involve feelings.

And I do enjoy those assets. Objectively, Kat is beautiful. It's not a secret. She's known as the Hot Professor among the undergrads, a fact that she must be aware of, even if she doesn't talk about it.

The dress she has on now is not only impossible to look away from, but it also makes me wonder if she's wearing the same lace underwear I caught a glimpse of, or something else. The dress hugs every curve, highlighting her hips and breasts and other areas my fingers are itching to explore.

Is she even wearing underwear? I can't see panty lines when I check out her ass—yes, I've done it more than once—but I know she's partial to thongs, or she was the one night we were together.

Besides stoking my curiosity about what's under it, the color of her dress complements her, offsetting her hazel eyes while bringing out the pink in her cheeks and making her light-brown hair appear almost chestnut in color.

Fuck, she's gorgeous.

I wonder if maybe I fucked myself over with this fake-dating thing. It seemed like a good idea at the time, and so far, it's having the intended effect—keeping Randi away from me and Adam away from her, while protecting our reputations and her promotion.

But at the same time, it's putting me through hell. Because the one woman I can't stop thinking about is the one I can't have.

I park the truck in a pay-by-the-hour lot, a rip-off if there ever was one, but infinitely easier than trying to find on-street parking at this hour. Opening Kat's door for her, I hold out my arm, and she takes it, steadying herself as she steps down from the truck.

"Where are we going to dinner?" she asks, looking around the area.

Sliding my hand down to cover hers, I gesture with my head and start walking. "Modern Mex. It's one of my favorite places, and if you're looking for tacos and margaritas, you can't beat them."

Kat mentioned she was in the mood for tacos. These are the best in the city.

"Do they have the fruity ones?"

"Oh, do they. Strawberry, mango, raspberry, pretty much anything you can think of. Trust me, you'll never find one that lives up to these."

I hold open the restaurant door. Inside, we follow the hostess to the table.

Kat looks around, taking in the place as we walk. The lights are low, the music just loud enough to create the perfect ambiance without overshadowing conversations. The scent of spiced meat and salsa wafts through the air.

"God, it smells amazing," she says. "All of a sudden I'm starving."

I chuckle. "Same. I could go for some chips and salsa."

Nodding, Kat slides into the booth and thanks the hostess as she hands over the menus.

As soon as the hostess leaves, Kat opens the menu and flips through. "What would you recommend?"

"You can't go wrong. I'm going with a mango margarita and a burrito. And chips and salsa."

She ends up ordering tacos and a raspberry margarita, and we munch on chips while we wait.

"So. What are your thoughts about the curriculum for this class?" Kat digs a legal pad out of her purse.

I shake my head. "Not yet. Let's enjoy the margaritas and then work on it. Plus, I want to know more about you."

I'm not lying. I'm burning to learn more about her now. I thought I had a handle on who she was after the last few weeks of lunches in the student union—

organized, on top of things, an alpha female. Takes no shit.

But seeing her home and just how different it is from the image she presents to the world at work—not to mention the ripped leggings and the spilled seltzer I almost stepped on in the living room—I'm realizing there's a lot more to this woman than I thought. And damn if I don't want to know more.

It strikes me that she hides that part of herself from most of the world. I'd imagine there are very few people she lets into the sanctity of her home and into that side of herself.

And fuck if I don't feel lucky to be one of them.

Her dark-red lips wrap around the straw of her margarita, her cheeks hollowing out as she sips the frozen concoction. What I'd give to have her lips wrapped around something else entirely.

Kat swallows and darts her tongue out to lick a drip of margarita from the corner of her mouth. "What do you want to know?"

I pick out a chip from the basket in the center of the table, dip it in salsa, and bring it to my mouth, chewing and swallowing as I think. I want to know a lot of things, but a lot of them cross the line from a business arrangement to something else.

"What made you want to teach? Why Anatomy?"

Her lips quirk to one side with a small smile, and I wonder what it would be like to kiss those full lips again, as more than a onetime thing.

"I originally wanted to go to medical school, but while I was taking biology classes as an undergrad, I became fascinated with how the body works. The human body, mostly, but also different animals, and how their anatomy works differently from ours." She takes another sip of her drink. "And I worked as a TA for a few lab sessions to bring in some money and found I was good at teaching. I liked seeing students' faces when things suddenly clicked."

"Makes sense. I had a similar experience." I decide to keep this conversation on the lighter side, at least for now. Until the alcohol starts to loosen her lips. "Where did you go to undergrad?"

"University of Virginia."

"Impressive. How about grad school?"

Kat chews on her straw. "Harvard."

"Ivy League. Damn." I raise my glass toward her. "You might be out of my league, Kat."

She rolls her eyes. "I've read your faculty profile, Blake. You went to Penn for grad school. It's quite literally the same league."

I laugh. "You've got me there. But you're still playing the game at a whole different level than I am."

By the time the waitress sets the food down, I've learned even more about Kat. She grew up in Virginia, on the outskirts of Washington, D.C. She's an only child.

"How about your parents?" I ask, reaching for a fork. "Are they still around?"

"Yes," Kat says, her eyes on her food.

Something about the way she says it makes me wonder if there's more to the story, but I don't have time to ask before she's moving the conversation forward.

"How about you? Any siblings?"

"I have a brother. Lawton. He lives out in Colorado."

"Ah. The coffee table book."

My heart warms a bit at the thought that she remembers seeing that on our first night together.

I nod. "We actually grew up in Chester Heights, though. Not too far from here. I love eastern Pennsylvania, so I was glad to get the job at Ardmore."

Kat bites into her taco, some of the filling spilling out the other side. "Oh, God, this is good. You were right."

"Told you. Just wait till dessert. We'll get the churros. They're out of this world."

We chew in silence for a little bit.

When Kat takes the last bite of her taco, she wipes the edges of her mouth with the napkin. "So what about your parents? Do they still live around here?"

And there it is. I knew this would come up when I asked about her parents, but I was still hoping I wouldn't have to talk about it.

It's not lost on me that Kat avoided this question, too. I wonder if we have more in common than I've realized.

"No." I shake my head and take a sip of my margarita. "They're not around anymore."

"I'm so sorry," Kat says, the way most people do, assuming that them "not being around" means they're both dead.

She reaches her hand out to cover mine in a gesture of sympathy. I don't correct her assumption about my parents.

Because as far as I'm concerned, my mother may as well be dead. She pulled away from Lawton and me after Dad's cancer took him from us back when I was in high school.

At first, we let her have her grief, but she never came back to herself, just getting more and more distant, to the point that I stepped in to act as a surrogate parent for Lawton.

Recently, she's been sending a card for my birthday

and for Christmas, but that's as much as I've gotten from her. I've never asked Lawton if he's in touch with her. I'm not sure I want to know.

"Thanks." I squeeze her hand gently.

"Any dessert tonight?" the waitress asks, interrupting the moment.

Our hands fall apart, and I try to regain control of the situation.

"I was thinking churros," I say, looking at Kat. "Do you want to split some?"

"Um. Sure." She takes a sip of her drink, nearing the bottom of the margarita.

I've never seen her look so uncertain, and it's reassuring in a way. It means I'm not the only one affected by our connection.

But the very fact that she brought up my parents reminded me of one crucial fact—I'm not looking for a relationship. It's just not in the cards for me.

Sex, sure.

Dating, maybe, at least for a little while.

Fake dating to reach a goal, absolutely.

Just nothing real and nothing long-term. Maybe my friends think they have something that will last, but I know the truth. Relationships end, one way or another, and I've seen the fallout when it does.

It's not something I want to experience. Ever.

As soon as I climb back into the truck after dropping Kat off at her house, I dial Lawton's number, the phone connecting through the Bluetooth in the car. The talk about parents over dinner has me needing to talk with him, to remind myself that I'm not alone in the world.

"Hey. What's up?" His familiar voice coming across the car speakers calms me somewhat.

"Not much. How are things out there?"

There's a slight hesitation before he says, "They're okay. Things with Kristina are...interesting."

I'd always rather hear about someone else's relationship drama than deal with my own. "Yeah? What's going on?"

Lawton and his long-time girlfriend moved out to Colorado when he took a job as a police officer up there. I always thought he was crazy for taking a job like that when he could have made more money as a cop here in Philadelphia, but he loves it up there.

"I don't think she's settling in as much as she thought she would. She's still struggling to find a job, and breaking into the social circles of a small town is hard, you know? I have built-in buddies from the force, but she doesn't have anyone but me." Lawton lets out a long sigh. "I'm worried she's going to leave, man."

His crisis overshadows mine, and I'm more than happy to spend most of my drive back home analyzing things Kristina has said or done and what she means by it and if it means anything that she refuses to buy a better coat for winter.

"I think it means she has no intention of being up here by the time winter comes," Lawton says, sounding dejected.

I agree, but I play the devil's advocate. I always have when it comes to me and Lawton. We debate both sides equally.

"Maybe she just hasn't found one she likes."

"Maybe." He doesn't sound convinced. "How are things with you? Settling into your job?"

"Yeah, it's—"

"Wait a minute!" Lawton interrupts. "Hold on. What about the girlfriend? The one you told me about?"

I did tell him about it. I wish I could tell him the truth, dissect all of it with him, but it's too risky with his big mouth.

"It's good. We went out to dinner tonight." And didn't talk about the curriculum once, for what it's worth, which means we're meeting tomorrow in my office. "I can't wait for you to meet her at Cam's wedding."

"I hope I can still come," he says. "What if I'm right and Kristina leaves? Do I just show up alone?"

"Addie can hook you up with Annika. I hear she needs a date."

"Maybe."

I pull into my driveway and kill the engine. "I'm home now, Lawton. Got to go. I'll call you soon. Keep me updated on the Kristina situation."

"Will do." He disconnects the call.

I sit in my truck, thinking. About Kat and the way she looked tonight. About the hitch in her breath and the hard nipples and dilated pupils that tell me she's interested in more. About just how badly I want to have her in my bed, taste her sweetness that I can't get out of my head, fuck her until she can't remember anyone's name but mine.

But beyond the obvious—fake dating and complicating all of that, not to mention the coworker status—it wouldn't work. Kat and I may be attracted to one another, but she and I would never be compatible long-term. She's too used to being the one in control, taking charge.

And in my bedroom, I'm the one in control. Maybe she was okay with it for one night, but in the long run? I'm not sure I can see Kat being okay with that, and it's not something I can turn off.

So for now, I'll settle for thinking of her in that little red dress, the feel of her body pressed against mine when I gave her that hug that I desperately wished could be more.

14

KAT

I'm never this nervous.

I regularly give lectures to over a hundred students. I've interviewed in front of panels, given talks at conferences in front of hundreds, if not thousands, of people.

And nothing has made me more unsettled than the idea of heading over to Blake's office in a few minutes.

My hormones were on high alert all through dinner last night. Actually, that's a lie. My hormones have been working overtime practically since I met Blake. And if there was any question about whether I was attracted to him, it was settled as soon as he pulled me into his arms for a hug.

I pull in a deep breath and straighten my spine.

Focus, Kat. This isn't a real relationship. Not only that, but it's a situation that's helping us out.

If we up the ante and turn this into something real, it has the potential to end badly. Which puts me right back in a position of having to turn down Adam's advances while balancing it with my goal of promotion. The same tricky situation that landed me in this spot in the first place.

Besides, we're not meeting to talk about relationships or how good Blake smells or what I wish he'd do with his hands. We're meeting to work on the curriculum for this new course. The thing we were supposed to do last night.

But despite not getting around to doing the one thing we had on our agenda for last night, I had a good time. A great time, even.

Blake is easy to talk to. So much so that I almost over-shared, although I'll blame that one on the alcohol.

God, that margarita was good. I'm craving another one already. Maybe I can get Angela and Naomi to come to Mod Mex instead of meeting at my house Friday night.

"How are things?"

I look up from my desk, startled to see Dean Kashman at my office door.

"Hi, Adam. Good. How are you?" I mentally groan as he steps into my office and takes a seat.

"Good, good. How are things coming with that course you and Grantham are working on? Will it be ready for next semester?"

Who develops an entire new course in a few months? It's nearing the end of October already. The likelihood of getting this hammered out as an outline by Christmas is fair, but having it ready to go in January? That's about as likely as me quitting my job to play the harmonica full time, or something like that.

Which is to say, between zero and none.

"Probably not," I say. "Next fall is a better bet. We want to make it a success."

Adam nods thoughtfully, and I mentally pat myself on the back.

Good answer.

"Well, then. Keep up the good work." He stands to leave but turns back just before he reaches the door. "If you're available, I'm having a few faculty over to my house. Cocktails and finger foods, conversation. That type of thing. Next Wednesday night, if you and Grantham are available."

I get the message loud and clear. I'm invited with Blake. And while I'm excited to be asked, I'm also pissed off. Because Adam's been having these little gatherings for as long as I've known him. People he invites—white men, typically, and their female partners—tend to end up on the short list for promotion or tenure or an endowed chair.

I've never been invited. But clearly, now that I have a man in my life, I'm worth socializing with. Or maybe it's Blake who's really invited, and I'm just coming along as his partner. The thought is infuriating, so much so that I almost don't want to go.

But promotion is what I'm after, and I'll do whatever it takes.

Within reason. I'll tolerate Adam and his smarmy smile and off-color jokes, but I won't go out with him. No way in hell.

I grit my teeth, careful not to let my smile falter. "I'll ask him. We'll let you know."

On the plus side, the anger is now overshadowing my nerves as I head to the Econ department to meet with Blake.

I practically stomp down the hall, enjoying the loud click-clack of my heels, until I realize that if I stomp too hard, I could break the heel off, so I slow down. I paid way too much money for the red-bottomed shoes to take my anger out on them.

"Ready to plan?" I ask as I walk into Blake's office without knocking and then shut the door behind me. "And then I have to talk to you about something. I'm too mad to do it right now."

He looks up from his desk, where he's writing something with a red pen, one eyebrow quirked. "Sure. Grab a seat."

I choose the one closest to the door and sit. Pulling out my legal pad, I say, "I had a few ideas. Do you want me to run through them?"

He caps his pen and looks me in the eye. "In a minute."

I get the sense he's about to say something I won't like. I mentally cross my fingers that he's not going to pry into why I'm pissed off, especially when I already told him I wasn't ready to talk about it. I was hoping he'd let it go and let me be angry before he asks me about it, but maybe not.

Blake leans back in his chair, the one I know he's obsessed with after having the department buy him a new one.

My requests for a new desk chair, on the other hand, have been ignored for the last three years.

Blake clears his throat. "So. I might be off base, but I sense there's some attraction between us."

The blunt way he puts it all out there throws me off at first. I open my mouth to deny the accusation, but I can't even summon the lie. And now that he's put this out there, the anger at scoring an invite to one of Adam's gatherings *only* because I'm with Blake is pushed to the back of my mind. For now.

"Let me clarify." Blake pushes a hand through his short, dark hair. "I'm attracted to you, Kat. That one night we had together was mind-blowing. Truly."

My pulse thuds so loudly I'm sure he can hear it, while a thrum of arousal courses through me. I swallow hard, hanging on his next words. Having him be so forthright about things is refreshing, sure, but somehow, it's also nerve-wracking. What is he asking?

"I'm sensing that it's not one-sided. Is that a fair assessment?" He studies me with that intense gaze of his, so confident and self-assured that I want to throw myself at him right now, consequences be damned.

"I suppose that's not entirely incorrect." Evasive? Maybe. But damned if I'll be the one sticking my neck out first.

Plus, we can't date, not for real. There's too much on the line to be dating a coworker.

"Kat." He frowns. "Cut the shit."

My eyes widen for a fraction of a second before I hide my surprise. Damn, he's blunt. It's freaking intimidating.

"Fine. Yes, I'm attracted to you. Just maybe not your personality all the time."

This garners me a smile. "Fair enough, although I think you like some parts of that personality."

A blush creeps over my face at his words. "Okay. So we're attracted to one another."

Blake gives me a brief nod. "Yes. But I want to get it out in the open that I don't do relationships. I don't do more than one night."

"Why?" The question pops out before I can stop myself.

He levels me with a stare. "Because of my career. Because I don't want to. Pick any reason you want."

I draw myself up as tall as I can while still seated. "Good. Well, that works out well because I'm focused on my career, too. So I'm glad we got that sorted. Can we work on the curriculum now?"

I look down at my legal pad, wondering why it feels like there's something he's not telling me.

"It's a good start." Blake taps the legal pad with his pen.

I have to agree with him. We've managed to outline a good chunk of the semester in the last few hours. I'll need to do a little more research to flesh out some of this, but this is more than I thought we'd get done.

And I'd like to point out that I managed to sit next to Blake through all that time, only occasionally imagining his hands on me. Now that I know exactly where he stands, I can concentrate on work without thinking of him like *that*.

I just need the rest of my body to get the memo.

I stand and stretch. "This was good. I'll get some more research done, and we can revisit the outline soon. Maybe next week?"

"Sure. Send me an email with what you're working on so we don't duplicate effort."

"Will do." I turn to leave, ready for a few minutes alone in my office.

"Kat?"

"Yes?" I look back at Blake, who hasn't moved from his seat.

He scratches the side of his face. "You were mad about something when you got here. Did you need to talk to me about something?"

Shoot. I'd almost forgotten. "Yes, thanks for

reminding me. Adam Kashman invited us to dinner. Me, technically, but it was clear he wanted you there. Both of us."

"When?"

"Wednesday night."

"Next week?"

It's Thursday. Is he asking if we're going back in time to yesterday?

I decide to leave the sass out of it. "Yes. Next week."

Blake picks up his phone and swipes through it. I assume he's checking his calendar.

"Sure. I'm supposed to meet up with my friends, but this seems more important."

I wave my hand in the air in a dismissive gesture, not wanting to be demanding. "Oh, if you're busy, it's no big deal. We can go another time. He does this like once a month."

Blake's finger pauses on his phone as he looks at me, his face dead serious. "This is important to you. To your career. Right?"

"I guess." Very important, in fact, for reasons that he probably won't understand.

He tilts his head, his gaze never leaving my face. "Why were you angry when you got here?"

"What?"

"When you got to my office. You said you needed to talk to me about something, but you were too mad to do it right then. And I'm assuming the dinner with the dean is the thing you wanted to talk about, yes?"

Damn him. How does he remember every little detail?

"Yes. I was just..." I blow out a long breath. "Adam's been doing this ever since I've known him. Dinner with select faculty. It's like an honor to be invited. The people he invites tend to end up with better committee assignments, on the shortlist for promotion, and things like that."

He rubs his hand over his jaw. "So yes. This is very important to your career."

"Yes. And it bothers me that until I was *dating* you, I've never been invited to one." The anger boils up again. "Like I'm not good enough on my own. Like I need you there with me to prove I belong. I don't know. It's probably not worth being angry over, but it's the same thing over and over. Older, white men get promoted, and everyone else gets left behind. And I've got more than one strike against me."

"Kat." Blake stands and crosses the room to me in a few long strides. He places his hands on my upper arms, strong but gentle, and looks into my eyes. "You have every right to be angry about that. I'm the one who should be coasting on your coattails, not the other way around. I'm absolutely coming to this dinner with you. And we're going to show them that Kathleen Fucking Milas isn't someone to mess with."

He folds me into his arms, hugging me close against his chest. The beat of his heart calms me, and a laugh bubbles up.

"What's funny?" Blake asks, not letting go.

"You called me Kathleen Fucking Milas."

"Yeah. Because you're a goddamn force to be reckoned with."

I pull back enough to see his face. "It's what my parents used to say. When I would worry that I wasn't good enough or something. They were always my biggest cheerleaders while I was growing up."

Until they let me down. But right now, we're going to focus on the positives.

"Well, then." Blake gives me another squeeze and lets go. "You give them a call and let them know they've got some competition for the title of your biggest cheerleader."

"Thanks, Blake."

As a smile spreads over my face, I realize that no matter how much I want Blake, like *want* him, I want him as a friend, too. I want this man in my corner, to bounce ideas off of him, to eat gelato in the food court. If I can only have one, I'd rather have his friendship than a physical relationship.

I just wish I didn't have to choose.

15

BLAKE

"Sounds like things are good with you and Milas." Jeremy saunters into my office, coffee in hand.

"You bring me one of those?" I've had two cups already, but the day is young. Caffeine is good for me.

"Nah. But there's more in the pot, and Randi just left to run something over to the Chem building, so you should go now."

I take my opening and head to the break room to pour myself a cup of coffee, grateful that Randi's office is still empty as I head back to my own office, where Jeremy has made himself at home.

"So? Things good with your girlfriend?" Jeremy leans back, his heels propped on a stack of textbooks that I've been meaning to put away.

"Sure. We're going to dinner at Kashman's place tomorrow."

"Really?"

I take a sip of the coffee. It's extra strong, just the way I like it. Hot and bitter. "Yeah. Why?"

Jeremy whistles softly. "That's a big deal. Your little arrangement with her is paying off."

I furrow my brows as I set the mug down on my desk. "That's what's strange, though. Kat says she's never been invited. Like Kashman only wants her there because she's with me."

"Huh." He takes a sip of his coffee, so much creamer in it that it's a pale tan. "Well, let me know how it is. I've never been invited."

I lean back, pushing a hand through my hair. "Part of me is wondering if we shouldn't go. Like if we go, are we reinforcing whatever game he's playing? She says it's the men who get invited all the time. I feel wrong taking advantage of that."

Jeremy shrugs, his hair falling over his eyes. He pushes it back into place as he thinks. "Straight white men, in particular. I think your heart is in the right place, but you've got to think about your career. And hers. She's no stranger to the politics of academia."

He's right, of course. Kat has been dealing with

this a lot longer than I have. She doesn't need me riding in like some white knight to fight her battles.

She'd probably have my balls if I tried.

Either way, I don't have time to dissect it right now.

I glance at my watch. "Don't you have a class to teach? I'm headed over to teach micro if you're going that direction."

Pressing his hands to his thighs, Jeremy stands. "Yeah. I'll walk with you."

I can't decide how I'm feeling about this dinner at Dean Kashman's house. It has the potential to do wonders for my career, and Kat's, if we can get in good with the dean. But it seems like so much pressure.

By the end of the day on Wednesday, I've run through the full spectrum of emotions and decided that I'm going to take this as an opportunity to make some new friends and to sell our relationship, especially to Dean Kashman.

He has no reason to question it. No one does. We've been the picture of a happy couple on campus for more than two months now. The only one who knows the truth is Jeremy, and so far, he's given me no reason to distrust him.

But there's something about the way Dean Kashman looks at us when we're together, Kat and me. Like he's sensing that there's something off, or like we're a puzzle he needs to solve.

It could be that he senses that our relationship is off somehow. That it isn't real.

And the last thing we need is his scrutiny.

Knocking on Kat's office door, I lean against the doorframe. "Hey. How are things coming?"

Kat looks up from the paper she's marking up with a red pen, tucking a piece of hair behind her ear. "Just finishing this up. I'll be done in..." She checks her watch. "Five minutes. Maybe ten. You want to wait here and then we can go?"

"Sure." Lowering myself into a chair, I pull out my phone and scroll through the text messages until I find the one from Addison.

ADDISON

When do I get to meet your wedding date?

When do you want to meet her? Maybe this weekend? I can bring her to the bar.

No!

I mean, sure, but I want some one
on one time with her. Or girls only
time.

Why?

Girl reasons.

What? What does that even mean?
Do you need to talk about tampons
and your cycles syncing up or
something weird like that?

If you must know, we need to talk
about you.

I don't approve of this plan.

Give me her number. I'll work out
the rest from there.

Sighing, I contemplate how to manage this. The last thing I need is Addison filling Kat's head with her opinions of me.

"Okay, ready to go." Kat's perfectly arched eyebrows pull together as she looks at me. "What?"

Standing, I shove my phone back in my pocket and hold a hand out to Kat. "Nothing really. My buddy's fiancée is still on the warpath about meeting you."

"I told you I don't mind." Kat slides her laptop into her purse and slings the bag over her shoulder in one smooth move. "When? I'm pretty open this weekend."

"Addison, the bride-to-be, is going to text you to figure something out. But what are you doing Saturday night? My buddies and I are meeting up at the bar. It'll be nice to have you there, if you're okay with a bunch of nosy questions. They want to meet you, too."

"I'd love to come."

We walk into the hallway together, making our way toward my truck as we talk.

"I think you'll like the guys. They're pretty laid back, most of the time. But Addie's the one who really wants to meet you."

Kat's heels click on the sidewalk. "You mentioned that a while ago. I can't wait to meet her."

"She's fun. She's...a lot, though, sometimes." I pull on my neck as we pause at the edge of the parking lot to let a car drive by. "She wants girl time to get to know you, she says."

To my surprise, Kat throws her head back, laughing. I stare at her as she gathers herself, still giggling.

"You're more nervous about that, aren't you? I can tell." She laughs again. "You can handle me meeting your friends. You just don't want me alone with her because we're going to talk about you."

"I'm not—" The denial dies on my lips, because she's dead on. "How do you know that?"

Still laughing, Kat pulls open the passenger door of my truck and slides in. "Because it's written all over your face, Blake. And that's what girls do when they get together. Especially girls whose only connection is through their significant others."

Sighing, she shakes her head as she pulls down the sun visor and flips the mirror open. "God, I needed that laugh. Thanks."

She wipes at imaginary bags beneath her eyes and applies a coat of lipstick, a coral pink color that brings out the gold flecks in her eyes.

I'm not really sure how to respond to that, so I just put the truck into Drive and pull out of my spot.

***

"It's got to be that one." Kat points to a yellow house with white trim.

Three cars are parked on the street in front of the house, and one in the driveway.

I check the street number as I park behind one of the other cars, verifying that this is Dean Kashman's house. "Nice place. Big for one guy. I thought you said he was single."

Kat pulls down the mirror and checks her makeup again. "He was married back when I first started at Ardmore. They got divorced...two years ago, I think? No kids."

Knowing Kashman, I'm not surprised his wife left him.

Kat puts her hand on the door handle, and I softly grip her other arm to stop her. "Hey. You ready?"

Kat smiles, but it doesn't quite reach her eyes. "Yeah. I'm good."

Shaking my head, I capture her gaze. "The truth."

She blinks at me slowly, pulling in a deep breath through her nose before she lets it out through her lips. "Okay, fine. I'm nervous. Is that weird? I'm not worried at all about meeting your friends, who are complete strangers, but the idea of walking into this house and socializing with colleagues has me tied up in knots." Her tongue darts out, licking her lush lips. "There's a lot riding on this. On *us*."

When Kat looks down, I move my fingers to her chin, tipping her face upward to meet my gaze. "We've got this, Kat. *I've* got this. Just relax and trust me."

Something in her softens. It's subtle, with the slightest relaxation of her shoulders, the ease of the pinch between her brows, the loosening of her jaw. If I weren't paying attention, I'd have missed it.

Kat may be a strong, independent woman, successful in her career, but there's another side of her. A side that can lean on a partner who she trusts.

And fuck if it's not the most attractive thing I've ever seen.

My jaw tightens. Nothing real. No feelings, nothing long-term. Because I've seen the fallout of "true love," and I'll be damned if I'm going to put myself—or someone I care about—in that situation.

Slipping her hand into mine, Kat follows me up the brick walkway to the two-story home.

Dean Kashman's house looks different from what I expected. For some reason, I pictured a bachelor pad, with a keg in the corner or something. Maybe because he hit on my girl, I expected it to reflect his single lifestyle.

Hold on. Scratch that. Not my girl.

Just for looks.

Anyway.

I've barely raised my hand to knock when the door opens, revealing Dean Kashman on the other side.

"Welcome, you two. Glad to have you. Feel free to grab a drink and mingle."

His house is tastefully furnished, warm, and inviting. A leather armchair sits next to a bookshelf packed full of books. An oriental rug in the center of the living room creates the illusion of a cozy space between the chair and a matching sofa, a coffee table sitting between them, in the otherwise large, open-concept home.

"I think his ex-wife did the decorating," Kat whispers in my ear, her warm breath tickling my skin.

We make our way to the bar, pausing to greet the other faculty members already in attendance.

Kat is in full career mode—charming, confident, a bright smile for everyone. It's the authoritative professor, but with an added dollop of charm.

I could get addicted to just watching her. I might be addicted already.

By the time we reach the bar, Dean Kashman is already there. I pour myself a glass of cabernet—a pricy one, from the taste of it—while Adam fills a glass with Sauvignon Blanc for Kat and tops off his own.

"I'm excited to hear how things are coming with the new course you're designing," Adam says. "I hope it's not too much stress to ask you two to work together."

His eyes narrow slightly.

How does Kat not see this? Adam is either trying to see through our ruse or, if he's buying it, trying to break us up. Or just showing his bias. I can't tell which, but I'll be paying more attention to figure it out.

Pulling Kat closer to me, I smile. "It's going well. And spending time with this woman is never a hardship."

I press a soft kiss to her cheek. Her skin warms beneath my lips.

Kat blinks up at me, looking slightly dazed, but she recovers quickly. "Yes, the curriculum design is going well. I think we'll have some preliminary outlines for you soon."

"Good, good." Adam lifts his glass to his lips and takes a long sip. "Now, Blake. Game theory is a fascinating subject. I've always wanted to know more. Does it give you a leg up with poker?"

I laugh. "Hardly."

I'm about to elaborate, talk more about my career as a professional poker player, but Kat stiffens next to me. I look around, but nothing has changed. Is it something about our conversation?

Looking down at her, I try to read her expression, but she's plastered a smile on her face. A fake smile, one that says she's uncomfortable with the subject. I don't understand how the idea of playing cards could provoke a sore spot, but you never know.

Changing the subject seems like the safest thing.

"Anyway, I think my subject pales in comparison to Physiology. I'd rather hear more about Kat's latest research project."

She perks up slightly, delivering her elevator pitch in practiced perfection.

I study her as I sip my wine, wondering if I just uncovered a new layer to Kat Milas.

16

KAT

I know I should hate this.

Letting a man take the lead, even my supposed boyfriend. I've spent so long striving to be seen as a professional. Some days it seemed like everything was working against me to get that recognition. It seems like as soon as I think I've made it, someone does something to knock me down a few pegs.

Like last semester, when I walked into the lecture hall for the first day of class and one of the students raised their hand to ask if the professor was running late and had sent his TA instead.

I'm pretty sure the student dropped the class. I introduced myself and started class, and after that first day, I never saw him in that lecture again.

So maybe I should be pushing back, making sure Blake and Adam and everyone else know that Kathleen Fucking Milas is here and that she doesn't need to lean on anyone. That I can hold my own in gatherings like this.

But as soon as we moved on from the course proposal, they started discussing the most boring topic you can imagine.

Golf.

I've tried golfing once. Driving the little cart around was fun, but the fun ended there.

And Adam knows I hate golf because he's in charge of organizing the annual golf fundraiser, which of course means his secretary does the work and he takes the credit. I've been asked every year if I'll participate, and after that one time I tried, I've made it clear that I'm not interested in trying again. In fact, I've tried to get him to consider ideas for the annual fundraiser other than golf, without any success.

I also don't know much about golf because the extent of my knowledge is that you hit a little ball with a stick. My one foray into golf taught me that there are many sticks with which to hit the ball, none of which worked particularly well in my inexperienced hands.

I start to zone out as the conversation veers toward which of the local courses is best. What I should be doing is wandering away, finding another conversation to join in, one that I can actually follow. Networking to take advantage of this evening.

But Blake's hand on my back, the warmth that emanates from his palm and spreads through my entire body, makes me think of other things entirely. And when his fingers gently trace circles, I relax even further into him.

Butterflies rise in my stomach at the casual contact, and a trail of goose bumps makes its way up my spine. With every slow caress, my body heats. Arousal starts to—

"Kat?"

I snap my head to Blake so fast I almost give myself whiplash. What the hell was I thinking? There's no arousal. *None.* Jesus, we're at a work function.

Adam and Blake are both looking at me expectantly.

Crap.

I clear my throat with a smile. "My mind was focused on some ideas for our upcoming course. Could you repeat that?"

Never apologize. Men don't.

"Do you play golf?" Blake asks, apparently for the second time.

I sip at my wineglass. "No, I don't."

Pretty sure Adam could have answered that one for me.

Blake tilts his head. "You ever want to learn, I'll take you. The season is over for this year, but maybe in the spring."

He's really committing to this fake relationship, and I appreciate it. Adam may rub some people—most people—the wrong way, but he's a smart guy. If we slip, he'll sniff it out immediately.

And then any chance I have at promotion is gone.

I step even closer to Blake and lean my head against his shoulder. "That would be amazing, babe."

His eyebrows lift for a fraction of a second, but he recovers quickly.

I look at Adam to see if he caught it as well, but he's focused on me.

"Do you enjoy other sports, Kathleen?" Adam asks.

Thankful to be back in the conversation, I bring my head upright. Leaning on Blake felt good. Too good, honestly. I'm trying to sell this relationship to everyone else.

I don't need to convince myself.

"Yoga is my go-to exercise. Part of the reason I love working at Ardmore. The classes in the fitness center are always fabulous." That may have been a little much on the I-love-Ardmore front, but there's nothing I can do about it now.

Adam drains the last of his wine. "They do have some great programming. Does anyone need a refill?"

I look down at my nearly full glass of wine.

"I think we're good, Adam. Thanks," Blake says.

Adam wanders off, and Blake turns to face me. I miss the warmth of his hand on my back immediately.

"I didn't know you liked yoga." He lifts his cabernet to his lips.

"It's good exercise, and I enjoy it." Shrugging, I take a sip of wine.

I limit myself to one alcoholic drink at work functions. Partly because I usually need to drive home after, but more importantly, because every work function is a chance to promote myself.

Blake's eyes are trained on mine. It's intense, the way he focuses, making me feel like I'm the only person in the room. Almost too intense. Those bright-blue eyes seem to look into my soul.

"I'd offer to join you, but...yoga's not really my thing."

I love the blend of strength, flexibility, and soul-centering I get from yoga. If I'm not taking a class, I like to be alone in a quiet space for my practice, but something tells me I wouldn't mind Blake being there.

"You should join me anyway. You don't have to be good at yoga to get benefit out of it." I nudge his foot with my toe. "You try it out, I'll go golfing with you."

Adam is still at the bar, and everyone else is at least five feet away, so I'm not sure why I'm keeping up this ruse.

Blake winces. "I, uh..." He tugs on the back of his neck. "Okay, if I tell you, you have to promise you won't judge."

"Pinky promise." Holding up my right hand, I extend my pinky finger and hook it together with his.

"I'm not flexible," Blake mutters, so low that I don't hear him at first.

"What?"

"My body doesn't bend in those ways. I always look like a flamingo trying to stand on its head when I try things like that."

The image has me laughing to the point that I almost snort.

I cough to cover it up. "We can start with the basics. You'll like it. I promise."

"Maybe." Blake doesn't look all that enthused.

I lightly shrug. "You try yoga, I'll learn to golf."

In my peripheral vision, I'm vaguely aware of another couple making their way toward us, but I can't tear my gaze away from Blake as one dark eyebrow arches.

"You're on, Milas."

<hr>

I tap the pen against my lips as I read through the answers on this week's exam. I know, I could get my TA to grade these, but I like to know how the students are doing and who needs more help grasping certain concepts.

My phone buzzes from where it's face down on my desk. I mark an answer wrong in red pen before I pick up the phone and swipe it open to check the text that just came in.

Unknown number

Hi, this is Addie, Blake's friend. Well, kind of Blake's friend's fiancée, but Blake is cool too. Did he tell you I want to meet you and hang out? Get to know you before the wedding? I'm going to be at the bar with the guys on Saturday if you'll be there. And I was thinking we could go shopping, maybe this weekend or next. I've got a wedding dress, but you can never have enough sundresses for the Bahamas! If you're up for it we can meet at the mall. I'll bring Holly. She's married to one of Blake's friends. Also she's my sister-in-law. It's a long story. I'll tell you the whole thing when we meet!

I stare at the phone in my hand, leaning back in my desk chair and doing my best not to stereotype based on one text message.

But holy cow, that's one long message. Kind of a stream-of-consciousness thing, which makes me wonder if that's what she's like in real life.

Chatty. Bubbly.

She reminds me a lot of Angela, actually.

Shopping isn't my go-to hangout, but she's right. You can never have enough sundresses. Or bikinis.

Hi Addie!

I throw in the exclamation point, trying to match her excitement.

> I'd love to meet up! I have plans this weekend, but maybe next weekend, or some evening if you want?

The reply comes back immediately.

> Yayyyyy! So excited to meet you. Can't wait to tell you all sorts of stories about Blake. I want to hear what he's like at work! He must be so different than he is with the guys.

> Sounds great!! Talk soon.

After hitting Send, I drop the phone on the desk and sigh. I'm not trying to be someone else with Addie. I just know it's important that she likes me, or at least tolerates me enough that I don't ruin her wedding.

When Blake first asked me, I figured we'd have "broken up" from our fake relationship by then. But as the wedding date is creeping closer, we're still committed to our ruse, so much so that we now have plane tickets to Nassau.

I'm actually looking forward to the wedding. It's in the Bahamas, after all, and who doesn't love a

Caribbean vacation? And more than that, it's a chance to spend time with Blake. We get along well. He's fun, and he's become a good friend.

I've tried to keep my attraction to him to myself, at least mostly. He doesn't need to know that I'm picturing him when I take care of my own needs.

I head up the stairs to Angela's office, needing some advice.

She's at her desk, a massive water bottle next to her while she writes something with a red pen.

I knock on the door frame and step into the office.

"One sec!" Angela calls, scribbling furiously for another few seconds before she sets down the pen and looks up at me. "Hey. What's up?"

Angela is outgoing, the type of person who can walk into a room full of strangers and suddenly be best friends with half of them. I'm hoping she has pointers for me, both on how I managed to land her as a friend when we're so different, and how to win Addie over.

"I'm supposed to meet one of Blake's friends next weekend. It's the girl whose wedding we're going to next month."

She studies me, her brow furrowed. "Okay?"

"I need them to like me. This is important to Blake. And it'll be super awkward at this wedding if everyone hates me."

Angela erupts with laughter. "Jesus, you're neurotic sometimes. I love you." She wipes her eyes, finally gathering herself. "First, Blake likes you, so not everyone will hate you."

"You know what I mean."

"Second," she says, continuing as though I didn't interrupt, "it's easy to make friends. Just be yourself." She sets her elbows on the desk, folding her hands and leaning forward to rest her chin on her fingers. "Kat, you're an amazing woman. You're a badass professor and one of the smartest people I've ever met."

"Yeah, but that doesn't mean that Addie is going to like me."

"Who?" Angela furrows her eyebrows.

"The bride. Blake's friend's fiancée."

"Ah." She stands from her desk. "Well, if she has any common sense, she'll love you. But let's go get some gelato to calm your nerves."

17

———

BLAKE

"Are you wearing makeup?" I stare at the woman holding the door open.

This is Kat's house, and the person in front of me vaguely resembles Kat, but...

"So? I always wear makeup." She bats her eyelashes.

I'm not sure she even realizes she's doing it.

"Yeah, but not makeup like this." I study her face.

If she always wears makeup, it's subtle. This, though, is bolder, but not overpowering. It somehow enhances her features in a way that's hitting me like a gut punch.

Her eyes are lined in black, the color extending beyond her lids. Her lashes are longer than usual, framing those eyes that I get lost in. Her lips are stained a dark red color, but now the peach blush staining her cheeks is more noticeable, and the full effect is enough to practically bring me to my knees.

With the dress she's wearing, the deep teal fabric molding to her body, she looks fucking incredible.

"Do you want me to take it off?" she asks, a slight pinch to her brow.

"Hell, no," I say, too quickly.

A smirk rises on those lips. Did they always look this kissable? My mind drifts back to that night we shared, memories of how soft and sweet they were. I'm itching to pull her to me, kiss her again, but I know better.

This is fake. And I don't do love. Or relationships. And we made a deal.

I reach a hand out to Kat. "Ready to go?"

She sets her hand in mine. I wrap my fingers around her delicate ones as I lead her to my truck. I round the front to the passenger seat and open the door for her.

She gives me a sweet smile as she climbs in, and the unexpected reaction goes straight to my dick. Fuck, she's perfect.

For the first time in a long time, I wish I weren't so fucked up. That I could open myself up to a relationship without the black cloud of negativity hanging over my head. If there were ever a woman who could make me reconsider my stance, it's Kat Fucking Milas.

I close the door softly behind her and round the truck, trying to get a grip. This is an arrangement. Nothing more.

Climbing into the driver's side, I look over at Kat and try for a neutral topic. "How was your day?"

"It was fine. I got a lot of work done."

"Exciting."

She shrugs, a small smile on her face. "It feels good to be done, at least. And I did some laundry."

"Whoa, you should have led with that. You can't match the excitement of something like that."

Kat laughs. I can't get enough of the sound, the one when she's really laughing, not just being polite. When it's real, she throws her head back with a wide smile and lets it out.

We talk more about her thrilling afternoon while I make the short drive to the bar, and then I share some of my excitement from the day.

Spoiler—it also includes house chores. Your thirties are an exciting time.

Now that Cam, Maddox, and I have all moved to the suburbs, besides the increase in chores with home ownership, we've changed which bars we frequent.

The ones out here tend to be more low-key, and parking is much easier.

Yeah, I heard it too. I'm old. I get it.

As we approach the entrance of McFadden's Bar, I reach out to grab Kat's hand.

"You nervous?" she asks, looking up at me.

A smile plays at her lips.

"Nope." I shake my head. "Should I be?"

"I'm just looking forward to hearing what they have to say about you." Kat gives me a playful nudge with her hip.

I pull her into me for a side hug, then let her go to open the door. "Eh, I'm not too worried."

Cam and Maddox are good guys. They'll keep it on the up and up.

"Blake!"

The second the door closes behind us, someone bellows my name, and I groan.

I didn't count on Miller. I love the guy, but he'll take pleasure in telling the most embarrassing story he can think of.

"Sorry about this," I mutter to Kat, just as Miller comes bounding over to us, weaving through the high-top tables scattered across the main section of the pub.

"Hey, man! It's good to see you." He pulls me away from Kat to engulf me in a bear hug. "And this must be Kat. Nice to meet you. How can you put up with this guy?"

Kat appraises him, then she sticks out her hand. "He's fun for now. Why, you have a better option for me?"

Miller chuckles and tucks Kat under his arm, leading her back to the table where Maddox and Cam have their arms wrapped around their girls. I trudge behind them, already regretting my decision to let Kat meet the guys.

"Did he tell you about Maddox's wedding?" Miller asks, bringing his beer to his lips.

I scowl into my pint glass, leaning back into the cracked vinyl of the booth. This is the third story Miller has brought up, and each is more embarrassing than the last.

The worst part about this one is that I honestly don't know what he's about to share. I may have overindulged slightly at Maddox's wedding. But it was the first of my best friends to get married off, and as one of his groomsmen, I spent the day throwing back beers and vodka shots. I remember drinking one glass of champagne at the reception, but beyond that, it's a little fuzzy.

Miller stretches his arms in front of him, fingers laced, clearly getting ready to tell this story with what will likely be a dramatic flair and a gross over-exaggeration. "So, we've been drinking all day."

Cam clears his throat while Addie smiles up at him.

"Except for Cam," Miller amends. "But the rest of us. Blake is keeping up, actually having a good time. I saw him smile, even. He was almost the life of the party. If I hadn't been there, he would have had a solid shot at the title. He holds it together through the ceremony, standing up there in his tux with the rest of us. He makes it to the reception."

This is where my memories fail me. I cross my fingers that it isn't too bad.

"He got into the dancing. I'm telling you, you've never seen moves like this. He was on fire. And then maybe on fire for real, because he must have gotten too hot."

Oh no. A hazy memory starts to creep up. Did I...

"He took his suit jacket *and* his shirt off and continued to dance topless."

Maddox rolls his eyes. Holly snorts, covering her mouth with her hand.

Kat dissolves into laughter. "Oh my God. I wish I could have seen that!"

She places her hand on my upper arm, her touch electric.

I suppose it could be worse, honestly. I never would have danced at all, let alone topless, if I'd been in my right mind. But it's not like I hit on someone inappropriate or threw up, or in some other way ruined the wedding.

"Oh, it gets better."

Hold up. There's more?

Miller looks gleeful as he continues to ruin my life. "He did the worm, then hit on Maddox's mom and offered to show her his worm."

What? That doesn't sound like me, even if I was completely blitzed.

Kat has one eyebrow raised, as though she's doubting the validity of this story. "Really?"

Miller's lips twitch. "Well, he did take his shirt off."

I'm going to murder him. Not tonight, though.

Instead, I brush my lips against Kat's ear, needing to regain some control here. "You play your cards right, you might get to see me topless again sometime."

"That a promise?" she asks, her lips twisted in a smirk.

"Hey, think we can get him to do the same thing at

Cam's wedding?" Maddox says, his mouth against Holly's hair.

She giggles. "I like the idea."

"Me, too," Addie chimes in.

Before I can open my mouth to object, Miller is getting into the idea.

"I bet we can. Anyone want to put money on it?"

Beside me, Kat stiffens, and I give her a questioning look. When she shakes her head, I lean in close again, whispering so only she can hear.

"You okay?"

A small nod. "Yeah. I just don't like anything about gambling." She shifts, sliding out of the booth as she raises her voice. "I'm going to run to the ladies' room. Be right back."

She disappears toward the back of the pub as I'm still processing her words. She doesn't like *gambling*? I mean, sure, lots of people don't like to gamble, or see it as a waste of money. But it seems like there's something more to it for her, the way her body turned rigid.

"Hey, I'll be right back." I stand from the booth, needing to follow Kat to find out more. "And, uh, by the way, Kat doesn't like gambling, so let's just stay away from that topic, okay?"

I turn around quickly, but it's not quite fast enough to catch the bewildered stares. I get it, honestly. We've all made a living as professional gamblers. So it's not exactly a taboo subject. If anything, it's our most common topic of discussion when we get together. But I don't know what's going on in Kat's mind right now.

I follow her path through the dimly lit bar to the restrooms, where I lean against the wall. I only have to wait a few minutes before the door of the women's room opens and Kat steps out, a fresh coat of lipstick applied. In the shadowy hallway, her eyes stand out even more, deep and huge and sultry.

"Hi. Blake," she says, sounding surprised.

"Hey. Just wanted to make sure you were okay." I gently grip her upper arms with my hands, steadying her. "What's up with the gambling thing? It seemed like more than just a 'not liking it' situation. Want to talk about it?"

Her shoulders lift beneath my hands then fall as she blows out a breath. "Not really, but it's not a secret. My dad was really into gambling. It got bad when I was in middle school, and then by high school, it had turned into an addiction, and it broke him.

"He got deeper into debt, and he ended up going through all of my parents' savings. Even my college fund. They'd worked so hard to save money for my education so I could follow in his footsteps at Yale, and then...there was nothing left.

"It's such a trigger for me. I'm sorry. Hearing about it, being around people who are into gambling, even as a joke... It's hard for me."

My heart twists. I've known too many people who've gone through gambling addiction. I'm well aware of how it can drag the rest of your life and your family and friends down with you. I know how important education is to Kat, how hard she's worked to get where she is now.

"I'm sorry, babe," I murmur, wrapping my arms around her. "Thank you for telling me."

Kat relaxes against my body. She fits so perfectly, her head right at the curve between my neck and shoulders. I slide my hand along her back.

A soft sigh escapes from her lips, the sound causing blood to drain from my head and flow straight into my cock as she presses more firmly against me.

This whole relationship may be fake, but I'm a man, not a saint. When a gorgeous woman's body is leaning into mine, control only goes so far. And when she's a smart, sassy woman like Kat, I forget the rules for a minute.

Tipping her chin upward just enough to meet my

gaze, I lower my lips slowly toward hers, giving her time.

And *fuck*, when her eyes drift closed and her mouth opens slightly? I'm a fucking goner.

My lips brush gently against hers, our kisses chaste at first. I catch a hint of the Guinness she was drinking earlier.

Then it's Kat who deepens the kiss, her lips growing firmer against mine.

I trace my tongue over the outline of her mouth, and it falls open, granting me entry. I slip my tongue inside, teasing and tasting and exploring.

Sliding my hand up her side, I reach the underside of her breast, brushing a thumb along the swell, and she moans into my mouth. I walk her forward two steps until her back is pushed up against the wall.

My fingers are itching to creep lower, to move down from the crest of her hip to her thigh, to slip down the crease where her leg meets her pelvis. I press one hand against the wall next to her head, our lips still tangled as I drag my fingers lightly down her hips.

"Hey!"

The sudden voice makes us fly apart.

I stifle a groan. "Miller, what are you doing?"

I really am going to murder him. Then I will bring him back to life so I can murder him again.

He shrugs good-naturedly. "Watching. I like to be a voyeur when I can't be with Becs."

We all know his girlfriend is up in New York, working hard in her final year of med school, so she couldn't make the trip down here with Miller. He won't shut up about it.

"Really?" Kat asks, looking far too curious about Miller's kinks.

"Maybe. Or maybe I just had to go to the bathroom." He steps past us and pushes the men's room door open. "Carry on."

Kat and I look at one another, our moment shattered.

"I'm sorry," I say quickly. "I shouldn't have—"

"Sorry," she says at the same time. "That was—"

We face one another, still breathing heavily. I'm hard as a rock, my cock pressing painfully against my jeans.

"Sorry," I say again. "I'm going to head to the men's room. I'll see you back at the table."

I duck into the restroom, running away like a fucking coward, because what the hell was I thinking?

This isn't a real relationship. We touch and we kiss *only* when we need to play the part.

Not in some back hallway of a bar. And a kiss sure as hell shouldn't affect me like this.

I use the privacy of the men's room to adjust myself, ignoring Miller, before I make my way back to the table.

When I slide into the booth next to Kat, she shifts slightly, so her thigh doesn't press against mine, and she doesn't meet my eyes.

I take a sip of my beer, but my stomach is in knots.

Did I just ruin everything?

18

———

KAT

"So, Kat," Addie says. "You work with Blake?"

I take a sip of beer as I nod, forcing my mind to stay in the present instead of replaying that kiss in the back hallway. What was I *thinking*?

"I'm a professor at Ardmore, too," I answer. "I'm in the Biology department, though."

"Oh, cool!" she says, lifting her cocktail. "What area? I teach math, but high school, not college. It must be so different."

I smile. "I focus on Anatomy and Physiology. I love it, but I'm a huge science nerd."

I shiver as I set my glass down. It's still warm for early November, in the mid-forties, so I'm in a short-sleeved top. I'm regretting not wearing a sweater.

"Are you cold?" Addie asks, her eyes large. "You

could go sit in the corner. Because it's...ninety degrees."

Her nose twitches before she bursts into laughter at the same time I do.

"Oh my God," I say, still smiling. "You're a math nerd. I love it."

Addie raises her drink across the table, and we clink our glasses together as she dives into a story about a teenager who didn't turn in his homework because, he claimed, his hamster ate it.

I snort when she tells me that the student then produced a nibbled-up worksheet and a textbook on which said hamster had relieved himself.

"At least my students don't usually have family pets to worry about," I say, helping myself to a handful of pretzels from the bowl in the center of the table. "The closest I've gotten is the emotional support dog one of my students has this year. But he's pretty well behaved and just sleeps through class."

Addie throws back her head with laughter. "I love that. What kind of dog?"

"Bassett hound. He drools a little, but he doesn't make noise. His name is Biscuit."

We trade stories about students while the guys have their own conversations around us. When Blake announces that it's time for us to head out, Addie reaches across the table and grabs my arm.

"Hey. I have a great idea."

"Yeah?" I ask.

We've only known one another for an hour or so, but Addie has wedged herself firmly into my heart. She'd get along so well with Angela and Naomi. I can't wait to spend more time with her.

"Come to my bachelorette party. It's next weekend."

I bite my lip. "Which day? I'm supposed to hang out with my two friends on Saturday, but maybe I could come if it's Sunday. It wouldn't be weird?"

Addie shakes her head. "Not weird at *all*. The more the merrier. It's Saturday, but bring them along. If they're anything like you, I'll love them."

I waver. "I could ask them."

Cam rolls his eyes, smiling. "She's going to bug you until you say yes, you know."

A laugh bubbles out of me. "Okay, then. I'll check with my friends and let you know."

Addie squeals. "I'll text you the details! Can't wait!"

"So what are we doing again?" Naomi asks from my passenger seat.

"Not sure. All I know is we're going to Addie's house. It should be right around...here," I say, approaching a driveway full of cars. "She just said it would be fun and that I should bring you. I think you guys will like her."

When Addie insisted on me bringing Naomi and Angela, I protested at first, but she insisted that the more people we had, the better it would be.

She refused to tell me what *it* was.

I park on the street and pick up my purse and the bottle of champagne that I brought for Addie, along with the gift that Angela, Naomi, and I went in on.

It's a gift card for one of the stores she listed on her wedding registry. I figured that was safest. Angela thought we should buy her a vibrator, but I've only met the girl once. Naomi and I agreed that I should probably get to know her better before I buy her sex toys.

Addie's house is a beautiful brick two-story with gabled windows and white trim on a quiet cul-de-sac not too far from my place.

"Do you think they'll have a male stripper?" Angela asks as we walk up the driveway.

I elbow her. "This is a nice neighborhood. I think it'll be classy."

Holly opens the front door when we knock. "Come on in! Kat, it's good to see you again."

I hand her the champagne. "Thanks for having us. This is Angela and Naomi," I say, gesturing.

Holly beams at them. "Glad to have you guys. Head on into the living room. Hope you're ready for some fun."

As we turn the corner to enter the living room, my jaw falls open.

"I told you we should have bought her a vibrator!" Angela whispers gleefully.

I don't answer her.

What does one even say when you enter a room to find a large table covered with brightly colored silicone sex toys?

An unfamiliar woman is arranging a pile of dildos into what I imagine is supposed to be an artful display. She turns as we enter the room.

"Come in, come in!" she trills. "I'm Cleo. Grab a glass of wine. Addie, doll, are we waiting for anyone else?"

Addie waves to me from the couch, where she's sitting with two unfamiliar women. "Hi, Kat! Thanks for coming. This must be Naomi and Angela."

I nod to confirm as she turns to Cleo.

"We're just waiting for Annika, and then we'll get started." Addie lifts herself from the couch and comes toward us, her arms wrapping around me in a hug. "This is going to be so fun! Cleo is a friend of Holly's former roommate. She does these parties. Like Tupperware parties, except with sex toys."

I just blink as Angela claps and giggles.

"Anyway, Cleo is going to show us her products, and we get a chance to buy stuff. If people buy a certain amount, I get freebies." Addie gestures toward the women on the couch. "That's my sister Josie and her wife, Chris, and you know Holly. My best friend, Annika, will be here, too."

I make eye contact with the two women and give them a smile as Angela hands me a glass of wine.

The dark-haired woman has her arm around the blonde woman.

"I'm Josie," she says. "Nice to meet you guys. You ever been to something like this?"

At least I'm not the only one blindsided here.

***

"Let's move on to dildos," Cleo says, setting aside the last clit vibrator.

We've been listening to her explain the different settings available for the last fifteen minutes.

After the initial awkwardness, I've settled in, getting more comfortable with the products she's been showing us.

Or maybe it's the second glass of wine that's hitting me now.

I'm no stranger to toys, but the idea of discussing them out in the open with people I don't know well is a new experience.

"Show us the big ones!" Holly says, cackling.

Cleo holds up a silicone penis that looks pretty massive to me, although it's smaller than Blake. "This one is one of our best sellers. It's a moderate size, with a lifelike profile."

That's *moderate*? I'm a little scared to see the largest ones. But then, I managed Blake, didn't I? And it was fabulous.

My pussy clenches at the memory.

"I've been ruined for life," Addie says dramatically. "That little thing isn't going to do it for me."

"Really?" Holly asks. "How big?"

It's like a car wreck. I watch in morbid fascination as Addie peruses the table of faux cocks and finally picks up one that's a little larger than the first one.

"He's like this," she announces, holding up the blue sparkly phallus for us to see.

Holly joins her at the table. "Maddox is more like... this." She shows off a dark-pink dildo that's about an inch shorter than Addie's, and slightly thinner.

"Ugh." Addie covers her eyes. "That's my brother. Just... no."

Holly giggles and ignores her. "How about you, Kat?"

I choke on my wine.

"How big is Blake?" Addie asks, clapping her hands with glee, disgust over the discussion of her brother's cock forgotten. "I bet he's big. Those broody types always are."

I cough, trying to recover from inhaling the alcohol.

"Um. About like that," I manage.

"Which one?" Addie asks, holding hers up next to Holly's.

Oh God.

"I thought you said it was small," Angela pipes up.

Naomi takes the opportunity to go to the table and selects her own dildo. "This is like my husband."

I'm not going to be able to look her husband in the eye for quite a while.

Everyone looks at me as my cheeks burn. But then,

does it even matter how big I tell them Blake is? We're not really dating, but I have seen his equipment. And it's not like anyone's about to fact-check me here.

I take a large sip of wine and stand. The table is spread with more fake penises than I've ever seen. I didn't even know they came in such extensive...variety, I guess. I spot one that looks similar to the one I own already. Compared to Blake, it's tiny.

After a minute or so, I pick up a jet-black cock and hold it up. "Like this."

It's heavy in my hand, solid, and thinking about Blake's dick is doing funny things to my head.

"That's a nice one," Cleo says, taking over. "This one is larger than some of our others, but it's also very popular."

"Does it work with a strap-on harness?" Chris asks with interest.

Josie smacks her, but she's smiling. "That is *way* too big."

Cleo takes every comment in stride as she presents a variety of dildos, in all different sizes, shapes, and colors, and I do my best to sink into the couch.

I still have my eye on that black one. I can't exactly admit that the only way I'll have a Blake-sized cock inside me is by using this plastic one, though. Or that I'm craving the feel of him.

Considering my options, I look around at what the other women have bought so far.

Angela has purchased three items—two vibrators and a clit stimulator.

Naomi has purchased a vibrating cock ring. Now I have two reasons I can't look Josh in the eye.

I get up from the couch and make my way to the side table to pour more wine.

While I'm there, I lean over to whisper in Addie's ear, "What if we want to buy something but not in front of everyone?"

She giggles. "We're practically like sisters here. But if you really don't want to do it in front of everyone, you can have someone else buy it. Or she has order forms over there so you can write down what you want."

She points to a stack of papers.

I breathe a sigh of relief. I'm all for the silent paper ordering.

Taking a sip from my refilled wineglass, I snag a paper from the stack and head back to my seat.

"Kat."

A deep voice calls my name, seeming to come from far away.

I squeeze my eyes tighter shut, not wanting to leave my dream.

"Kat." Again, insistent.

A hand settles on my shoulder. Large, warm, firm.

"Blake," I mumble, because this dream is so vivid, I think I can smell him, that spicy, woodsy scent that I can't get enough of.

The couch beneath me shifts. "Kat. Wake up."

Finally, I force my eyes open, blinking against the light.

I'm still in Addie's living room, but it's quiet now. The table of dildos is empty other than a few boxes.

"Hey, girl," Addie says, leaning over the back of the couch. "You good? You fell asleep, and we didn't want to wake you."

Oh my God. I am mortified. Who goes to a friend's bachelorette party—a new friend, nonetheless—and falls asleep?

"Angela and Naomi got a ride home with Annika. Blake is going to take you home." Addie nods toward something.

I turn toward the direction she's indicating and realize why I can smell Blake.

He's here.

Sitting on the couch next to me, his face a mask of concern.

"Let's go home," he says, holding a hand out.

How did he get roped into this? Obviously, I had enough to drink that I fell asleep, so I'm in no condition to drive, but he shouldn't have to rescue me here.

"Addie called Cam, and Cam drove me over," he says, answering my unasked question.

I place a hand over my eyes. This could not be going worse.

Blake reaches over and takes my hand, tugging me into a seated position. "Do you need to get any of your things?"

Addie heads to the table, grabs a box, and hands it to me. "Here you go. Your Blake-sized dildo."

Yep, it just got worse.

Blake does his best to hold back his laughter, but he can't hide the smirk on his face. "Come on, babe. Let's get you and your dildo home."

19

BLAKE

Kat's eyes close as soon as we start driving, and I can't stop looking over at her.

She's different this way. Softer, more vulnerable. Completely different from the hard exterior she cultivates at work.

I drive her Honda Accord back to my house. My truck is in the garage since the guys were at my place when Addie called Cam, and he gave me a ride. Kat may freak out at waking up at my place, but at least she can just get in her car and drive back home once she's sobered up.

"Kat," I say, tapping her leg.

No response.

She's either really tired or really drank too much, or a combination of the two. Addie said that Kat had three glasses of wine, and I've never seen Kat have more than one, so my money's on a drunk Kat.

I try again, this time getting a groan from her, but she's no closer to waking up.

"All right, babe," I say, unbuckling her seat belt. "Time for bed."

It's 7 p.m., too early for me to go to bed, but it's late enough that I think she's out for the night. I climb out of the driver's side and round the car to her door, where I scoop her into my arms.

I snag her purse with one hand, but I leave the dildo on the floor, despite the fact that I'm dying to see it. Apparently, Kat told them it was the same size as me. I'd love to know how she pictures me after that one night.

It better be damn big.

As we walk through the house, Kat settles her head against my neck. The scent of her shampoo tickles my nose, something floral and coconut, and *fuck*, this is killing me.

I haven't wanted more than a one-night stand with any woman in years, so my self-imposed ban on relationships hasn't been a problem. But now my need to protect myself and the people around me from hurt is directly clashing with my desire for *more*.

I want more of everything Kat has to offer.

Her gorgeous smile.

Her quick wit.

Her dirty mind and luscious body.

The way she gets me in a way that so few people do.

I carry her into the guest room and place her gently on the bed. Kat immediately rolls to one side, pressing her face into the pillow. I slip her shoes off and set them next to her on the floor.

Now what? She's wearing jeans. It's not the most comfortable sleepwear, but she may murder me if I undress her while she's asleep.

I push a hand through my hair. There's no right option here.

I stare at her sleeping form for a few minutes, trying to decide, and all it does is make me hard.

Fuck.

I grit my teeth and reach over her to carefully unbutton her jeans, then I peel them down her long legs. She rolls to her stomach as I pull a blanket up and over her, but not before I get a good view of her ass, her thong nestled between the two round globes.

My cock strains painfully against my jeans. This woman has no idea what she does to me.

I manage to fold her jeans neatly and set a pair of

shorts and a soft T-shirt on the bedside table, along with a bottled water, before I lose all control.

Once I make sure Kat is settled, I move to my bedroom, where I strip out of my clothes and head straight for the shower. There's a bead of precum already forming at the tip of my cock.

I step into the shower and brace my hand against the tile as the hot water streams over me. My dick is so hard it's painful. I grip the base and squeeze. Why can't I let this arrangement with Kat be what it is?

This is a business deal. An agreement.

Not a goddamn relationship or even friends with benefits.

But fuck if I can't get her out of my mind.

I reach for the body wash, squeeze some into my hand, and use the liquid to coat my fist as it glides along my length.

The pressure builds as she consumes my consciousness. I grit my teeth, moving faster as need coils inside me. My head falls back as my chest tightens and my breaths get faster.

Her sass. Her confidence. Fuck, there's nothing about this woman that doesn't turn me on.

And when the edges of my vision blacken, when my legs shake as I come, it's her face I'm picturing.

The humidity hits me square in the face as soon as we step off the plane in Nassau. Cam promised me that November is the perfect time to visit the Bahamas.

"Not too hot and not too humid," he said. "It'll be gorgeous."

I call bullshit.

It's got to be at least eighty degrees, and the air is so thick with humidity that I could cut it with a knife.

It doesn't help that I'm wearing jeans and a button-down Oxford shirt. I was comfortable in Philadelphia and on the plane, but now it's a different story.

Kat, for her part, looks effortlessly beautiful and breezy. She wore a dress with a sweater on the plane, and now that we've stepped outside, the sweater has been tucked into her tote bag, leaving her in just a sundress. The yellow of the fabric looks perfect against her tan skin. It's almost glowing.

Her face is glowing, too, a smile stretched from ear to ear. It doesn't fade as we pick up our luggage, as we slide into a taxi, or even as the receptionist at the hotel drops a bomb on me.

"I'm sorry, what was that?" I say, just in case I didn't hear her correctly.

"We have you and Miss Milas in room 402. Would you like any help with your bags?" The woman behind the counter—Jenny, her name tag says—smiles helpfully.

I'm about to put Jenny in her place, point out that we should *obviously* have two rooms and that someone messed up the reservation. But even as I open my mouth, a finger taps my shoulder.

"Thank you. Room 402 sounds great. We can handle the bags." Kat steps up to the counter from behind me, sliding closer to me and then, when I don't expect it at all, elbowing me in the ribs.

"Ow!" I protest, wondering what I did.

Kat glares daggers at me.

"Here are your keys," Jenny says, clearly ready to be done with us.

"Thank you," Kat says.

She grabs my arm and hauls me toward the elevator, luggage in tow.

As the elevator door slides closed, she finally lets me go.

"What was that about?" I ask.

Kat rolls her eyes. "You doofus. We're here as a couple. Of course Cam and Addie only booked us one room. They think we're a real couple. Plus, how much do you want to bet there's only one bed? How did you not think this through?"

Uh, good question. I didn't, obviously. When I first decided to bring Kat to this wedding, it was mostly an attempt to avoid being set up with Addie's friend. And then Kat and I got along well, so I figured it would be fun to hang out with her.

And despite my PhD-anointed brain, I didn't put any thought into where two people who are supposedly dating might spend the night while on vacation.

I'm not all that surprised that she thought it through, actually. She's smarter than I am, in plenty of ways. What *is* surprising is that she anticipated the one-bed situation and still agreed to come along.

The elevator opens on our floor, and Kat strides toward room 402.

"You coming?" she says, holding the door open.

I step into the room, and once again, I momentarily forget our situation. This place is beautiful. It's not so much a hotel room as a suite, with white walls and curtains accented with a beige the color of sand. Framed artwork of flowers and the ocean provide pops of color.

I slip off my shoes just inside the door and let my toes curl into the thick white carpet. Keeping this place clean has to be a colossal task, but it's absolutely breathtaking.

I push back the gauzy curtains, revealing a view of the beach that's so freaking gorgeous that I suck in a breath. "Kat. Come here."

"Huh?" she calls from deep inside the suite.

I turn around to see her poke her head out from the bedroom, which is its own separate room from the sitting room that we entered. I cross my fingers that when I finally get around to checking it out, there will be two beds. Because there's no way I'll be able to share a bed with Kat and keep my hands off of her.

"Come see this." I beckon with my hand.

Kat saunters over, dropping a pillow on the love seat as she passes.

"What are you doing?" I ask, curious about the pillow.

"Uh, coming to see something. You called me." Kat looks at me like I've grown a third head.

I need to rein this in. I'm used to being in control, confident, the one people can lean on. But the idea of sharing a room with Kat has thrown me for a loop, and I'm floundering here.

Jesus, I can't believe I didn't see this coming. It sounds like the plot from one of those romance novels

Miller is always reading. Oh no, they go on vacation, and there's only one bed, and now they have to bang.

I straighten my shoulders. There will be no banging. This is a professional arrangement.

"With the pillows, Kat. Are you redecorating?"

She looks past me to the beach, her eyes growing wide as she takes in the massive expanse of coastline that's visible and the ocean that stretches as far as I can see. "This is beautiful. I could just look at this view all day."

I could, too, although my view is one of Kat's tight ass and long legs in that sundress, her hands pressed up against the window. What would it be like to fuck her just like this? Her looking out at the ocean, watching the waves crash on the sand as I drive into her over... and over...and over...

"Blake?" Kat's eyebrows form a line as they pull together.

Fuck.

"I'm good. What's going on with the pillow?" Maybe if I redirect this, she'll ignore the fact that I was staring at her ass.

"Oh. That. I figured I'd sleep on the love seat. It's not huge, but it'll be fine for a few nights. I know you were kind of thrown by sharing a room."

I turn to look at the sofa. "Love seat" is an accurate

description. "Oversized armchair" may be even more accurate, actually.

"You can't sleep there."

"Why?"

The love seat looks like it could fit maybe half of Kat's body comfortably. If she pushes her head up against one arm, her legs will hang off the other end. There's no chance that would be comfortable for anyone but a four-year-old.

I gesture to the seating, which looks smaller by the minute. "It's nowhere near big enough. Your legs are going to hang over the edge."

She studies the furniture. "It'll be fine for a few nights. Besides, what's the other option? Are you going to sleep there?"

"We're adults. We can share a bed without it getting inappropriate. Right?" I take a step toward the bedroom, but I look over my shoulder at Kat. "Right?"

At least, I sure as hell hope she can. Because my willpower is growing really, *really* thin.

This may be a king-sized bed, but right now, it feels smaller than the love seat where I originally planned to sleep.

Everything was fine when we went to sleep. Blake settled on his side, I stayed on mine, and we had plenty of space between us.

So why do I feel like I'm being squished between two walls?

I wiggle my butt, trying to make some space, and a sound makes me freeze.

What was that?

"Mmmm." It comes again, low and rumbling.

As if someone has flipped a light switch, my brain suddenly starts functioning. I'm lying on the very edge of the mattress, at risk of falling off the bed entirely, while Blake has managed to make his way over to my side during the night. He's pressed up against me, my back to his chest, and one heavily muscled arm is wrapped around my midsection, holding me close.

"Blake," I hiss, trying to wake him up.

I wiggle my hips again and immediately wish I hadn't.

Or maybe I wish I'd gotten a better feel.

Because my back may be pressed against his chest, but my ass is up against something else entirely.

Something hard.

Big.

Really big.

My body heats as I remember our night together, the way he felt inside me. The way he commanded my body, allowing me to surrender my control to him.

The kiss we shared in the bar.

There's something between us, more than just an arrangement. Blake has even admitted it.

What I don't understand is why he's so against turning this into something real. It certainly feels real right now, with him holding me close and both of us turned on.

Okay, maybe it's just me, and his erection is just morning wood or in response to a dream.

But that kiss? He wasn't faking.

"Mmm." Blake mumbles something unintelligible and pulls me closer, and dear God, I have to actively stop myself from grinding my ass up against his groin.

When did I become such a sex-crazed hussy?

Actually, don't answer that. I can guess. It was probably around the time that this man gave me the best sex of my life and then declared that we'd spend all this time together with "no intimacy at all." It's like I've been edged for the past three months. I'm about to explode.

"Blake," I whisper.

His only response is another muffled sound.

I'm so sexually frustrated that I'm about to scream. I press my thighs together, searching for some relief, but it's not enough.

Why did he have to sleep practically naked?

I followed the rules. Everyone knows that if you're pretending to be someone's girlfriend, you're inevitably going to end up sharing a bed at some point. Right? So I planned ahead and packed for any option —flannel shorts and top to be cute but comfortable, a T-shirt and shorts if we're going casual, and a nearly see-through negligee. Just in case.

Blake, on the other hand, didn't plan ahead. Or maybe he did, and he's intentionally torturing me. A pair of boxers that does nothing to hide his sizable bulge with nothing else? That's what you wear when you're in your bed alone. Or when you're sleeping with your *actual* girlfriend.

Not when you insist that there can't be anything real between you and the person you're sharing a bed with.

I shift again.

Blake is dead to the world.

But maybe it's not the worst thing. I slide my hand down, moving beneath his hold, to tease the waistband of my flannel shorts. When he doesn't show any sign of waking, I let my fingers slip beneath the elastic and down to find my clit.

I'm hot and wet just from being next to Blake, and even the lightest touch on my clit has me biting my lip to keep from moaning out loud.

I press harder, my fingers sliding over the sensitive spot.

There's something about Blake's hard body against mine and the fact that he's asleep and could wake up any minute and catch me. It's just taboo enough to drive my arousal higher. I move my fingers faster, rushing toward an orgasm.

I hold my breath, trying not to make noise as I near the peak, climbing closer and closer until I tumble over, my body tightening and shaking with the force of my release.

As I come down from my climax, I listen to Blake's breathing. Is the pattern different? Now that I'm thinking slightly more clearly, I'm hoping I wasn't loud enough to wake him. He's in the same position, his arm around my waist. I turn my head to peek at his face—eyes still closed.

Breathing out a sigh of relief, I relax into the pillow.

Then, with no warning, Blake pulls his arm away from me, rolls to the other side of the bed and off, stands, and heads into the bathroom in one swift movement.

I roll over and stare after him, listening. The shower starts.

Crap. He must have heard me, or I woke him up somehow. My face flames with embarrassment.

I'm about to bury my face in my pillow and just fake sleep for the rest of the day. That's the best course of action here, right? If my fake boyfriend did, indeed, catch me masturbating while in the same bed as him—while *cuddling* with him, even—the only acceptable solution is avoidance until this has disappeared from our memories.

But then, maybe I shouldn't be embarrassed. He's

the one who may have caught me, but he's the one who ran off. For all he knows, I was thinking about someone else.

I mean, I obviously wasn't. But he doesn't know that.

Blake has got to be the most frustrating human I've ever met. He says he doesn't want a relationship, but then he proposes this fake-dating thing. He says no real feelings or intimacy, and then he kisses me in the back of a bar and finds every possible opportunity to touch me.

There's more to this than he's told me. I can tell.

A sound from the bathroom catches my attention. I strain to hear, but it's muffled through the door.

So, like any normal sneaky person, I slip out of bed and tiptoe across the room to press my ear to the bathroom door.

The running water from the shower is the loudest noise, but Blake's deep groan is unmistakable. I'm about to knock and ask if he's okay, when the sound comes again, long and low.

And then, "Kat. Oh, fuck."

I gasp, a hand flying up to cover my mouth as I spring back from the door to make sure he doesn't know I'm snooping.

A smile spreads over my face, and I feel much better about him catching me masturbating.

Because while I'm almost certain now that he did hear me, I know what he's doing in the shower. And he can say all he wants that there can't be anything real between us, but he wants me.

I just have to convince him to give it a chance. And since he was in control the first time we were together, this time, it's all up to me.

***

"What are you doing?"

Blake glares at me from his lounge chair. "Nothing."

Well, maybe not *glares*. But his look suggests that he's either annoyed with me, on edge, or displeased with some situation.

I'm inclined to think it's all of the above.

I give him a bright smile as I lean on my elbow, letting my boobs press together into some pretty impressive cleavage.

We're relaxing by the pool, both of us in swimsuits. Blake wanted to just keep things low-key today before the rehearsal dinner tonight.

From my perspective, things are about as opposite of low-key as they can get.

Ever since I overheard Blake taking care of himself in the shower and muttering my name while he stroked himself, I'm on a mission. To prove to Blake that we have a chance.

Did this start as an arrangement? Yes. But there's so much more here. I know it, and he knows it. And I'm not talking about the *attraction* that he pointed out in the blandest way.

I want him. I'll admit it. Since our one-night stand, I've fantasized about having a repeat of that evening.

But it's more than just lust, I've realized. I've gotten used to being around Blake. When something happens, he's the one I want to tell.

I've never been in love. I'm not even sure I know what love is, if I'm being honest. But Blake is the first person I've been with—even if I'm not really *with* him —who makes me want to see if love can really happen.

And I'll be damned if his hard-headedness stands in the way of that. I'm Kat Fucking Milas. I'm a catch.

To drive home the point in my internal debate, I lean farther toward him, squeezing my breasts together with my upper arms until I look like some kind of *Sports Illustrated* swimsuit model.

Heat flares in Blake's eyes as his gaze rakes down my neck and to my breasts.

I give them another squeeze, just in case.

"Do you want to get a drink?" I ask innocently.

A muscle ticks in his jaw. "I'm good. Do you need me to go grab you something?"

I tilt my head, giving him another few seconds to take in my pose. "No thanks. Was just seeing if you wanted something."

I roll onto my back, resting an arm over my eyes.

The bikini I chose today was strategic. It's a pale blue, the tiny triangles of fabric leaving plenty of cleavage on display, and the bottoms cut high on my hips, and I'm loving the appreciation in Blake's gaze.

While I might dress conservatively when I teach, I work hard for my body, and I'm proud of it.

The key to seducing a man, though, is to leave him wanting.

I sit up, swinging my legs over the side of the lounge chair. "I'm going to head in and get cleaned up for the rehearsal dinner. You coming?"

"I'm going to stay here." Blake has been a man of few words today, his communication consisting mostly of heated stares and one-word answers.

I smirk as I walk away, swaying my hips a touch

more than usual. If I'm already getting to him, he's in for a surprise.

Leaning toward the mirror, I add a touch of lipstick to freshen my look. Everything is going according to plan this evening.

My makeup is on point. My dress hits at exactly the right spot to showcase my calves, long and lean in the nude heels that give me an extra three inches of height. The jade green fabric complements me perfectly, making my hazel eyes a shade warmer somehow, and the neckline strikes the perfect balance between high enough to wear to a classy event like a rehearsal dinner and low enough to attract attention.

Not just anyone's attention. Blake's.

And I can tell I have it.

His gaze has been on me practically every second, so heated and heavy I can feel it. I'm taking every opportunity to touch him. We're seated next to one another at the dinner table, and I'm using the proximity to its full advantage.

Leaning over to whisper something directly in his ear.

Touching his muscled forearm to get his attention.

"Accidentally" tapping his foot with mine.

From the way the muscle in his jaw jumped the last two times I brushed my fingers over his arm, I think we're in a solid position. When we make our way back to the room tonight, I'll make my move. He won't be able to resist it.

I give my boobs a squeeze and drop the lipstick back into my purse.

Heading down the hallway on my way back to dinner, I see Blake approaching from the opposite direction. My stomach clenches with nerves even as a sly smile crosses his face.

I put extra sway into my step and lift my chin as I get closer. But instead of passing me, he stops and faces me, halting me in place, and then closes the distance. I take a step back, then another, until I'm practically up against the wall.

My breath is ragged as I look up into his eyes. The pupils are so dilated that the blue is only a sliver around the black.

He leans in. I dart my tongue out to wet my lips, parting them slightly.

But instead of meeting my lips, he brushes his mouth along my jawline to my ear. "I know what you're doing, Professor."

The term sounds almost mocking.

A shiver runs through my body as the short hairs of his five-o'clock shadow scrape along my skin.

I pull in a shaky breath. "And what is that?"

His voice is a low rumble. "You've been teasing me, Kitten. All day."

"You think so?" The heat coming off his body tells me I'm treading on thin ice here, but fuck if I don't want to poke the bear.

He's been so aloof until now, despite our obvious connection. I need to get a reaction out of him, even if I'm playing with fire.

He chuckles darkly. "You want to do this, Kat? We're going to do it my way."

21

BLAKE

My cock throbs, pressing painfully against my slacks. Despite my session in the shower this morning, I've been hard most of the day.

And Kat is the entire reason.

Starting first thing this morning, when I woke up to her fingering herself.

Fingering herself.

Not just in the same bed as me, but while I held her against me.

It took every ounce of strength to not move my hands down next to hers and help.

I prayed that she'd chalk my erection up to morning wood—it may have started like that, but when I woke up to her heavy breathing, it was entirely because of her.

How did I end up cuddling with her? No idea. We went to sleep on opposite sides of the bed, our backs to one another. But however it happened, it set something in motion.

Kat has been on a mission today. It's obvious that she's doing everything in her power to make me want her.

The joke's on her, though. I've wanted her since the minute I saw her, and it has nothing to do with the cleavage she's had on display today.

Okay, it has something to do with her cleavage. But there's more to it than that.

The night we shared was barely enough to whet my appetite for not only her body but her mind, and since that day, I've been wishing there was a chance for more between us.

I've been hanging on by a thread. My resolve to keep this fake relationship...well, fake, is fading. If nothing else, I've been getting closer and closer to throwing out the rule about no intimacy.

Kat may be a strong, independent woman, used to doing things her way.

But this time? We're doing things my way.

I draw back from Kat to study her face. Emotions war in her eyes. Excitement. Trepidation.

Lust.

"Yes," she breathes, and it takes everything in me to keep from claiming her mouth right here.

"Good girl," I say, my voice low, my control so tight it's about to snap. I don't miss the way her shoulders relax at my words, the way her eyes widen for half a second. "Let's go."

I take her hand and lead her down the hallway, taking long strides that eat up the space between the dinner and the elevator.

"Should we say goodnight to everyone?" Kat asks.

I don't answer. I already spoke with Cam and Addie, along with anyone else who'd ask where we were, letting them know both Kat and I were turning in. When I left the rehearsal dinner and headed down the hallway, I knew exactly what my plan was. There was never any intention of returning to the party unless she turned me down.

And after her teasing all day, there was no chance of that. She wants this as much as I do.

The elevator door slides open with a soft *ding*. I wait for Kat to step in before I follow her and press four. We stand in silence, her hand gripping mine until the doors slide open on our floor.

From her expression, it's obvious that she expected me to kiss her in the elevator, that classic move from all the rom-com books and movies. But because it's classic, it's cliche, and the last thing I want to be is predictable.

The hallway from the elevator to our room seems longer than usual. Kat's breathing gets shallow as we approach the door, and my own pulse starts to ratchet up.

I take my time, though, sliding my key card into the slot and pushing the door open slowly. We're on my time now.

I'm controlling every second of this.

Kat steps past me into the room, turning back to face me only a few feet beyond the door.

I give her a slow smile as the door closes behind us, but I stay far enough away that she'll question everything.

The confusion is obvious in her eyes as she looks from me to the door, then deeper into the suite and back. When her eyes meet mine again, she runs her tongue over her lips almost hesitantly, like she's waiting for me to pull her to me and kiss her.

I place a finger under her chin and tilt her face upward. "My way, remember?"

She nods, her lips parting, her sudden submissive nature sending every drop of blood in my body to my already-hard cock.

"Turn around."

Kat does, and I grasp the zipper of her dress and pull it down to her waist, exposing her back and a lacy bra. As I slip the sleeves off her shoulders, the deep-green dress puddles around her high heels. I walk in a slow circle around her, taking in everything.

Her soft skin.

The way her pulse hammers in her neck.

The jade-green lace of her matching bra and thong.

The sharp edge of her hipbones and clavicles.

The sheen of moisture already visible through the sheer fabric of her underwear.

Behind her once again, I unclasp her bra and let it fall to the floor. Circling to stand in front of her, I set my hands on her hipbones and run them up her sides until my thumbs brush along the sides of her breasts, drawing a gasp from her lips.

I hold back a groan at the way her body responds to mine. Fuck, she's absolutely perfect. Her breasts are small, round, and firm, her dark nipples beading into points that beg me to take them in my mouth.

We have all night, though. And Kat has spent all day teasing me. It's time she gets a taste of it herself.

I drop my hands from her body and gesture with my chin. "Get on the bed."

A soft sound escapes from her lips, almost a protest at the loss of my touch, but she obeys, kicking off her heels as she walks through the suite toward the bedroom. The lights are off, only the faint glow of the resort shining through the window. A sliver peeks through the space where the curtains part and falls across Kat's stomach, illuminating her glowing skin.

"Touch yourself." I cross my arms over my chest, watching her from the foot of the bed.

Just like the one night we shared together, her breath hitches at the dominance in my voice. Kat Milas may be a strong, independent woman, but she gets off on being told what to do. And the fact that she is so confident in every other setting makes her submission to me even hotter.

Her fingers move tentatively down her body and pause at her breasts. She rolls one nipple then the other between her fingers, a moan slipping from her mouth.

"Pinch them." My voice is dark, deep, commanding, and she's responding to it like no one I've ever met.

She tightens her fingers around one nipple until her lips part with a gasp, then she moves to the other.

I give her a minute to play with her nipples then focus her attention back on me. "Now touch yourself. Just like you did this morning."

Her sharp intake of breath confirms that she didn't realize, or at least didn't know for sure, that I knew exactly what she was doing in our bed this morning. Her hand moves down, her fingers pushing aside the fabric of her thong to reveal a perfect pink cunt dripping with arousal.

Is she wet at the thought of being caught touching herself this morning? At being told what to do, giving up control?

Or is it the attraction that's been building between us since the very first night we met?

I move to the side of the bed, leaning over her to speak into her ear, my jaw scraping along her cheek. "You want this, Kitten? Be sure, because if we do this, that pussy belongs to me. No one else touches it without permission. Including you, baby."

Kat throws her head back with a moan as I cover her hand with mine, directing her fingers exactly where I want them.

Sliding over her clit.

Teasing her entrance.

Her body tightens as her fingers move and she gets closer to a climax.

I remove my hand, letting her take what she needs.

"Come for me, Kitten," I say, as her back arches and a fine sheen of sweat covers her body.

At my words, she explodes, her body shaking with the force of the orgasm as her moans fill the room.

While she breathes heavily, her eyes half closed, I undo my shirt buttons one at a time. I pull the shirt off my shoulders and toss it to the floor, then I reach for my belt as she smiles slowly at me.

"That was..." She licks her dark lips. "Yeah."

I've never known Kat Milas to be at a loss for words. "It was beautiful, Kitten."

"Why do you call me that?" she asks, her gaze dropping to my hands as I undo the belt buckle.

I shrug. "You're Kat, but for me, you're my little Kitten. You're not as hard as you show the rest of the world."

Her eyes widen as I shed my pants and boxer briefs in one movement, my cock hard, precum beading at the tip.

I chuckle at her expression. "You didn't think we were done, did you?"

Expressions flit across her face.

Lust.

Anticipation.

Need.

Kat slips off the bed, dropping to her knees in front of me, and takes my cock in her hand, her confidence doing as much for me as the sight of her dilated pupils and her hard nipples. Her delicate fingers don't even touch as she grips my girth.

Keeping her eyes on me, she leans forward and swirls her tongue around the head of my cock.

I groan at the sensation. "Fuck, Kitten, you do that so well."

Her hand slides to the base of my cock as she guides me into her mouth. The wet heat surrounds me, and when she hollows out her cheeks to take me deeper, I see stars.

I grasp a handful of her curls and twist it around my hand, guiding her as she moves back and forth until the edges of my vision blacken and I'm dangerously close to coming.

I pull back, fisting my cock as I look down at her. "Get back on the bed, Kitten."

Kat looks up at me, not moving. "I wanted to make you come."

Fuck, that's hot, and a part of me wants nothing more than to watch her on her knees like this. But we're doing this my way tonight or not at all.

"When I come, it's going to be inside you, baby. Get that ass on the bed."

Her cheeks are flushed and her eyes are dark with arousal as she takes my hand to climb to her feet. She gets back on the bed and lies back against the pillows. She's so gorgeous, so vulnerable, and it does something to my heart.

She slips her thong down, its fabric soaked, and throws the underwear to the floor. "Then fuck me, Blake. Like you mean it."

I laugh as I pull my wallet from my discarded pants and remove a condom. It's cute how she thinks she can gain control here. How she thinks she wants to.

"Don't worry, baby. You'll know I mean it." I rip open the foil and sheath myself in one motion, then I settle on the bed over Kat.

She pulls in a breath as she looks at my cock, thick and heavy between my legs.

I glide my cock along her slit, taking my time. "You're so fucking wet, babe," I say, and she moans in response.

Then I shift my hips and bury myself inside her in one thrust, her pussy gripping me like a vise.

And I realize that not only is this the biggest gamble of my life, but that we just upped the ante once again.

22

KAT

Blake slides into me, so thick and hard and long that it takes my breath away.

I tilt my hips, needing more, but he holds himself steady.

"You're so fucking amazing, Kitten," he says, pulling back and thrusting in. "I could spend every night buried deep inside you. It would never get old."

All I can do is moan as he starts to move, fucking me harder and faster. I arch my back, lifting my hips, needing to take him deeper.

Blake pulls back, though, teasing my entrance with just his tip as I whine for more.

"You need more, Kitten?" he says, keeping his thrusts shallow.

I need everything he'll give me. I've never felt so

full, so completely consumed by another person, and I need him back inside me like that.

"Yes. Fuck yes," I pant, tilting my hips again.

He doesn't give in, still teasing me with nothing more than the first two inches of his cock.

"Hmm," he says, his hips moving slowly. "I'm not sure. Because from where I'm standing, Kitten, you've been teasing me all day. Trying to get me to this point. You've had me hard as a fucking rock all day, and I think you need to be punished for it."

Those words shoot straight through me, my pussy clenching. Dirty talk shouldn't do it for me. I hold a PhD, for crying out loud. But reason has no place here. It's nothing more than feeling, seduction, lust.

"How?" I manage.

I want nothing more than for him to bend me over the side of this bed and pound into me. I'm realizing, though, that he's completely in charge now. I may have had a moment while I was going down on him. I literally had him by the balls there for a few minutes.

But this is all him. We're playing his game, on his terms.

And I fucking love it.

Blake doesn't respond. He pulls out completely, and in one swift move, he has me bent over the bed, my torso on the mattress and feet on the floor. I'm tall enough that it's a comfortable position, and as he positions himself behind me, I push my ass back against him.

"Oh, Kitten, you still think you're directing this?" Blake chuckles, and then I gasp as his hand comes down hard on my backside. "That's for teasing me today, baby. Because the joke's on you. I don't want you for your body, as fucking delicious as it is."

His hand connects with my ass again.

"I want you for you. For your sass, your confidence. Your looks are just a bonus, Kitten."

His words make my heart clench, because it's the first time anyone has ever said anything like that.

I know I'm attractive. I put myself through college by modeling. And I've gotten used to the stares, the comments, the unwanted attention.

No one has ever wanted me for what's beneath all of that.

Blake guides his cock inside me, thrusting forward to bottom out in one move that steals my breath. He pulls back, only to thrust deep once again as his palm lands on my ass cheek a third time.

The sensations are overwhelming. The stretch and fullness and pleasure of his cock inside me. The sting of his spanks—not hard enough to hurt, but enough to leave a delicious tingling sensation in their wake.

The overwhelming sense of being owned.

"So good, Kat. So. Fucking. Good." He punctuates each word with a hard thrust. "This is my cunt, baby. Got it?"

An orgasm cuts off my air, and the only sound I make is a strangled cry, my body shuddering beneath him.

He slows but doesn't stop as I recover, and when my breathing normalizes, he picks up speed. "You've got another one for me, don't you?"

I'm still recovering from the last orgasm. Another one may kill me.

I shake my head, my face rubbing against the soft cotton of the hotel sheets.

Blake's hands grip my hipbones, and he uses them as leverage to pull me back onto him as he thrusts forward, setting up a rhythm that's hard and fast and punishing.

"I think you do, Kitten. Another climax just for me."

Before I can protest, my body betrays me, spasming around his length as my body starts to build toward another orgasm.

Blake swells inside me, burying himself deep. "Fuck, baby. Fuck."

One last climax rips through me, leaving me

shaking as he comes, too. He collapses on top of me, his body pinning me to the bed as we try to catch our breaths.

I'm quivering when he pulls out of me.

Blake helps me back onto the bed, where I duck under the covers, pulling them up to my chin to warm my shaking body while he takes care of the condom.

My confidence in the moment trembles in the vulnerability of the aftermath. This is the part they don't show in movies. They show the buildup, the hot sex, and then cut to the morning after. And maybe this is why.

Alone in this big bed while Blake is in the bathroom, I start questioning if this was the right move. If it was as good for him as it was for me, because it was fucking mind-blowing. Wondering what he's thinking.

And God, I hate when my mind does this. It's not a feeling I'm used to.

Blake is smiling when he emerges from the bathroom, though, and my heart melts again.

"You're fucking amazing, Kitten," he says, sliding into bed next to me and pulling me close.

He nuzzles his nose in my hair.

Sleep beckons, but I need to know. "Are we doing this, Blake? Really doing this?"

His arms curl around me, holding me tight. "Yeah, baby. This is real."

There's raw vulnerability to his words, but strength, too.

I relax into him, my back to his front as he holds me tight.

You'd think twice in one night would be enough, but I wake up still wanting Blake again.

Not wanting a repeat of yesterday, I slip out of bed and tiptoe to the bathroom. I'm going to be spending the day getting ready with the bridal party—Addie assures me there will be mimosas.

Unlike the bridesmaids, though, no one is coming to do my hair and makeup, so I need to be practically ready for the wedding when I head to Addie's suite.

I turn on the shower and study myself in the mirror as I wait for it to warm up. My lips are puffy, the edges chapped, a remnant of all the kissing we did last night.

Kissing may be putting it lightly. At one point, it was a full-on make-out session, the kind high schoolers have behind the bleachers at the football field.

The area between my legs is sore but still aching for more.

I think I'm addicted to him.

I slip into the shower, letting the hot water wash over me. The water pressure is perfect. Steam rises in the glass enclosure as I take my time, lathering the body wash richly over my skin. The humidity down here is doing nice things for my skin, which is a bonus, so I almost don't need the moisturizing body wash. It makes me smell nice, though, so I wash a second time.

When a blast of cold air hits me, I let out a short scream.

"Jumpy this morning, huh?" Blake says, stepping into the shower with me.

He ducks his head under the spray.

"Only when someone invades my shower," I retort, but aside from the cold air, which is already fading, I'm not that upset.

In fact, this is the first time I've had a full, unobstructed view of Blake completely naked, and I don't hate it.

Water runs in rivulets down his chest, dipping into the valleys between his chiseled muscles. His abs are defined, forming a V that points down to his...

I swallow hard, remembering last night.

"I'm just happy to see you," Blake says, smirking.

It would seem so. His cock is hard and ready. A bead of precum at the tip washes away as he steps under the water again.

I wasn't expecting him to join me in the shower, but I'm not at all upset by his presence.

He pulls my back into his front, palming my breasts as he bites my shoulder.

"Don't leave a mark," I gasp out. "My dress is strapless."

That's the last thing I need, a hickey on full display at a wedding.

"Then I definitely want to leave a mark. Make sure everyone knows who you belong to." He growls the words.

His hands slide down my wet skin, over my hips, and to my core. He slips a finger inside me as his cock presses against my ass, and I know he can feel how wet I am.

"Fuck, Kat." He spins me around to face him, pressing my back against the hard tile of the shower. "I want you so bad right now, Kitten."

"Then take me," I breathe, no longer caring that he's interrupted my shower.

Nothing matters but the two of us.

Blake lifts my leg, bending it at the knee and

pulling me closer, so that his cock presses against my center. "Are you on birth control?"

I nod. "I have an implant. I'm good."

"You sure?" He pushes against me, the tip of his cock teasing my clit.

"Yes. God, yes." The last word ends on a gasp as he pushes inside me.

He hooks a hand behind my other leg and lifts it so I'm straddled around him. He's holding me in place, back against the shower wall, while he fucks me. In this position, I can't control the pace or the depth.

It's all him.

He thrusts hard and fast, reaching the brink of orgasm in minutes.

"Touch yourself," he orders, as his cock swells inside me.

My muscles tighten as I find the bundle of nerves, touching myself with just the right amount of pressure, and when he comes inside me, I explode right along with him.

Blake lowers me carefully to the ground, his cum running down my leg.

"Nothing like a shower quickie to wake you up," he says, smirking.

"It's definitely new for me."

I've never had sex in the shower. I didn't even think it was a thing people did. I thought it was like multiple orgasms or having an orgasm just from sex. Something that just happens in movies and romance novels.

But then, those turned out to be possible for me, too.

Talk about a sex education.

Blake picks up a bottle of something called 5-in-1 and squirts gel onto his hand. As he lathers his hair and then continues with the suds over his face and down his body, I peek at the label. Apparently, it's shampoo, conditioner, body wash, face wash, and—I squint— full-body deodorant.

I have approximately eight products to fulfill those five functions. No wonder men don't need as long as women in the shower.

It smells good, though, and I take a long sniff as he rinses.

"All yours," Blake says. "Thanks, babe."

He winks as he opens the shower door and steps out.

I wash my face before I turn off the water.

Blake has left a towel within easy reach, which I wrap around myself before I squeeze the extra water out of my wavy hair.

I rub some product between my fingers and comb

it through my hair. Hotel hairdryers never seem to have a diffuser, so I'll have to grab mine out of my suitcase if I want to try to play up the curls.

I layer on my moisturizer and sunscreen before I pull out my makeup kit.

"I'm going to head over to Cam's suite," Blake says, walking into the bathroom in nothing but gray sweatpants.

"Are you going to wear a shirt?"

He grins. "Of course. They don't appreciate my body like you do."

I roll my eyes, but I'm smiling as he lands a chaste kiss on my lips.

"Have fun with the girls. And Kat?"

"Mmm?"

He leans in close. "That was just a quickie in the shower. I'm saving up for tonight. I'm going to be inside you all night long."

23

BLAKE

Getting hard in a room full of your best friends is not ideal.

But that's what's going to happen if I can't get the thoughts of last night out of my head.

We're in Cam's suite, getting ready for the wedding. It's ironic that none of my best friends—not even my brother—know the whole situation with Kat. Jeremy and I are friends at work, but we don't have the same deep bond I do with these guys, and he's the one who knows how everything started.

I yawn, doing my best to hide it behind my hand, but I'm not quick enough for Miller, who smirks in my direction.

"Late night?" he asks, fiddling with his cuff links.

"Something like that." I slip my own cuff links into the holes of the dress shirt and fasten them.

"How come they can't just use buttons for these monkey suits like normal people?" Miller grumbles. "We should see if we can get someone to go get us coffee. Becca kept me up late last night, too."

Probably not as late as Kat and I were up. We barely slept, just napped here and there between having sex. Plus this morning in the shower, before I headed to Cam's suite to get ready and Kat went off with the girls. It was fucking amazing, better even than the first time we were together, and even though it's been less than an hour since I saw her, I'm craving her already.

It's not like the fact that we're sleeping together is a secret. If anything, the fact that we weren't fucking before this weekend is the secret. It's calming in a way to know that we won't have to pretend today. Our relationship is real.

The thought scares the fuck out of me, and I'm still uncertain it's a great idea. I'm sure something will happen to fuck this up. Isn't that what always happens in relationships?

Maybe I shouldn't mention that to Cam, who's grinning like an idiot in his tux.

"Getting cold feet?" Miller elbows Cam.

It does nothing to dim Cam's smile. "Hell no,

man. I've been looking forward to this day for as long as I can remember."

"Probably not as long as Addie has." Miller wiggles his eyebrows.

Maddox looks murderous. Maybe fair, since Cam first met Addie when she was thirteen, and I'm pretty sure Maddox's little sister used to write *Mrs. Camden Allen* on her notebooks throughout high school.

Talk about manifesting your future.

"Can we not talk about my sister like that?" Maddox asks. "I might need a beer for this."

Lawton abandons his efforts at tying his bow tie for a minute to cross the room to the mini fridge. "Who else wants one?"

He pulls out two bottles of Kalik, the favored island beer, opens them, and hands them to Miller and Maddox before grabbing his own.

I shake my head. My thoughts are jumbled enough without adding alcohol to the mix.

Lawton lifts the bottle to his lips and takes a long swig before he looks at me. "How are things with your girl?"

I want to growl at him. I'm trying my best not to think of her at all right now, and that's a losing battle. There's no chance I want to talk about my relationship with Kat.

Maddox claps me on the back. "I'll admit, I never thought I'd see the day you went out with a woman more than once, let alone you in a relationship. But maybe you just needed to find the right one."

Miller eyes me over the top of his beer. "I'd say he found the right one. Have you seen the way they look at one another?"

Lawton chuckles. "I've seen the way they can't keep their hands off each other."

"That's not—" My denial dies on my lips as I realize that they're right.

Even when we were convinced we were just *pretending*, there's been an undercurrent of something there, the electricity simmering between us.

"What's she doing today?" Cam straightens the collar of his shirt.

It seems crazy that we have to put on these penguin suits so early in the day. Why can't we just get dressed half an hour before the ceremony, you ask?

Because pictures.

They want plenty of time to get posed photos of the bride and groom, the bridal party, all of it.

I'm not as annoyed by the outfits as Miller seems to be, but I'd much rather be in a pair of swim trunks, sitting around the pool.

"Kat's hanging out with the girls."

Kat seems to have fit in perfectly with Addie, Holly, and Becca. Addie's best friend, Annika, is here as a bridesmaid, as are Addie's sister, Josie, and her wife, Chris. Every time Kat wasn't with me last night, she was chatting with one of the women.

I'm glad she's enjoying herself. I just worry that they're going to fill her head with their opinions of me. And now that this is something real, I don't want someone else to mess this up.

I can do that all on my own.

Maddox, Miller, and Lawton finish their beers just as someone knocks on the door. I pull it open to find a short woman with red hair that rivals Addie's, a determined expression on her face, and far too much energy.

"Let's go, boys!" she says, clapping her hands.

Her tone manages to hit the unique cross between a cheerleader on helium and a drill sergeant.

"That's the wedding coordinator," Cam mutters to me, seeing my perplexed expression at the tiny dictator. "Zinnia."

He has got to be joking. Zinnia?

I don't have time to contemplate her name, though, as Zinnia herds us toward the door. Apparently, it's time for pictures. She's mentioned this three times in the span of two minutes.

I can see how Addie would get along with this woman. But while Addie is bubbly and chatty, Zinnia is more...like a mosquito, if one could bark orders at you.

Not in the mood to get scolded by Zinnia, the wedding dictator, I follow the other guys toward the door, Lawton and me bringing up the rear.

"Lawton," I say, motioning to him just before we exit the hotel suite.

He pauses and turns to me. "Yeah?"

"I told the other guys this already, but don't bring up poker."

His eyebrows pull together in confusion. "Don't bring up *poker*? It's not exactly a taboo topic. And in this group?"

I pull on the back of my neck, the starched collar of the shirt already starting to bother me. "I'm not trying to be shady or anything. It's just that Kat's dad had a problem with gambling. So poker and any talk of things like that could be a trigger for her."

Understanding washes over his features. "Got it. That makes sense. But how are you going to keep this from her forever?"

"I won't. Really. I'm planning to tell her when we have time to talk about it. I want her to be secure in what we have." As I say the words, I realize they're true.

I want Kat to know everything about me, including how I started playing poker to make ends meet and realized I could make a living doing it.

Lawton moves toward the door then hesitates, turning back to me. "For what it's worth, I think she's good for you, Blake. You seem happier."

Deep inside, I think he may be right.

As expected, the bridal party is an interesting collection.

On Cam's side, we have his best friend, Maddox, who is also his soon-to-be brother-in-law. There's also me, Miller, and Lawton. Rounding out the group is Julio, Addie's newly adopted brother, who turned twelve last week. Standing next to Addie are Holly, Josie, Chris, and Annika.

I'd always thought the tradition was for the groom to not see the bride until the ceremony, but Zinnia assures me that this is "how things go nowadays," with a staged photo shoot of Cam seeing Addie in her wedding dress and then pictures with the wedding party "before things get crazy," she says.

I'm not sure there's such a thing as *before* crazy with this crew.

James and Leo, Josie and Chris's twins, are rolling on the sand in front of us, completely ruining their tuxes. I gather that Zinnia told Addie she needed either a ring bearer or a flower girl, and she went with the only little kids she knows, the two-year-old terrors. I can only imagine what they're going to do with the baskets of flower petals they're going to carry down the aisle, let alone the rings.

I'd trust an actual bear to handle the rings before I'd trust these two. Or a hyena.

Holly and Maddox are taking turns holding their son, Rhys, who is maybe...half a year old? She told me his age in months. I'll just give him credit when he hits one year old, and we'll call it good. As far as I know, he has not been entrusted with any wedding duties.

Kat stands with Becca, Miller's fiancée, the two of them next to Zinnia, who has a clipboard in her hand that she consults every two minutes.

Kat sips from a glass of champagne while she watches the antics, her expression somehow staying between neutral and mildly amused.

It's impressive, especially when Leo feeds James a mouthful of sand.

The photographer takes shot after shot of the

group in every possible permutation, Zinnia directing us into position. All the guys with Cam. The guys with Cam and Addie. The girls with Cam and Addie. The girls with Addie. And so forth.

Zinnia finally waves most of us aside to get family photos, Cam and Addie with her siblings, then with the couple with Addie's parents.

Cam's parents aren't in the picture. But Judy, Addie's mom, has known Cam since he was in college and will be standing in while Robert, Addie's father-in-law, walks her down the aisle.

It's the perfect mash-up of natural and found family. Adding in the fact that Addie and her siblings are all adopted, it's a beautiful mix.

A pang hits me deep inside. I've never wanted to get married, so it's never been a problem that I won't have parents at a wedding. It's been me and Lawton on our own since high school. So why does it suddenly seem to bother me?

Zinnia clucks at me to move, and I make my way toward Kat.

"How are you holding up?" I slip an arm around her waist. "This dress is gorgeous. Are you wearing this to the wedding?"

Kat leans into me, just enough that I can feel her touch all along my side. "I'm having fun, actually.

Maybe it's the champagne, but the girls are fun." She takes a sip. "And no, this is just for now. I'm going to change before the ceremony."

I look down, enjoying the view of her cleavage from this angle. "You can keep this dress if you want. I like its assets."

Giving me a playful shove, she snorts. "I can imagine which *assets* you like."

"I'm a simple man." I shrug, grinning.

Still smiling, Kat tips the rest of her champagne past her lips and swallows, making her delicate neck ripple.

God, I want to bite that neck. Right where her neck meets her shoulder. Brand her as mine.

She looks at her watch. "Speaking of changing, I should get going." Kat hands me her empty glass. "I'll see you after the ceremony."

The remainder of the picture taking is much the same, like a game of musical chairs.

At one point, Josie kicks off her high heels and hitches her dress up to wade into the water after Leo, who has decided to take a dip in the ocean.

At another, James tries to climb beneath the full skirt of Addie's dress.

I thank God that no one has asked me to babysit.

There's not a snowball's chance in hell that I could handle those two hellions.

Zinnia, for her part, seems unfazed, continuing to direct the poses and at one point, holding Leo under one arm like he's a sack of potatoes to keep him from running into the frame. Her ease with the toddler makes me think she has experience with kids. I wonder briefly if they teach those kinds of moves in parenting classes.

"I think that's good," she says, finally. "There's enough time to touch up your makeup before the ceremony starts, and then we're on!"

I don't have makeup to fix, nor do I want to shotgun a beer with Miller and Maddox, so I sit in the lounge with Lawton.

As he sinks onto the couch next to me, he blows out a breath and pushes a hand through his hair, leaving it just slightly disheveled.

Time to address the elephant in the room, then. Or the elephant that's conspicuously *not* in the room.

"So. What happened with Kristina?" I ask.

He flinches at her name. "Nothing good."

Normally I don't pry, but "nothing good" doesn't seem to cover it when you've moved across the country to a small town together, and she just seems to disappear.

"Did you...break up?" This seems like the obvious question.

He leans back on the couch, shoulders slumped. "You could call it that. I came home from pulling a double shift, and she was gone. Didn't answer my calls. I just got a text a few days later."

Ouch. "Did she say why?"

"Fuck if I know. Something about not feeling like High Lonesome was the place for her and how I was holding her back."

My heart aches for him. Between the two of us, he's always been the hopeful, optimistic one. The one who believes in love, even when he saw just how shitty things can end up.

Looks like he's seeing it again.

"When?"

Lawton's jaw clenches. "Last week. So I had the pleasure of sitting next to an empty seat on the plane that she should have been on. And now I'm sleeping in a huge suite alone. Her timing is impeccable."

This is the point when most people would offer some kind of support or consolation. Tell him that he'll find someone new, that everything happens for a reason, that something good will come out of this.

I have no such words of wisdom.

"That sucks, man."

"Yeah."

We sit in silence until Zinnia pops her head in to tell us to line up.

The ceremony itself is taking place on the beach next to the resort, and then we'll head back inside for the reception.

Most of the ceremony flies by in a haze. It's simple and beautiful, with white folding chairs arranged in rows and a flower-covered arch at the front where Cam and Addie stand.

I search the small, gathered group for Kat, finding her in the third row. She was right about changing her dress. The white sundress was gorgeous, but what she has on now is radiant.

A pale-teal strapless gown, showing off her toned shoulders. The silky material reflects the light, and next to her deep-tan skin, it's the perfect color palette for the Caribbean, the blue almost matching the color of the ocean.

"Addison and Camden, please read the vows you have written for one another." The officiant's voice pulls me back to the ceremony as he looks at Cam.

Cam clears his throat. "I, Camden Joseph Allen, take you, Addison Jane Anderson, to be my wife. To love you through thick and thin, in good times and bad. To always order pineapple on half of the pizza and to ensure that nothing you want is ever out of reach."

Addie giggles as he slides the ring on her finger, then she sobers as she holds her vows in front of her and reads.

"I, Addison Jane Anderson, take you, Camden Joseph Allen, to be my husband. To walk with you through the pleasures and trials of life, to stand by your side when fate leaves us stranded, and to love you for who you are, from this day forward." Her smile is radiant as she slips a ring onto Cam's finger.

I steal a look at Kat. Her eyes are bright, a small smile on her face, her head tilted to the side, and a lump grows in my throat.

My breath hitches as I look at her among the flowers and wedding guests.

I can see this with her. Not today, not for a while, but someday.

When I look back at Cam and Addie, their hands are clasped, their gazes locked on one another.

"You may now kiss the bride!" the officiant announces.

24

KAT

My eyes prickle with tears as Cam and Addie read their vows. They wrote their own, which is what I've always wanted to do for my own wedding, and they were beautiful.

And yes, before you ask, I've planned my entire wedding out in my head. Plenty of people do.

It'll be small, classy. My dress will be a simple strapless dress with a full skirt. Bouquets and decorations of dusty lavender and yellow roses, accented with lavender and veronica. My cousins as bridesmaids.

I always pictured my daddy walking me down the aisle, but we don't always get the wedding of our dreams.

But in all of it, the only thing I've never actually

pictured when it comes to my wedding is who the groom will be.

I lock eyes with Blake as Addie and Cam kiss, and something rises in me.

Hope, maybe.

Or maybe it's a combination of lust, champagne, and the fact that we're surrounded by so much love it could make you sick.

It's also terrifying. Things between me and Blake are real now. What's going to happen when we get back to Ardmore? And more importantly, what happens if this doesn't work out? Do we break up publicly? How will we work together or teach a class?

It was stressful enough when it was fake.

Blake gives me a wink as he walks down the aisle, his arm hooked in Annika's, and a sense of calm rushes over me.

Annika gives me a small wave, which I return.

It's like instant friends. Despite how nervous I was to hang out with Addie and Holly, the two of them accepted me instantly, making me feel like I belong without having to change anything about myself. And meeting Becca today, along with seeing Josie, Chris, and Annika again, is making me feel like I have a whole new group of people around me.

I cross my fingers that I can keep these friendships

going once we get back to Pennsylvania. I've never been good at keeping in touch with people that I don't see on a daily basis. I get so wrapped up in my work, and suddenly I realize months have gone by, and I haven't reached out.

The small crowd makes its way into the resort, most of us stopping to dump sand out of our shoes just before we enter.

One of the event spaces is set up for us with a cocktail hour on one side of the room, with waiters passing trays of champagne, mocktails, and small bites, as well as a bar in the corner. The other side is set for dinner, with a dance floor in between.

I take a glass of champagne and a conch fritter from two of the trays and sip at my drink slowly as I take in the space.

It's magical, all fairy lights and sparkling accents. I note with relief that there's one table set for two, clearly Cam and Addie's. I was worried that Blake would be stuck at one of those wedding-party-only tables, and I'd be sitting alone, but it looks like I'm safe.

Out of curiosity, I wander to that side of the room and peruse the place settings, looking for my name. I find it quickly, at one of the tables closest to the dance floor. I'm sitting next to Blake, which I expected, but it's nice to confirm. The other six seats at our table are designated for Miller and Becca, Holly and Maddox, Lawton, and someone named Kristina.

Hmm. I wonder who Kristina is. This is a fairly small group, only about forty or fifty people, and I haven't met anyone with that name just yet.

You never know, though. Holly and Maddox have a baby, and they're often pulled away to change him, or so Holly can nurse. Maybe Lawton also has a kid with this Kristina, and she's in the hotel taking care of it.

I'll have to ask Blake about it. I haven't spent enough time with Lawton, even though he is Blake's brother, to feel comfortable asking personal questions like that.

I dart a glance around the room before I snag Becca's name tag and swap it with Miller's, leaving them still sitting next to one another but with Becca sitting next to me instead of Miller, for a couple of reasons.

First, I like Becca. She's in her final year of medical school, and we bonded over the similarities between grad school and med school and our shared love of biology. Plus, she's sweet. Quiet at first, but after a couple of hours, we were laughing together like old friends.

Second, Miller loves to pull pranks, and I'm not what you would call the best audience for jokes like that. I don't love being the target of anything, even harmless pranks. So a little space between us is a good thing.

"Ooh, are we sitting together?" Holly asks, coming up behind me.

I point to her seat. "Yeah. Me and Blake, you and Maddox, Miller and Becca, Lawton, and someone named Kristina. Do you know her?"

Holly's brows furrow. "I think that's Lawton's girlfriend, but I've never met her. I started dating Maddox after Lawton had already moved to go to the police academy, so I haven't had a chance to get to know him well."

"He seems fun," I say.

I haven't interacted a ton with Lawton, but he's always been nice to me and seems like he's always smiling.

"Oh, they all are," Holly says, studying the name cards. "I'd love to be a fly on the wall at one of their tournaments, you know? I bet they all get super intense when it's a real game of poker."

I swear the blood drains from my face, my heartbeat rushing in my ears. "They play poker? For money?"

Holly gives me a strange look. "Well, yeah. I figured you knew. Blake doesn't do much now that he's teaching at the college, and Lawton doesn't have much time for tournaments. But that's how they all met, mostly. Maddox and Cam in college, and the others formed a little group because they were all playing professionally."

Hold it together, Kat.

I swallow hard, setting my nearly full glass of champagne on the table. "Interesting. It hasn't come up before, but I'm interested to learn more."

I'm always amazed when I can lie this smoothly.

Out of the corner of my eye, I see Blake heading toward us. "I'm going to run to the restroom. Be right back."

I manage to keep a neutral expression as I make my way as fast as I can go without arousing suspicion to the door to the hallway. Once I'm sure no one in the reception can see me, I squat against the wall, focusing on my breathing.

In...

Out...

In...

Out...

"You okay?" Blake's deep voice cuts through the haze.

Spots still dance in my vision. But as they clear, red takes their place, fury filling my veins.

I push myself up to stand. "How could you lie to me, Blake?"

The look on his face tells me everything I need to know. He knows exactly what I'm talking about.

"Kat, I'm sorry. I wasn't trying to lie to you or hide —"

"I told you about my dad. About how I didn't want to be around gambling or anyone who gambles. It's not a joke to me, Blake. It ruined his life. It almost ruined *mine*."

I'm hyperventilating, on the verge of tears. The fact that not only is Blake involved in this world, but that he used to gamble *professionally*?

"I just didn't want to bring it up. I know you don't like to talk about it." He reaches for my hand, and I flinch.

"It's not just that he had a gambling addiction, Blake." A tear escapes from the corner of my eye and traces a path down my cheek. "He gambled away my college fund. I was going to go to Yale. It was where he went, and I was going to follow in his footsteps. We even went together to look at the school."

I swipe at my cheek. "It was only when I got the acceptance letter that he told me that there wasn't any money for college. That I'd have to take out loans or finance it myself. And Yale isn't cheap."

"Kat." Blake traces my face with his hand.

My body wants this man. That much is obvious. I was starting to have feelings for him, too. Maybe even starting to fall for him a little.

But I can't let myself fall for someone who has this in their life. I know what gambling does to a person and to their family. We'd be doomed before we even started.

"I have to go." I try to step past Blake, but he blocks my way with his broad body.

"Kat. Wait."

"Let me go, Blake." I shove at his chest, but I may as well be pushing at a brick wall for all the good it does.

"Please, Kat. We need to talk. But not here. This is Cam's wedding. I don't want to mess anything up."

A pang of guilt hits me because he's right. No matter how betrayed I feel right now, I'm not going to be selfish enough to ruin their wedding reception.

I have plenty of practice putting on a brave face.

I grit my teeth so hard I'm surprised I don't crack a molar. "Fine. I'll put on a good show. Just like old times."

He winces at that, and I know it cuts deep. Old times. Like when it was all pretend.

"And then tomorrow, I'm leaving. You can stay

here with your gambling buddies and have fun." I don't give him a chance to respond as I spin on my heel and head back into the reception.

Holly is still at our table, so I head there first to do a little rearranging.

"You okay?" she asks, her eyes wary.

Leave it to the social worker to sniff out trouble.

"I'm good," I say, surprising myself with how easily the lie comes across my lips. "Just chatting with Blake for a minute. I was thinking, though, what if we girls sit together?"

Holly doesn't argue, and soon the two of us have the table arranged perfectly—the boys on one side, girls on the other, with my seat flanked by Holly and Becca.

I head for the bar to grab another glass of champagne. Or maybe a whiskey. It's going to be a long night.

Sitting between Becca and Holly seemed like a good idea.

But it's done nothing to insulate me from Blake's glare.

Even a few hours ago, that dark stare would have

had my stomach fluttering, my core pulsing. It's that dominant look, the one that says he owns me. The look that makes me want to ignore all the impulses that said not to get involved, that there could be a future for us.

But now I know there's no chance of a future. And I'm too pissed off to be turned on.

I meet his gaze across the centerpiece of wild sage and yellow elders, the vivid orange and yellow hues warm in contrast to the pain I see in his eyes.

I've got patience. I've sat through plenty of things that were long, boring, or just painful.

But none as bad as this.

Because it's not just putting on a brave face and bullshitting my way through a faculty meeting or even a funeral.

My heart is ripping into shreds.

I thought sitting away from Blake would help, but seated like this, I have a clear view of his face. It's even worse.

A waiter places a salad in front of me. I stab a tomato with my fork, lift it to my mouth, and chew.

This is going to be a very long reception.

25

———

BLAKE

She's done with me.

Last night, after what I can only describe as stony silence from across the table during the dinner, Kat went to our room early, before any of the dancing, and I went with her.

Only to be treated to more silence while she went through her skin- and hair-care routines, then slipped under the covers in shorts and a T-shirt and rolled onto her side facing away from me.

Of all the possible punishments, the silent treatment is the worst. It brings up memories of my mom, the way she was after Dad died, and those wounds run deep.

What's even worse is that Kat's quick dismissal is just proving what I already knew—relationships never end well. Even those that are "till death do us part" end eventually, with death parting the couple and the survivors left to shoulder the aftermath.

Maybe there's hope for some. My friends seem happy with their women. But I've known for a long time that it's not in the cards for me.

"So what exactly happened?" Lawton asks, sipping his umbrella drink.

When I booked the plane tickets, I pictured spending the weekend relaxing by the pool or on the beach, sipping cocktails with Kat. It's a perfect setting, with temperatures in the low eighties, a light breeze off the ocean to combat the humidity, the smell of salt in the air along with the hints of floral scents from the flowers across the island. We're sitting on lounge chairs by the pool. The chairs are arranged in pairs of two, scattered across the pool deck, with some daybeds on one side. It's the kind of place you relax with a wife or a girlfriend.

Not with my asshole brother.

Okay, he's not an asshole, but I'm in a foul mood, if you can't tell. Everyone is pissing me off.

I just grunt in response to his question. "Don't want to talk about it."

"Okay." He sips again and leans his head back on the lounger.

"Fine. She's got issues with gambling. Her dad was a gambling addict and got in too deep. She said she didn't like talking about it. So I fucking didn't talk about it. I told the guys not to, either. Remember?"

"Yeah. I listened." His brow furrows. "Who the fuck told her?"

"Fuck if I know. She was talking with Holly at the reception, so my money's on her."

"But Holly wouldn't say something if she knew it was an issue. Did she know?"

I drag a hand down my face. "I thought everyone knew. Figured Maddox would have told her."

Lawton looks doubtful. "I'm guessing either he didn't, or she forgot. Pretty sure neither of them is sleeping that well with that kid of theirs."

I grunt. "Kids are evil."

"Right there with you, man." Lawton reaches over, tapping his plastic cup against mine. "So what are you going to do?"

What am I going to do? This is the question that kept me up all night. Kat's the one who wanted this to be more, but it felt so right. It was different than any other woman I'd been with, and even being with her the other night was different than the first night we were together. There was more of a connection, maybe. More trust.

I guess that's what I get for thinking I could have a real relationship.

I just shrug, keeping my gaze on the blue of the pool in front of us.

Lawton lets out a heavy sigh. "I'd normally say fight for her, love is worth it, and all that shit, but I just got dumped over a text. So I'm not in the best state, either."

I grab the opportunity to talk about something other than my own shitty life. "Was it out of the blue? Or was this something that was coming for a while?"

He shakes his head. "It seemed out of the blue for me. Who the fuck knows, though. Maybe looking back, there were signs, but God knows I didn't pick up on them. Maybe the new town, new house, new job all at once were keeping me so busy that I didn't have a chance to realize that she wasn't happy."

I can see that. They'd been together for a while, but completely changing everything about your life can upend a relationship pretty quickly.

"You think you're going to stay up there?" I ask, swirling my drink.

The frozen strawberry daiquiri is melting and turning into an overly sweet cup of juice. I take another sip, trying to enjoy what's left of it.

Lawton stares off into the distance. "Maybe. I love

it up there. The guys on the force are like my family now, and I've got the house. It's just..." He takes a breath and then blows it out. "I thought I was there, you know? The house, the girl. Next comes family. And now I'm just starting over."

"Thought you didn't want kids."

Lawton has always flip-flopped on this one. He'll see a kid and think it would be fun to be a dad, then see the reality, like with Maddox and Holly's son, and swear off procreating. I think deep down he does want the whole family, kids, white picket fence thing. He's a romantic little shit, even with everything that happened to us as kids.

"You never know." He levels a look at me. "Back to you, though."

Fuck. This isn't what I want to talk about, and he knows it.

"There's more to the story with Kat, isn't there? I know why she left. But what made you want to have a relationship with her in the first place? You've said you don't do girlfriends for years. Since like high school, if I remember. I thought you wanted to be a player." He gives me a smirk.

He's partly right. I don't do girlfriends, but it has nothing to do with being a player.

"She was just..." How do I explain this? "Different,

I guess. There's something about her that I couldn't walk away from."

As I say the words, I feel the truth of them. Kat *is* different. She's smart, funny, beautiful. She can hold her own in any situation, and faced with my blunt, in-your-face attitude, she gives it right back without being intimidated like most people I know.

There are so many layers to her, and I want to get to know every one.

But I've lost my chance.

And I feel like a fucking idiot. I never wanted to lie to her. She said she didn't want to talk about gambling, so I made sure she wouldn't hear about it. It was never supposed to be about lying or keeping something from her.

"Hey!"

A too-cheerful voice behind me makes me turn my head.

I curse under my breath.

The happy couples are here, all of them looking bright and shiny and way too fucking pleased with life.

"What's wrong with you guys?" Miller asks, taking the lounge chair next to me. "You look like your puppy just died."

Becca smacks his arm. "Leave them alone. They can be in whatever mood they want."

"Fair enough." Miller turns to Becca with a shit-eating grin on his face, and the second she slips her sandals off, he sweeps her into his arms while she shrieks.

"Miller! Put me down!" She's in a one-piece bathing suit with her shorts still on over it. She kicks her legs wildly.

"As you wish," he says, and dumps her in the pool before shedding his T-shirt and cannonballing into the pool.

I can't even laugh at his antics today. I'm in that shitty of a mood.

For a while there, I actually thought that Becca and Miller were the perfect example of someone being out there for everyone. Miller's an acquired taste, always joking around, but he's a good guy. And somehow, Becca completes him.

Maddox pulls off his shirt and plucks Rhys from Holly's arms. He holds the baby on his hip as he wades into the shallow water, bouncing him around while the baby babbles and laughs beneath his little sun hat. Holly watches from the edge of the pool, a serene smile on her lips.

Cam and Addie, meanwhile, have claimed a daybed and are already making out.

I exchange a glance with Lawton. I love my friends.

We both do. But being surrounded by this much love is making me sick.

"Think we can ask them to go away?" Lawton mutters.

"Eh, they already think we're grumpy assholes. It wouldn't change their opinion of us." I suck down the last of my daiquiri.

Lawton sits up on his lounge chair. "I'm going to go wallow in my room. Meet you at the bar later?"

I've never been one to wallow, but I've got to say, it's underappreciated. I've told people to stop wallowing in their pain in the past, but never again. Because when your life is shattered into pieces like this, it feels damn good to wallow.

Or to be more accurate, it doesn't feel good at all, and I feel so shitty that I don't want to be happier. What's there to be happy about?

I've spent the afternoon sprawled across the bed that Kat and I shared. Her scent is still on the pillow, a combination of her perfume and her lotion and the products she brushed through her hair before bed. Not that we slept much that second night.

I can't bring myself to do anything more than

clutch her pillow to me, wondering why I let myself get this far into things.

I pride myself on being in control in every area of my life. In the classroom, in the bedroom, in relationships. It's part of the reason I've stayed away from getting entangled in a romantic relationship at all.

I never should have given in. I should have stuck to my guns, to do exactly what I told Kat the first time I realized the attraction was mutual.

That we couldn't give in to it, that we needed to keep things for appearances only.

But I cracked. I let myself slip, give in to Kat's teasing, and now look where it got me.

Absolutely fucked.

And the worst part is that not only do I have to see her when I get back to work, I still have to figure out a way to work with her to create and teach this class that the dean asked us to do.

If she's still willing to talk to me.

26

KAT

"Wait, what?" Angela's voice rises two octaves. "No. I didn't hear you right."

"We broke up. Close the door."

Angela shuts my office door behind her and sits in one of my chairs. "Tell me everything. Wait. Should we wait for Naomi? She's teaching a class right now."

I bury my face in my hands. "I don't care."

"I thought you were going to a wedding together and then having a romantic weekend in the Bahamas? What the hell happened to change all of that?"

"It's a long story." My voice is muffled as I speak into my hands.

The story is one I don't want to completely get into. No one at work knows about my family drama, and I'd like to keep it that way.

Well, no one but Blake. So much for trusting someone.

"I have time."

Of course she does. I swear, Angela must have some kind of time machine or other magic because she seems to get about thirty-six hours' worth of stuff done every twenty-four hours.

"Well, we went to his friend's wedding. The Bahamas are beautiful, and the rehearsal dinner was a lot of fun." I leave out the details of the night after that dinner, but a hot flush makes its way through my body as I remember how he commanded my body. "His friends are a lot of fun. But then..."

Angela leans in, waiting for the juicy details, but she's about to be disappointed.

"I found out something about him that made me lose trust in him." That sounds tactful. "And we decided to break up. So, that's that."

Her brows pull together. "Um, it doesn't sound like that's all. I don't understand. You guys seemed like such a good match. And this is really sudden."

If only she knew how sudden everything was. She knows that this whole thing started as an arrangement, but she was convinced that we've been sleeping together almost since it started. In reality, we went from fake relationship to real relationship to no relationship in twenty-four hours.

So it shouldn't be that big of a deal, if you ask me. We were barely together, as far as the two of us are officially concerned. To everyone else, it may look like a breakup after a few months, but it's not. So it shouldn't hurt.

That's what I keep telling myself anyway.

"Anyway, we're over. It's inconvenient, but it is what it is." I set my palms on my desk. "I just have to figure out what to do about this class we're supposed to design and teach. I can do it. I'm just not in the mood to work with him as extensively. Maybe I'll send Adam an email."

Angela frowns. "Are you sure?"

"Yes? I mean, it seems reasonable to let the dean know if we can't follow through on a project he gave us, right?" I'm not sure Angela is making much sense right now.

She rolls her eyes, tapping a perfectly manicured finger against her dark lips. "No, not that. Obviously, if you're sure you're giving up, let him know. But maybe you're being a little hasty. It's not going to paint you in the best light if you back out of this, either."

I narrow my gaze. Hasty is not a word people use to describe me. Nor is giving up.

Methodical.

Driven.

Perfectionist, sometimes.

But hasty? Never.

I think things through, weigh the pros and cons of everything before I decide.

For example, continuing to work on this course with Blake. Pros—get a new course on my CV, make Adam happy, points toward my promotion. Cons—have to see Blake. Have to work with Blake. Have to talk to Blake.

Obviously, the pro-con list here tilts heavily in favor of abandoning this course.

"I'll think about it," I concede.

I'll ask Naomi. She's always the logical one. Maybe she'll be on my side.

"Good," Angela says. She lifts her arm to peek at her watch. "I'm going to get some work done. Lunch at 11:30?"

"Sure." I check the time, too, and do the math.

I have a class to teach in an hour, so that gives me plenty of time beforehand to figure out how to word this email to Adam, letting him know I'm out.

"See you then," Angela says, tossing the words over her shoulder as she exits my office.

I stare at my computer and open up a blank email.

To: Adam.Kashman@ardmore.edu
From: Kathleen.Milas@ardmore.edu
Subject: Economics of the American Healthcare System

Dean Kashman,
I really want to teach this class, but Blake is a dickhead.

Hmm. Maybe not the most professional. I backspace and try again.

Dean Kashman,
Thank you for thinking of me to teach this proposed class.

This is a good start.

However, I will be unable to take this on, as

I tap my fingers on my desk. As what? As Blake is a dumbass? As I slept with the esteemed Professor Grantham, but now I don't like him, and I don't want to see him? I try to come up with something less inflammatory.

However, I will be unable to take this on, as Blake and I have broken up.

Nope. That sounds like I'm a high schooler quitting the cheerleading team because she broke up with the quarterback. Remember, mature, professional woman here. A woman who deserves tenure and a promotion to associate professor. I erase everything I've written so far and try again.

Dean Kashman,
Thank you again for thinking of me to teach this proposed class with Professor Grantham. While I remain excited to develop and teach this class, creating and co-teaching with Professor Grantham will not be a possibility. I am open to exploring other co-teachers, as my background in Biology does not lend itself to teaching the Economics portion of this class.
Let me know your thoughts. Happy to come by your office to discuss.
Kathleen Milas

I re-read the email. Good. No emotion, no wiggle room. No apologies.

I look up at the clock on the wall. It's five minutes until my class starts, so I need to get moving.

My mouse hovers over the Send icon. Something has me hesitating, though, and instead, I click Save. I'll see what Naomi thinks about this situation before I decide whether to send it.

———

Human Anatomy and Physiology is a mixed bag. A good portion of the class are pre-med majors, taking the course to gain some background before applying to medical school.

But there are usually some non-science majors taking it just to fill their graduation requirements, or the occasional art major looking to get a better understanding of the human form and, usually for the first week only, the asshole jocks hoping to see pictures of naked people.

This far into the semester, the less interested parties have been weeded out, and this year's class has been particularly enthusiastic and engaged.

I click forward to the next slide in my PowerPoint, a drawing of the human abdomen filling the screen. Lines point to different organs, and I've removed the identifiers.

I step out from behind the podium, using my laser pointer to hover over one area. "Who can identify this organ?"

Hands shoot up. Pre-med students are usually prepared, meaning they've often studied the course material before class.

I point to a girl in the third row. "Allison. What am I pointing to?"

"The liver," she says confidently.

"Correct. And nestled just under the liver, what's this?" I move the pointer down a hair to hover over a dark-green blob.

I'm pretty sure it's not that color in real life, but then I've never seen inside a living human. I leave that to the real doctors.

I point to a boy with glasses who has his hand raised.

"The gallbladder."

"Exactly." I click to the next slide, zooming in on the area. "We're going to focus on this area today, how the liver and gallbladder function, and how disease processes can disrupt the function and even the anatomy. First, tell me something the liver does."

There's silence for a minute, and I give them a smile. "Call it out. There are a bunch of right answers."

"Process alcohol?" one calls out, to a giggle from the rest of the class.

He's not wrong. My liver got a workout over the weekend, after I returned early from the Bahamas.

"Indeed, and I believe that function is important to a lot of students. Those over twenty-one," I say, smiling. "What else?"

Now that they've gotten that one out, the answers come quickly.

"Drug metabolism."

"Making bile."

"Glycogen storage."

I switch to a slide listing all of the liver's functions, allowing the students time to copy down the information, even though I'll be posting my slides to the class portal tonight.

We move through gallbladder function and then pictures of the liver when things go wrong. The bumpy scarring of cirrhosis, the blackened liver of biliary atresia, the yellow waxy appearance of fatty liver. I wonder briefly what my own liver looks like right now after the vodka I consumed trying to forget about Blake.

I manage to focus on teaching, doing my best to push thoughts of Blake and vodka and hangovers out of my mind.

"Now, what does the gallbladder do?" I point to the small green sac on the screen.

"Stores things," one student says.

I nod. "What kind of things?"

A kid in the back who has a neck thick enough to suggest he plays either football or rugby raises his hand.

"Piss," he says loudly, not waiting for me to call on him.

I frown. "Nope. Want to try again?"

He shakes his head. "No, it's definitely piss. Pee. Urine. Whatever you want to call it."

I raise an eyebrow. "The gallbladder stores bile. It comes from—"

"No, it's piss," he says, cutting me off.

Are you fucking kidding me? Who does this asshole think I am?

"Bladders hold piss," he says again, doubling down. "How do you not know this?"

I grit my teeth, forcing myself to hold it together. This isn't the first time a student has challenged me. But it's the first time it's been so brazen, so offensive.

The rest of the class is buzzing, their attention divided between me and the asshole jock, and I know I have about nine seconds to get things back under control before I lose the class entirely.

I clap my hands loudly, three times. "That is it for class today. I'll send additional clarifying material out, and slides will be posted on the portal. Lab this week will focus on the *biliary* system." I emphasize the word as I point at the jock. "Please come see me during office hours this week."

After I've had time to cool down and won't want to murder him. At least my TA will run the lab sessions, where the students are dissecting cats this month. I don't think anyone wants me to be near this kid with a scalpel in my hand.

I was afraid to ask where the animals came from my first year of teaching, but I've since learned that they're typically feral cats that are found already dead or those who were euthanized due to their health and donated by shelters or families.

It feels a little better knowing that none of the cats died just for the purposes of teaching college students about the biliary system, but I'm still glad my TA and lab instructor manage most of the animal labs.

Students file out of the room as I pack away my laptop and papers, ignoring the fact that we're ending class about twenty minutes early.

Normally, I stay after class for students to ask questions or for those who want to chat about something. But today, I need to get out of here.

Between Blake and the jock challenging me in front of the class, I'm rapidly losing all control. I can feel myself spiraling. I don't want to be anywhere on campus when I completely lose it.

So I shove my laptop and papers into my tote and rush out of the room along with the students, running away yet again.

27

BLAKE

I'm in a foul mood, which isn't usually how people return from a vacation to the Bahamas.

But after spending my last two days there getting drunk and commiserating with Lawton about our shitty love lives, or lack thereof, I'm in no mood to head back to work where I may run into Kat.

What would I even say?

I suppose it doesn't matter anyway. She made it clear that she doesn't want to talk to me or hear anything I have to say.

We still have this course to work on, and God knows how that's going to go. I was questioning the feasibility of continuing to work together after the night of the rehearsal dinner, wondering if I could work objectively with someone I had feelings for, but the feelings weren't new.

Giving in to them was.

"Need some coffee?"

The high-pitched voice makes me rub at my temples.

"No." I'm in no mood for Randi's shit.

"Oh."

I look up. She's in my doorway, twirling a lock of hair around one finger while she chews on gum with her mouth open.

"Randi, what do you want?" I ask bluntly.

I've tried to be friendly, but it's really not in my nature to be anything other than blunt, and niceties require too much energy for me to summon right now.

She shrugs, her too-obvious cleavage bouncing above her low-cut top. "It's clear you're not in a great mood, that's all."

No shit. She should be a fucking detective.

"And I wondered if maybe you wanted some coffee. And..." She steps into my office. "I wondered if maybe it had to do with Professor Milas. If you two broke up and maybe you were looking for someone to cheer you up."

Points for perseverance, I guess.

I blow out a breath. "Randi, I'm not available. Please don't ask again."

"Okay," she says, tossing her hair over her shoulder and snapping her gum, seeming completely unaffected by my dismissal. "But if you change your mind, you know where to find me."

Yeah, I know where to find her. It's why I avoid walking past her office.

I have no interest in talking about Kat to Randi, but I do want to talk to someone, and Jeremy knows the whole story.

I shoot him a text, and he appears in my doorway three minutes later.

"What's up?" he asks. "How was the wedding?"

"Shitty. Come in and close the door."

He does and takes a seat, his legs crossed. "I'm listening."

I take a deep breath and then blow it out, scrubbing a hand down my face. "I fucked up."

Jeremy's expression doesn't change. "Continue."

"Kat and I are no longer together. She has something in her past that she didn't want to talk about, so I didn't bring it up as it pertains to me, and now she feels like I hid something from her."

His eyebrows pull together. "That's...cryptic."

"It's something personal, and it's her thing. But the point is, I didn't try to lie to her or deceive her or anything. She won't give me a chance to explain, though. And now everything is fucked."

He nods slowly, his hand rubbing over his chin. "Well, it's a good thing the relationship wasn't real, huh? That would be a lot messier." He looks at me, his gaze intense. "Or is there more to the story?"

That's the problem with working with a bunch of smart people. They know too much and can read into things.

"Fuck. Okay, yes, things got real. You happy?"

A grin spreads over his face. "I knew there was something between you two."

"It was just last week. While we were in the Bahamas. Before, it was all pretend."

He shakes his head. "You can tell yourself that, and maybe that's when you made it official. But there's been something between you since the very beginning. Chemistry, a kind of electricity. You could see it when you talked to one another."

He's right. I could feel it, too.

But it doesn't matter. It's over now.

"So?"

"So when things get messy in a relationship, you

talk about it. Fix it. Maybe give it time, but I think there's something worth saving. Just my two cents, though."

He's right, but I'm not sure it's up to me. Kat's the one who needs convincing.

But maybe there's a chance that she's had a chance to process everything, that maybe she'll listen now that we're back at school and not in the frenzied excitement and high emotions that make up a wedding.

I push back from my desk. "Yeah, you have a point. I'll go talk to her."

Jeremy stands. "Good luck. Let me know how it goes."

"Sure thing. Talk soon."

As he exits my office, I look down at my watch, my plans coming to a halt as I realize the time. It's 10:45, which means Kat is in class right now. This isn't a college rom-com movie, where I could bust into her classroom in the middle of lecture and make some proclamation of love or something like that.

First, that move is reserved for jocks and overly confident twenty-somethings, and is aimed at another student, not the professor.

Second, she'd probably cut my balls off for interrupting her lecture. Kat doesn't fuck around when it comes to her job. And I'm rather attached to my balls, thank you very much.

So in the interest of coming across as a non-asshole who plans to keep all of his genitalia intact, the best option is to wait.

I sink back into my chair, both deflated and relieved. In my head, I start to plan out what I need to say to her. Apology for the whole poker thing. Try to explain that it was never meant to be a secret, that I was just trying to be nice and respect her triggers.

I'm tempted to explain how professional poker playing works, how we take precautions and check on one another to make sure no one ends up falling into the spiral of addiction, but I'm not sure she's ready to hear that.

Most of all, I need for her to hear that I don't gamble anymore. If it's important to her, I'll give it up forever. She's more important than any poker tournament or anything else.

I realize the truth of the words as I plan them out in my head.

Even though Kat and I started as an arrangement, she's grown on me. Her little quirks, her humor, the sound of her voice. I miss all of them. And while my younger years made me swear that I'd never be in a serious relationship, let alone get married, maybe things can change.

As the clock ticks down to 11:20, I pace in front of my door. It's closed just in case anyone walks down this hallway. I don't need anyone to know just how neurotic I am.

Like Kat, I pride myself on taking work seriously. On being in control and competent.

This image may not jibe with that reputation.

I wipe my sweating palms on my slacks again.

11:18. Almost time to head over there. The lecture hall her class is in isn't too far from her office, so I'm going to try to catch her while she's walking between the two. She's too much of a professional to blow me off in front of students and other faculty. And yes, I'm fully taking advantage of it.

11:19. Time to go. It'll put me right at the door when she dismisses class.

I push a hand through my hair and reach for the doorknob, only for a knock from the other side to startle me.

I jump back. This wasn't part of my plans.

"Come in," I call, managing to make my voice sound almost normal.

I'm not sure who I expected, but Dean Kashman wasn't at the top of the list.

"Professor Grantham," he says by way of greeting.

"Dean Kashman."

What the hell is he doing here? When the dean stops by your office, something usually isn't right. It's like being called to the principal's office.

Or more accurately, it's like the principal couldn't even wait for you to come to his office, so he's coming to get you out of class himself.

"Mind if I come in?"

I do my best to ignore the sinking feeling in my gut. "Of course. What can I do for you?"

"Everything okay?" His expression is unreadable.

I try to smile, but my poker face fails me. "Yep."

He furrows his brows. "Did something happen between you and Professor Milas?"

Unfortunately, while something *did* happen between me and Kat, I have no idea where we stand right now. And fuck if I'm going to discuss it with Dean Kashman. Besides being my boss, I know he's interested in Kat. It's the entire reason she agreed to this harebrained scheme in the first place.

My analytical brain runs through the various options, gauging the likely outcomes.

One—I admit that Kat and I broke up. Likely not much fallout for me, other than Randi trying to sink her claws into me, but Adam will take that as license to ask Kat out again, putting her back in the precarious position of having to balance not wanting to date him with his influence on her chance at promotion.

Two—I tell him we're still together, that nothing happened. If he's talked to Kat, he'll know this is a complete lie. Best-case scenario, I'll be on his shit list; worst case, I'll be looking for a new job before my first year at Ardmore is even done.

Three—I tell him that we're talking through things. This is only true if Kat agrees to it, but it gives me some plausible deniability if Kat has already told him we're done. He may relate to the struggle and see my perseverance and unwillingness to give up just because things are tough.

Yep, that last one seems like a winner.

"We're having a bit of a rough patch," I admit, "but you know how it is. Good things take work."

His face doesn't give anything away. "I understand. My ex-wife and I did go through some very bumpy bumps during our relationship."

I'm not sure if he's showing support for us

working this out or trying to tell me that relationships can fail even after trying to make things right.

And I'm not sure "bumpy bumps" are exactly the best description for what Kat and I are going through.

I smile, though, giving him the benefit of the doubt. "So you know how it is. I need to go meet up with her now, actually. Is there anything else I can do for you?"

Adam shakes his head. "No, not really. Was just stopping by a few offices to say hi. I'll let you get going."

"Thanks. I'm sure I'll see you soon."

He gives me a wave and heads down the hall.

Checking my watch, I realize Adam's impromptu visit has ruined my plan to catch Kat between her lecture and her office, but our conversation has made me even more certain that I need to talk to Kat and work things out, for both our sakes.

My steps are quick as I walk to the lecture hall, then to Kat's office, but she's nowhere to be found. I try the food court and even Angela's and Naomi's offices.

Nothing.

Fuck.

I need to talk to her. I was hoping that giving her time to cool off would work in my favor, but I'm not going to get anywhere with explaining my side of things if she won't even talk to me.

There's no sign of her at the library or in the labs, either.

My stomach sinks as I walk slowly back to my office.

I'm too late.

28

KAT

I've never cut out of work early. But I'm barely holding it together.

This relationship with Blake… I'm not even sure it *was* a relationship. We only made things real for a day before everything got shot to hell. Twenty-four hours may be an entire marriage for some celebrities, but for the rest of us, it's barely a blip.

So it really shouldn't hurt so bad.

Logically, I'm doing my best to convince myself that it's not that bad. That it wasn't meant to be. That I'm not devastated or betrayed or completely destroyed.

Now that I'm alone in my house, though, I only have myself to lie to, and it's hard to do that when I know the truth.

It's also the reason that I'm sitting on my living room floor, clutching a bottle of vodka.

I keep telling myself that it's better than curling into a ball on the floor of my office since one of my students or a coworker could walk in—or worse, Blake —but I'm not sure it is, if I'm being honest. Either way, I'm spiraling because of a man.

And Kat Fucking Milas doesn't do that.

I take a swig of vodka, grimacing as it burns its way down my throat. I hate the taste, but there's something about the less-than-pleasant experience that makes me feel somehow in control of my wallowing, even though the very act of drinking like this practically guarantees a loss of control.

I'm sure my therapist could have a field day with that.

In the spirit of regaining control, here's what I've decided to do:

First, I'm going to drink enough that I forget why I feel like crap.

Second, I'm going to eat half a pan of brownies. I baked them before I started drinking—no oven fires today, thank you—and they're cooling in the kitchen in the special brownie pan that makes every piece have edges. No squishy middle pieces here.

Third, I'm going to...something. I haven't figured that part out yet.

I lift the vodka to my lips again, bracing for the taste, when my doorbell rings.

Great. Just what I need, someone to see me in this state.

I stay on the floor, hoping that whoever it is will go away.

The doorbell rings again.

Persistent, but I'm more stubborn than they are. I remain exactly where I am.

"Kat," a voice calls. "I know you're in there. I can see your feet through the window."

I pull them in, tucking them beneath me, like maybe that will make my visitor disappear.

Instead, I can hear the sigh through the door. "I'm not leaving. Open the door."

It's a man's voice, one that's vaguely familiar, but I can't put my finger on who it is. I wait, but he doesn't say anything else.

A full minute goes by.

Maybe he left.

I set the vodka on the ground and crawl across the living room to the window. Hiding behind the curtain, I push it aside slightly to see if the coast is clear.

Fuck. It's not.

My gaze is squarely met by a pair of bright-blue eyes that are far too familiar. The hair is different, and he's not as tall as Blake, but there's no way to miss that Lawton is his brother. They even dress similarly, Lawton in a pair of blue jeans and a blue button-down with the cuffs rolled to his mid-forearms.

In contrast, I'm wearing my leggings and an oversized long-sleeved T-shirt that has a hole in the armpit. At least my crotch is covered this time.

He's standing on my doorstep, arms crossed over his chest, a grim expression on his face. "Let me in, Kat."

The dominant personality seems to run in the family.

I huff out a breath and climb to my feet, the vodka bottle clutched in one hand as I make my way to the front door.

Pulling the door open, I plant my free hand on my hip. "What do you want, Lawton? Why are you here?" I let out a hiccup. "I thought you lived in Colorado. And how did you even know my address?"

He reaches out and plucks the vodka from my hand. "I came back to Philadelphia to hang out with the guys for a few extra days. And Addie gave me your address. Water, please."

I gape at him. "You stole my drink, and now you want me to get you a water?"

He steps past me into the house, pulling the door shut behind him. "I'd like *you* to drink some water. We're all done with the alcohol for tonight."

"I don't like you." I hiccup again.

He may have a point.

Normally, I'd never let people see me like this. I don't even like to see myself like this. But I find myself not caring what Lawton thinks. He doesn't live here, he doesn't work with me, and now that Blake and I aren't dating—or even fake dating—I'll never have to see him again, so I don't care what he thinks.

It's quite freeing.

"I'll take care of this and the water. Go wait in the living room. Maybe sit on the furniture this time instead of the ground." Lawton walks toward my kitchen like he owns this place.

A few minutes later, he walks into the living room with a glass of water. He must have found my nice dinnerware. The glass he hands me is dark blue to complement the design on the matching plates that I rarely use.

"Thanks," I say, taking a sip.

I've only been wallowing for half an hour or so, but the vodka went to my head quickly.

I gulp down a few more swallows before I set the glass on the side table and sit back on the sofa. "So. Why are you here?"

Lawton settles into the chair across from me. "I need to talk to you about Blake."

Nope. Hard pass. I start to stand up, ready to tell him just where he can shove his talk about his brother.

"Kat. Sit down." His voice is deep when he gives commands, just like his brother's, but unlike Blake's voice, Lawton's doesn't send electricity pulsing through my core.

I lean back and fold my arms over my chest. "Fine. What?"

He folds his hands, unfolds them, then twines his fingers together again. "Blake doesn't know I'm here. But you need to know something about him."

The fact that he's a professional gambler and hid that fact from me when he knew it was a problem is all I need to know, but I let him continue.

"Our dad died when I was twelve. Blake was seventeen."

"I'm so sorry," I murmur.

Blake told me his parents were gone, but not the details.

"Thank you. But that's not the main thing." A flash of pain crosses his face. "Our parents were deeply in love. High school sweethearts, married young."

I can almost picture Blake and Lawton as kids, losing their dad at such a young age. It tugs at my heartstrings.

"My mom was devastated when Dad died. She shut down completely. We thought it was a phase, but it didn't get better."

A lump grows in my throat.

"I was a kid and didn't understand what was going on, why she couldn't get out of bed or take me to baseball practice or make my lunch." His shoulders hunch slightly. "Blake was a kid, too, but as the older brother, he took on everything. Driving me to practice, doing the grocery shopping, making sure I did my homework and brushed my teeth and studied for my math tests."

Tears prick at my eyes. "That must have been really hard on him."

Lawton shrugs. "It was. But he never complained or made me feel like a burden, not even when he had to put off going to college to stay home and make sure I was okay through high school.

"Dad's life insurance money covered a lot, but it ran out. Blake was always good at poker, and he started playing professionally to make ends meet. And then he kept playing to cover the cost of our tuitions. Even so, Blake didn't start college until after I graduated from high school."

It makes more sense now, why Blake is just now finishing his PhD and starting teaching. I assumed he'd just done something between college and grad school because so many people do. I never imagined it was something like this.

And I never thought he'd chosen gambling because his back was against a wall thanks to a parent's actions. It's exactly the reason I took those modeling jobs in Japan, working just enough every summer to cover my in-state tuition at UVA.

I have a pang of sympathy for him, deep inside.

"Thank you for telling me," I say, because I'm not sure what else to say.

Knowing these details of Blake's past changes him in my eyes. But what we had is broken now. I'm not sure there's a way back.

Maybe the idea of turning this into a real relationship was all a fantasy.

Lawton shakes his head. "It's not just that. It's..." He thinks for a minute, rubbing a hand along his jaw. "The way my mom responded to my dad dying shaped his perspective on a lot of things. Relationships, especially."

I take a sip of water, focusing on his words.

"He got it in his head that relationships always lead to heartbreak, one way or another, and that they have negative effects on people around them when they end. So he's never wanted a relationship. It's always been one-night stands for him."

I wait, silent, as Lawton runs a hand over his jaw before continuing.

"I was surprised when he told me he was dating you. He's never mentioned a girlfriend before. But when I spent time with you at Cam's wedding, it made sense. You're good for one another. You bring out the best in him, and you make one another happy."

A tear slips out the corner of my eye, and I swipe it away with the back of my hand before he can see. "Not anymore, though. We're done."

Lawton pins me with a stare. "I think you should talk to Blake before you make that decision. He never would have done anything to deliberately hurt you. He might have made dumb decisions, but they were made out of caring and respect for you. Not to hide anything."

I lift my shoulders and then drop them. "It's too late, Lawton. It doesn't matter anymore."

"It's never too late to do the right thing. And if it helps, it definitely matters. Especially to him."

A spark of hope lights in my soul at his words. But if it matters to Blake, why is Lawton the one here? Why isn't Blake here, explaining all of this and apologizing?

"He's scared," Lawton says, like he can read my mind. "He comes across as this confident guy, but he has scars. Everyone does. And relationships ending are a big one for him."

Probably like gambling is for me, I realize.

"Just think about it," he says, standing to leave. "Talk to him. Everyone has things in their past that make them scared about facing those things in the future. But it's easier to face things when there's someone beside you."

It dawns on me that he's right. And I wonder, for the first time in a long time, if carrying around the scars from the past is causing pain in the present.

I haven't talked to my dad about the gambling thing. I've gone back home for holidays here and there, but we've always kept things surface level. We don't talk about the past.

He's texted me and called me, but there's always been an excuse to keep him at an arm's length.

In a couple weeks, the students will have their winter break, and the faculty get the time off too. I'd planned to just stay here, like the last couple of years, but maybe it's time.

Lawton waits patiently while I pull out my phone and send a text.

Dad

> I'm going to come home for Christmas this year. I'd like to talk with you about things.

I wait, holding my breath, and a reply comes back almost immediately.

> I'm looking forward to it, pumpkin.

We usually think of scars as permanent, but it's not entirely true. A scar is just a collection of collagen, laid down by the body as it rushes to fix a wound. Some scars are there for life. Others stretch, get lighter and less prominent as the years go by.

They don't fade overnight, but they're not the same from year to year. And maybe emotional scars are a lot like physical scars.

Lawton nods as I look up from my phone. "You want to go now?"

I nod, standing unsteadily from the couch and head to my bedroom.

I peel off my leggings and T-shirt and drop them into the laundry basket. Wanting something other than my usual pencil skirts, I pick up the flowy skirt I bought a few weeks ago. The lightweight hem flutters around my knees.

I top the skirt with a white T-shirt; more casual than I'd usually wear to the university, but it's not like I'm headed there to teach.

A quick look in the mirror, a coat of lipstick, and I'm on my way.

29

BLAKE

I was too late.

Guilt and desperation weigh heavily in the pit of my stomach as I make my way back to my office.

I've looked everywhere on campus, and Kat is nowhere to be seen. Her office door was shut, with no answer when I knocked.

There's been no answer to the text I sent asking where she is. Finally, I stopped by their department admin office. Their secretary, a round gray-haired woman named Wilma, let me know that Kat hadn't been feeling well and left after her lecture, cancelling her office hours for this afternoon.

Bullshit. Kat's hiding. I'd bet anything.

But my plan for getting her to talk to me has stalled, at least for now. I was banking on the fact that she wouldn't yell at me at work. Plus, if there were students and other faculty around, she's unlikely to blow me off because it would look bad. All of that setup is gone now.

If I go to her house, I don't have that angle. She can just ignore me and refuse to answer the door.

And I honestly don't know if I can take that.

Pushing the door shut behind me, I lean my back against it. My shoulders are heavy.

I should have known that getting into this in the first place was a mistake. It wasn't something I thought out, and from the minute the words flew out of my mouth—*I'm dating Professor Milas*—I've regretted them.

Honestly, though, that's not entirely true, even though I've been trying to convince myself. There have been good moments. Great, even. Kat is funny, intelligent. Beautiful. She's the whole package.

I guess what they say is true: you can't have everything.

A knock at the wood behind my head makes me want to groan.

"Just a minute."

It has to be Jeremy. He's the most frequent visitor to my office, and while he's been a voice of reason through this whole harebrained scheme with Kat, I need to be alone right now.

"I can wait."

It's not Jeremy.

It's a familiar voice.

A clear, sweet voice I'd know anywhere, one that goes straight to my cock.

"Kat?" I turn around, pulling open the door to find her standing there.

She laces her fingers together in front of her, looking more nervous than I've ever seen her. To anyone else, it would be an innocent move, one that doesn't mean anything.

But I know better.

I know everything about this woman. The way her voice changes when she's excited, how her eyes dance when she's teasing. The way she plays with her fingers when she's nervous.

"Can I talk to you?" she asks, finally meeting my gaze.

I move to the side so she can enter my office. "Of course. I was trying to find you earlier to talk, actually."

"I...had to leave campus for a bit." Kat steps past me into my office.

I don't miss the way she gives me a wide berth. It stirs up my regret.

This isn't how she'd be acting around me if I hadn't kept the whole poker thing from her.

Or were we always destined to end up like this, dancing around one another at a distance? If I'd told her about my past as a pro poker player, maybe we never would have gotten to that point in the Bahamas. Would she care if the guy she was in an arrangement with had a past with gambling, rather than the guy she was really dating?

Either way, I need to make her realize that's what poker is for me. The past. I'll give it all up right now. It started out of need, and I grew to love the thrill of winning, the challenge of trying to guess who has what hand based on how they play, the puzzle of estimating the chance of winning based on the cards I can see.

But now, there's something I love more.

It's too soon to tell her I love her, but it's what I've realized. She's grown on me the past couple months, getting deeper into my heart every time we shared gelato in the student center or threw ourselves into planning this course or walked across campus together. She's become an inextricable part of my life.

Poker I can live without. Kat, I can't.

I close the door behind her, giving us some privacy.

There's a window in my office, but I pulled the curtains earlier, so the light is just a warm glow from the lamp on my desk.

"Lawton came to talk to me," she starts, standing by my desk but not taking the seat nearby.

I stiffen, wondering what my brother would have told her. He's the only person who knows the full story of what happened when we were younger.

I don't mind Kat knowing. Of everyone I know, she's the one I want to tell everything. And honestly, she deserves to understand why I'm fucked up.

"He told me about your dad dying, and about how hard your mother took it." Her eyes meet mine. "I'm so sorry, Blake. That must have been so tough on you."

I can't get words past the lump in my throat, so I just nod. There's concern in her gaze, caring, but no judgment or pity.

"I'm sorry about the way things...ended." Her gaze goes to the floor as she tucks a piece of hair behind her ear. "I didn't know about your mom or everything from the past. I hope you can forgive me."

The only thing she needs forgiveness for is thinking that we're done. It's going to take a lot more than that for her to get rid of me.

"Kat." I deepen my voice to get her attention. "I don't care about all of that. Did seeing the way my dad's death affected my mom fuck my views on relationships for a while? Yes. But being around you... It's changed all of that. You make me want to try, even if it hurts sometimes. I don't want to give up on us."

Her eyes are bright with tears. "The gambling thing is hard for me. I'm working on it. I texted my dad today. He's been trying to talk to me about things for years, and I haven't been ready to listen. But...now I am. Even so, it's not just the gambling. It's that you kept it from me."

If I could go back in time and undo anything in my life, I'd tell her about poker the minute I met her. I'd give up any kind of gambling just for her. It would be worth it.

"I never meant to lie to you or keep anything from you, Kat." I swallow hard, hoping it's enough. "It's not a big part of my life anymore. It's not a part of my life at all now, actually. The friendships I have with the guys started that way, but those relationships are deeper now. They don't need that common thread anymore. And I don't need gambling in my life. But I do need you."

She draws in a deep breath, her eyes fixed on me.

I take in a breath, too, as I get ready to lay it all out on the line. "I promise you, Kat. I'll never keep anything from you ever again. Starting right now. It's too soon for this, but...I'm falling for you, baby."

Her lips part softly, her hazel eyes sparkling with unshed tears. "This is real, isn't it?"

I can't wait any longer to touch her. "This is more real than anything I've ever known."

I pull her toward me and crush my lips against hers.

She meets me with the same fervent need, our kisses demanding. She bites down on my lip, causing me to groan before I take her mouth with my tongue, savoring her taste.

Kat presses her body against mine, and fuck, I don't care that we're at work right now. I have to have her.

In one movement, I spin her around and move us until we're standing next to the desk. "Bend over."

She looks over her shoulder at me. There's a question in her eyes, but her pupils are dilated with lust.

"Over the desk," I say again, giving her ass a light smack.

Office sex isn't the reason I keep my desk clean with very few things on top, but it's coming in handy right now.

Kat presses her upper body against the dark wood

as I shove my pants and boxers down in one movement, only pausing to grab a condom from my wallet. I usually keep one in there, but the way Kat and I are going through them, I may need to find a way to have more available at any given time.

I sheath myself, then I lift Kat's skirt, taking in the shape of her gorgeous ass. The black thong she's wearing doesn't cover much, but I don't want anything between us now.

I take hold of the lace and yank, ripping it off her body.

Kat gasps, but I don't care. I'll buy her a new pair. Hell, I'll buy her a hundred of those thongs, if I'm the one who gets to look at them.

I reach between her legs, finding her center hot and slick. *Fuck.*

"This is real, babe. This is so fucking real." I surge forward, driving all the way home in one movement. "Don't ever. Fucking. Doubt. It."

I punctuate each word with a hard thrust.

I can't get enough of this woman.

She matches me thrust for thrust, pushing back against me to take me deeper.

I grip her hips, pulling her as close to me as I can get her.

I'm never letting this woman go.

After one of the best orgasms of my life, we lie on the floor of my office, staring up at the ceiling, both of us still breathing heavily.

"You should have someone paint over that water damage," Kat says, pointing.

"Mmm?" I pull her closer to me.

The carpet may not be the most comfortable, but it beats lying on the hard linoleum. Next time, though, I'm having her in a bed. My bed, preferably. Every night from now on. Or her bed, for all I care. As long as I'm with her, it doesn't matter.

"There's a water spot on your ceiling."

This time, I follow where she's pointing. There's a brown spot in the center of the white paint.

"Huh. I never noticed that before."

"You missed it all those times you fucked someone else on your office floor?" she asks, a teasing lilt in her voice.

"You're the only one I've ever fucked in my office, Kitten." If I have my way, she's the only one I'll fuck ever again, in my office or anywhere else.

"Huh. Well, missed opportunity. This carpet is pretty nice." She runs a hand over it. "Did you see where my underwear went?"

Folding her thong wasn't exactly high on my list of priorities at that moment, and it's destroyed now anyway. I tossed it somewhere, but after looking around, I don't see it. The black could be camouflaged against any shadow, though.

I sit up to look for it as the squeak of the doorknob turning makes Kat gasp.

The door pushes open before we can react, and in that moment, all I can do is thank my lucky stars that we were in too much of a rush to actually take our clothes off.

"Oh!" Randi lets out a startled gasp. "I, um, brought your mail. I was going to put it on your desk, but, uh…"

She looks from me to Kat and back again, crimson staining her cheeks.

I climb to my feet. My pants are up, but my belt is still unbuckled. There's no point in pretending she didn't just walk in on us, so I buckle it as I walk toward the door to take the pile from Randi's hand.

"Oh, and, um." Randi stoops down to grab something from the floor and adds it to the mail pile. "You might need this. Sorry again."

She hands me the pile of interdepartmental envelopes with Kat's thong on top.

"Thanks."

She rushes away without another word. As soon as I close the door, Kat dissolves into giggles, and I start laughing, too.

"A few minutes earlier, and she would have..." Kat says, getting to her feet. "I'm betting she won't bug you anymore about going on a date with her. That was about as much proof as we could offer her that we're dating."

I snort with laughter. "As long as the gossip doesn't spread all over campus, it'll be fine."

She adjusts her skirt, takes the thong from me, and stuffs it into her purse. "Ready to work on that course outline?"

As long as Kat is next to me, I'm ready for anything.

30

CHRISTMAS

Kat

My emotions are all over the place. Excitement, joy, anxiety. The last one isn't a familiar feeling when I'm on my way to my parents' house for Christmas, but this year is different for a couple of reasons.

First, I'm not going home alone. Blake is coming with me and meeting my parents for the first time.

I sneak a glance at Blake, whose focus is on the highway in front of us. "Are you nervous?"

He shakes his head. "Not really. I want to make a good impression, but I'm pretty sure you're going to do whatever the hell you want when it comes to relationships, regardless of their opinion."

"I value their opinion."

He looks at me quickly with an amused expression then back to the road. "I know that. And I'll be on my best behavior. I'm just saying that while they're important to you, they're not going to come between us." He reaches over and grasps my hand, keeping one hand on the steering wheel. "Plus, I think they'll be more focused on other things than our relationship."

Right.

Because I'm ready to talk to Dad.

To tell him about the effect his gambling addiction had on me, but more than that, to forgive him for it.

I grip Blake's hand as he knocks on the door. "Ready?"

He just gives me a wink as the door opens, my dad standing there with a wide smile on his face. There's uncertainty behind it, but he looks genuinely happy to see us.

"Hi, Dad," I say.

Normally, we tiptoe around one another, but things have changed.

"Hey, honey." Dad holds his arms out, and for the first time in years, I fall into them, letting him hold me close. "It's good to see you."

When he finally lets me go, I give him a shy smile as I gesture to Blake. "This is Blake. My boyfriend."

The term doesn't seem to do him justice, given everything we've been through, but it's nice to use the term without feeling like a fraud.

Blake takes Dad's outstretched hand and shakes it with a smile. "Good to meet you, sir. You have a very special daughter here."

"That I do. Come on in. Mom is making something in the kitchen."

"A mess?" I supply the punchline to the joke Dad has told for years.

Truth be told, Mom is a fantastic cook, but she does tend to leave a pile of dirty dishes in her wake. The two of them had an agreement when they first married that Mom would cook and Dad would clean. It's the perfect example of their partnership.

It also explains why Mom never really bothered to minimize the number of dishes and utensils involved in her creations because she didn't have a stake in the cleaning process.

Dad chuckles. "As usual."

He leads the way to the large kitchen.

The room is exactly how it's been since I was a kid. Pale-yellow walls and white cabinets contrast with the dark hardwood floor and the speckled black granite countertops. The familiarity is comforting, especially after staying away for a few years.

I pull out a chair at the island and motion to another for Blake. "It smells amazing in here, Mom."

The aroma of whatever she's cooking in the pan on the stove in front of us makes my mouth water.

She laughs, her shoulder-length hair bouncing. There's more gray than the last time I saw her.

"So far, it's just butter and onions. Just wait. I found this recipe online. It sounds amazing." She wipes her hands on a towel. "And Blake, lovely to meet you. I'm Diana. Thanks for taking care of our girl."

"The pleasure is mine, ma'am."

Boy, can he turn up the charm when he wants.

"And Kat is pretty darn good at taking care of herself. I'm just lucky to be able to spend time with her."

I kick him beneath the counter, the movement almost making me fall off my own chair.

"Suck-up," I whisper.

"I like this one," Dad declares.

I smile, looking between Mom and Dad as Dad steals a piece of bread from the baguette Mom is slicing.

Mom hip-checks Dad out of the way. "Those are

for the dip. Get out of here before I slice your fingers off."

I laugh at their easy chemistry as Blake wraps an arm around me and kisses my shoulder.

Dad clears his throat. "Kat, would you like to talk for a minute?"

Blake squeezes my shoulder. "I need to talk to my brother. Do you mind if I use the bedroom?"

I nod, grateful that he's read the situation and recognizes my need for privacy. "Of course. Up the stairs, and it's the first door on the left."

Blake makes his way out of the kitchen, and I face my parents.

Dad twists his fingers in front of him. "Kat, I want to apologize."

"It's—"

He holds up a hand to cut me off. "Let me finish. Please. I have an addiction to gambling. You know that, but I've accepted it over the last years. I've gone to meetings, something called Gamblers Anonymous. And with their help, I've accepted that I'm not able to handle any gambling without it getting out of my control. Part of my recovery is making amends to those I've wronged."

He blows out a long breath as Mom gives him an encouraging nod.

"Kat, I know I deeply impacted your life when I lost your college savings through gambling. I can't change any of that now. I just hope you can forgive me and know that I'll do anything I can to support you now and in the future. And please know just how proud I am of you that despite everything I did, you've succeeded on your own. You make me so proud every day, pumpkin."

Tears prick my eyes. Looking back, I wonder if I'd be the same person if I'd had my college degree completely paid for. If I hadn't worked to put myself through school to be where I am now.

I step around the island and wrap my arms around Dad. "It'll take some time for me to get there completely, but I want to forgive you, Dad. I love you."

Blake

I head up to the bedroom to make my phone call, giving Kat some privacy.

Sitting on the edge of the queen-size bed, I pull my phone out and pull up Lawton's number.

He answers on the first ring. "Hey. What's up?"

"How's your Christmas?"

It's technically the twenty-third, but since

Christmas is on a Monday this year, this counts as part of the holiday weekend, at least in my mind.

"Eh, it's okay. I signed up to work the next three days so people who have families can celebrate with them." There's a hint of bitterness in his voice.

"Any word from Kristina?"

"Nope. Gone and out of my life." He lets out a sigh. "Maybe I can send a letter to Santa asking for a new woman in my life. I love it up here in High Lonesome, but the pickings are slim. Most people don't move up here for the single life."

His mention of relationships brings up the question I've wanted to ask him for years.

I look around the bedroom. It's cozy, with a thick white comforter on the bed and a multicolored blanket that looks homemade. The walls are a deep orange, accented with colorful paintings. It reminds me a lot of Kat's house, and I wonder if this was her room growing up, or if she and her parents just have similar taste in decorating.

The warmth and comfort surrounding me makes me think I need something like that in my life.

"How do you do it?" I finally ask. "Stay optimistic. Believe that relationships can work out. Ever since Dad died, I can't get past the impact his death had on Mom. And how her reaction to his death impacted us."

"Honestly? There are a few reasons," he says. "I was younger than you when it happened. The biggest memory I have from all of it is you taking over and taking care of me. That kind of love is what I want, Blake. The kind that makes a family stick together, even when things don't go well."

I swallow past the lump that grows in my throat.

"And...I never told you this because I know you resent Mom for how she handled it. The impact taking care of me had on your life and your career."

"I don't resent it," I say automatically, but I realize that maybe I do.

Isn't that what I've been avoiding all these years? Putting someone in the same position I found myself in?

"But what I didn't tell you," he continues, ignoring my denial, "is that I've talked to Mom. I visit her every couple years. She's in Florida now, living in a condo. She misses you, Blake."

I miss her, too. I wonder if I can move past everything. If there's a chance to have a relationship with her again.

"Anyway, a couple years ago, we finally talked about Dad. About why she shut down so completely. I asked her if she regretted any of it, if the love they had was worth the pain. She regrets putting so much on you, Blake. But she doesn't regret the years she had with Dad. She told me she'd go through it all again to experience what they had together."

We talk for a while longer, but his revelation spins in my mind.

She'd go through it all again to experience the love they shared.

Maybe the chances of getting hurt are worth the chance to experience something amazing.

Something like I have with Kat.

***

Dinner is every bit as delicious as promised.

The company is just as good. I've learned more about her parents, who set the bar high for education. Diana is a corporate lawyer, while Tom has a PhD like Kat, although his is in government and public policy. He teaches at a university in D.C. while also advising several government think tanks in his spare time.

We don't talk about his past, but from the ease in Kat's body, the warm way she looks at her dad, I can guess that their talk went well.

Conversation flows easily as we eat lasagna with

garlic bread and red wine, and Kat wasn't kidding about her mom's cooking ability.

"Did you get your mom's cooking skill?" I ask Kat as I take another helping.

Her dad winks. "Let's just say she got the brains but skipped the cooking gene."

Kat elbows him. "Hey, you never know. I might have learned to cook in the last few years."

"Did you?" he asks, looking interested.

"Maybe," she mutters.

Unfortunately for her, she told me a few of the stories of her kitchen mishaps.

"I thought you set the stove on fire a few months ago," I say.

"Oh, look at the time. I have to get Blake to bed."

Her parents laugh as Kat hauls me out of my seat because it's not much past 7:30.

I take one more large scoop of lasagna and shove it into my mouth as she pulls me from the table.

"What about dessert?" I ask after I swallow, as Kat leads me toward the stairs.

"They won't have dessert tonight. Mom does a big thing on Christmas Eve with cookies and cake and all sorts of stuff, so she won't serve anything tonight."

After what Diana managed to do with the lasagna,

I can only imagine how her baked goods will taste. My mouth is already watering.

And when Kat locks the door and turns to look at me, my mouth is watering for an entirely different reason.

"Come here," I say, unbuttoning my shirt.

She pulls her sweater over her head as she walks toward me and drops it to the floor.

I add my shirt to the pile then unbuckle my belt. When she steps closer to me, I reach for the waist of her pants and unbutton her jeans before pushing them down.

Kat smirks as she steps out of the pants, kicking them toward her sweater and leaving her in just a thong and tank top. She's not wearing a bra, something I didn't know until this moment. Her nipples are hard, prominently on display through the thin fabric of the mauve top.

"You still mad that I made you leave dinner?" she asks, her lips curved up.

I shed my own pants, leaving me in my boxer briefs, and pull her tank top over her head. "Not at all. I think I'm still hungry, though."

I kiss her, long and languid, exploring her mouth as I walk her backwards toward the bed. When the backs of her legs hit the mattress, I pull back and brush the pad of my thumb over her lower lip.

"Get up there."

She climbs onto the bed and lies back against the pillows, parting her legs slightly, and Christ, I'm a goner.

I pull her thong off before I position myself between her legs, spreading her open just for me. I enjoy the view for a few seconds. Her skin is smooth, begging for my touch.

I kiss her neck then her collarbone, making my way down her body. When I reach her breasts and swirl my tongue around each nipple, she sucks in a breath.

"You like that, Kitten?" I bite down gently, just enough for her to feel my teeth.

"Blake," she groans, lifting her hips.

"Shh. Your parents are downstairs. It's been an emotional night already. If they know we're having sex up here, that might be the last straw." I trail kisses down her flat stomach, my hands tracing a line down both sides.

She has the perfect body, if you ask me. Toned but not so skinny she's going to break. There's a softness to her hips, and her ass? Round, tight, amazing.

As I reach the lower edge of her abdomen, she parts her legs farther. Her pussy glistens with moisture.

I swipe two fingers along her slit and hold up the evidence for her to see. "You're soaked, babe. This all for me?"

"Fuck yes," she pants out.

Bringing my fingers to my lips, I taste her arousal. "Fucking delicious. Taste how sweet you are, Kitten."

I gather more on my fingers and tap them against her mouth.

She opens her lips and pulls my fingers into her mouth, sucking them clean.

"Good girl," I say.

My already-hard dick stiffens further as I imagine her sucking on something else entirely.

Kat bites her lip as I slide my fingers from her mouth. "I don't know why that's so hot."

"It's because you love letting me take control in the bedroom." I kiss the apex of her thighs, just above her clit. "You get off on doing what I tell you to."

I flick my tongue over her clit, earning a moan.

"I shouldn't."

"Fuck that." I flatten my tongue and run it along the length of her slit. "What you like in bed has nothing to do with you being a badass in every other area of your life." Another long swipe. "You can be the boss bitch in the classroom and on your faculty committees and have the dean by the balls and still love coming home to let me be in charge here."

A shudder runs through her body. She grabs a pillow and holds it over her face to stifle her moans as I alternate between short, quick movements and longer strokes.

When her thighs start to quiver, I know she's close. I pull her clit into my mouth and suck as her hips buck and she comes, the pillow muting her cries.

I stay between her legs, my tongue laving her with slow, gentle pressure as she comes down from her orgasm. Her muscles go slack, and she tosses the pillow to the side.

That's when I finally pick my head up. "How you doing, babe?"

She tosses her head back. "So fucking good, Blake. So fucking good."

I reach for the nightstand next to the bed, where I stashed a box of condoms earlier. I shed my boxers and roll one on. My dick is so hard it's painful.

I squeeze the base as I settle back between her legs.

"Take me, Blake," Kat whispers.

Shaking my head, I notch myself at her entrance. "This isn't fucking, Kat. It's more than that." I slide into her, slow and steady. "I want to make love to you."

She wraps her legs around me, pulling me closer. "Make love to me, Blake."

"All night long, Kitten. All night long."

I move inside her, slow and sweet, our eyes fixed on one another, and it's so different from how I usually have sex. Before Kat, it was just fucking, and while it was good, there was something missing. I thought I'd found it with Kat.

But this is better even than the other times Kat and I have been together.

We're not just physically joined.

It's deeper.

More real.

And I never want to lose this feeling.

This time, we come together, clinging to one another as simultaneous orgasms wash over us, and we stay like that, even as my cock softens inside her, neither of us willing to break the connection.

"Blake?" Kat says softly as we lie together.

"Yeah?" I kiss the top of her head.

"I love you." She says it simply, without fanfare, like it's the most obvious thing in the world.

And maybe it is. Because I've realized that I love her, too.

"This is real, babe. And I love you. No matter what

happens, I'm here for good." I roll to my back, pulling her with me so she's cuddled against my side.

She sets her head on my shoulder.

When her breathing slows, I kiss the top of her head again and pull the cover over both of us before I wrap myself around the most perfect woman I've ever known.

EPILOGUE

KAT, NEXT OCTOBER

My cheeks hurt from smiling as I wrap up today's lecture.

As usual, the students have been engaged in the topics, moving the discussion forward with insightful points and thoughtful questions.

The last students filter out of the room as I pile my papers together and slide them into my tote. Blake stands from the front row, grinning.

"Nice job, babe," he says, giving me a side hug. "As always."

When we finally managed to work on the proposal for Economics of the American Healthcare System, we knew we had a winner. The level of excitement both of us had to start teaching this class was above anything I've felt for any of my other courses.

And it's translated into a hugely popular one among the students, especially the pre-meds. The fact that so many of them are in my classes, between Anatomy and Physiology and this one, has made me a sought after advisor for undergrads hoping to apply to medical school.

I slip the tote over my shoulder and slide my gaze over the empty seats, coming to rest on the lone remaining figure sitting way in the back.

"Nice work," Dean Kashman says, standing. He walks down the empty aisle to meet us at the front of the lecture hall. "I knew this class would be a hit, but you two have taken it to a level I couldn't even imagine."

"Thanks," I say.

Blake gives him a nod, "Thanks. Appreciate your support."

"Of course." Adam looks at me. "Can I have a minute with Professor Milas?"

"Sure thing. Kat, I'll meet you in the student union for lunch." Blake gives us a wave as he heads for the door.

Dean Kashman turns toward me. "Again, great job. I, uh..." He adjusts the cuffs of his shirt. "I wanted to apologize. For asking you out. It's clear that you and Professor Grantham are meant to be together."

"I appreciate that."

"And I wanted to also let you know, unofficially, that your promotion was approved. The committee met yesterday, and the official notification will come next week, but they unanimously voted to promote you from assistant to associate professor. Congratulations." He reaches out a hand, and I shake it, my brain still reeling.

I did it.

Blake is waiting for me when I leave the lecture hall, and I manage to contain my excitement for all of three seconds before I blurt it out.

"I got the promotion!" I whisper-shout. "It's not official until next week, but it's happening. Thanks to you and this whole arrangement."

Blake picks me up and twirls me in a circle. When he puts me down, he's shaking his head, but he's smiling.

"Not me at all, babe. This was you. All you. And so deserved." He leans closer to speak directly in my ear. "And I can't wait to fuck an associate professor."

BONUS EPILOGUE

BLAKE, THREE YEARS LATER

"Fuck. Fuck, fuck, fuck." Lawton's voice on the other end of the phone is frantic.

"Slow down. What happened?" I pour coffee into one of the colorful, eclectic mugs that Kat collects.

Since I moved into her house a year ago, things are much more colorful—I've always decorated in neutrals and minimalist style, while Kat loves colors.

It's cheerful, actually. It's hard to keep a frown on your face when you're surrounded by paintings and artwork in every color.

"I don't— Fuck. This can't be happening."

Lawton's job as a police officer requires him to stay calm in the most stressful situations, so I can't even imagine what has him this rattled, especially this early in the morning. He's two hours behind us in Colorado, so it's barely 5 a.m. there.

"Okay. Take a breath. Whatever it is, we'll figure it out. Do you need me to come out there?"

Please say no. I have plans for tonight.

The box with the ring is in my sock drawer.

"I might." He starts hyperventilating again.

I will murder him if he messes this proposal up for me, but family comes first, even if you have to murder them afterward.

"Tell me what you need."

"It's...it's Kristina."

His girlfriend from like four years ago? He hasn't mentioned her since Cam's wedding. I thought they were over.

"What about her? I thought she was ancient history."

"She's dead."

I should probably feel worse about this news, but she did dump my brother in a rather unceremonious way.

"I'm...sorry?" I venture.

He finally takes a deep breath and gathers himself. "I mean, not to speak ill of the dead or whatever, but she was kind of a bitch. I'm not that torn up about her."

Not judging him at all. "So why are you freaking out?"

"She has a kid."

"Oh."

I guess that's not surprising. We're in our thirties. People get married and have babies all the time. Maddox and Holly have two now, with one more on the way. Cam and Addie have one, and Becca is pregnant with her and Miller's first. According to them, Kat and I need to catch up.

Maybe once I get her to marry me. It's taken a few years, but her parents have finally given their blessing, or at least acquiesced to the idea that I'm not going away, so they have to get used to me.

"He's four."

"What does that have to do with anything?"

He's silent for a minute. "Do the math, Blake."

I think back to four years ago. I'd just started at Ardmore. I'd just met Kat. And Lawton had just...

Now I understand the panic in his voice.

"It's mine."

Look for **Hitting the Jackpot**, the final book in the Betting on Love series, coming early 2025.

My small town life gets flipped on its head when a child I never knew about is suddenly mine to care for; now, falling for his nanny may be a mistake that will cost me everything.

I thought I'd move on from the heartbreak of the past, until a part of it came back. Finding out I have a son and learning to be a father is stretching me thin. When I add in my job as a small town police officer, it's more than I can handle alone.

Hiring a nanny seemed like an obvious choice, but when I placed the ad, I never pictured *her* coming into my life. And if I thought being a single dad was tough, that was before I added in the complication of trying to keep my feelings to myself while living in the same house as the woman I shouldn't be falling for.

I'm not sure how long I can fight these feelings. But soon, I'm fighting for something else entirely, and even my time as a poker player didn't set me up for stakes like this: something that could have me hitting the jackpot... or losing everything.

www.ingramcontent.com/pod-product-compliance
Lightning Source LLC
Chambersburg PA
CBHW031514010826
48973CB00013B/1288